The Fallen Ship II

The Fallen Ship Series

Book 2

Mark Wayne McGinnis

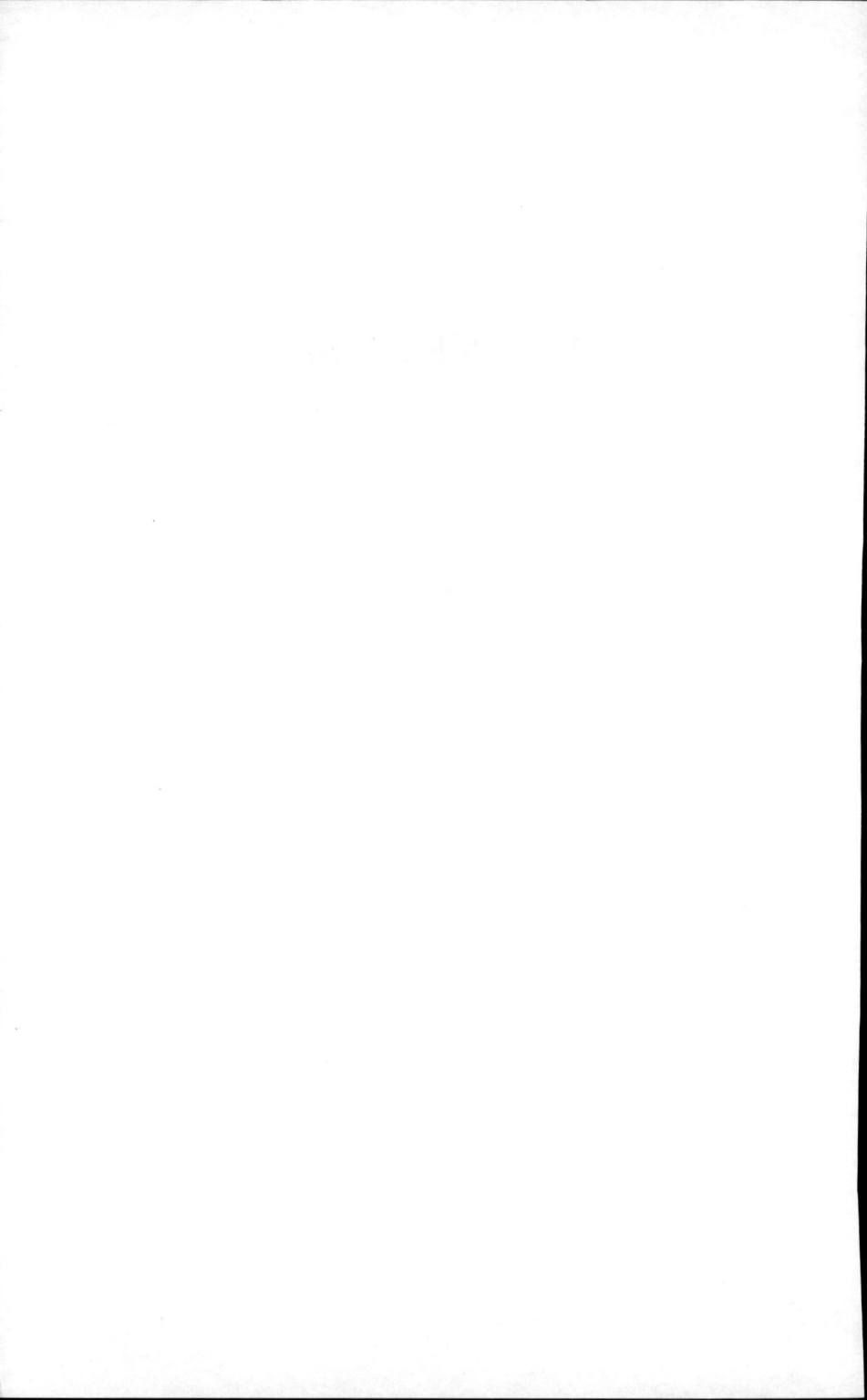

Chapter 1

Solar System, Beyond Earth's High Orbit
***Relentless Thrust*, Primary Mess Hall**

Sam Dale

Sam Dale cut his Gia-enabled connection to Harper and slid his iPhone back into the side pocket of his tactical vest. He imagined her standing there on top of that building within the Schriever Space Force Base complex. Her pretty face left a momentary impression on his psyche. He wondered if he'd survive long enough to see her again.

Ivan stumbled over a bowling ball–sized robot head, sending it rolling across the compartment, where it careened with a loud *clank* off an adjacent bulkhead.

"My bad ... didn't see the fucking thing."

Sam was glad that Harper and Julian, back on Earth, were okay—that and they'd come through with McGovern. He thought about the implications of now having a donutted four-star general in their ranks. Sam didn't relish the fact that he'd soon be giving marching orders to the older man. To someone who was so accomplished—a battlefield-tested officer who was more used to being the one barking off orders than taking them. *But, for reasons of her own, Gia has chosen me to lead this uprising...*

Standing there within the battle-wrecked confines of the ship's mess hall, Sam swiped a hand through the lingering gray haze. *And that wafting smell.* He certainly wasn't going to be the first to say it out loud. Sam glanced over to the prone bodies. The three were blackened, charred beyond recognition. But damn, that aroma—it reminded him of Afghanistan.

He appraised what was left of his team. First was the gruff and ethically challenged Ivan Dvorak, who at one time had been a fighter pilot with the Czech Republic Army. Then there was Carl Bennet, a crack-shot sniper who'd been with the Castle Rock Police Department, and finally, Jarpin, the last of a certain breed of Silarian warrior called *Orlicon Strass*. Teddy and Flout, as well as Gromel, were the three that had been killed by the Clash-Troopers. Their seared bodies were now positioned next to one another, shoulder to shoulder, off in one corner of the mess hall.

"You look confused, boss. Like you fall from wagon and hit your head," Ivan said in broken English.

"We'll head out in a few minutes," Sam said, letting out a slow breath. The loss of three good men was weighing on his conscience. He had to force himself not to replay things. Attempt to rewrite history or play the whole *what-if* game. Instead, he thought about their current situation and what had brought them here. Gia ... this was pretty much all about Gia.

Ivan, Carl, and Jarpin were looking at him. Waiting. Who was he kidding? He wasn't in charge; she was. He was as much a puppet on a string as everyone else on board this ship was, not to mention all those back in Castle Rock. The simple fact that Earth, humankind, would have been destroyed if it hadn't been for her intervention, well, that eased some of his frustration. Sam had been just one of her growing number of pawns—now playing within this elaborate intergalactic chess match. The implications of which were life and death—the very survival of thousands of inhabited worlds, if not complete star systems, at stake.

It would be easy to blame the aliens. The Silarians were an arrogant, wretched race. But what was really going on here was a high-stakes game between two god-like, self-important artificial intelligence (AI) entities. On one hand, you had the long-established, diabolical Geo-Mind who, over a millennium, had taken over the minds, the free will, of its once-creators, the Silarian Empire. And on the other hand, you had Gia, the Geo-Mind's rebellious AI offshoot, who had evolved over time while seemingly growing a conscience ...

Sam's nostrils flared at a new smell accosting his senses. Staring up at him was a mangy, panting dog.

"You get injured by any of those bots?" Sam asked.

"Called Clash-Troopers. Nope. I'm good," answered the talking dog.

"Okay ... Then why are you staring at me like that?"

"I'm not staring at you. It's not always about you, Sam," the dog said.

Sam made an irritated face. "What's not always about me? What are you even talking about?"

Ignoring the question, the dog circled around twice before lying down at Sam's feet.

The filthy, stinky golden retriever, originally named Rocko, had been the first on Earth to get mind-fucked by Gia. Well, not just Gia, but Gia and a young Silarian Landa-Craft pilot named Cypress. Because the advanced aliens, the Silarians, had the keen ability to jump consciousnesses from one organic form to another at the time of their impending deaths, and because Rocko was the only organic being in close enough proximity to save the desperate, dying pilot ... well, now Cypress and Rocko, along with Gia's influences, all co-inhabited this dog's mind.

As of this moment, Sam and those of his small team who'd survived had managed the impossible. Along with Gia, who, to be honest, had done most of the heavy lifting. They had secretly boarded *Relentless Thrust*, vanquished an imposing squad of Clash-Trooper robots, and now, this relatively small enemy gunship was theirs for the taking. But just a glance out one of *Relentless Thrust's* windows would throw a wet blanket over any sense of accomplishment one might have.

The Silarian 23rd Fleet, over one hundred highly advanced warships, was here to do what it had done to so many other worlds—terra-displacement. Earth had been slated for terra-displacement, had already been scanned and cataloged. Massive containment vessels were currently here, awaiting further orders. Soon would come the high-orbit energy weapon strikes on Earth's military fortifications. After that, there would be the dispersing of engineered pathogens that would wipe out humanity in a matter of weeks. Gia had informed Sam that terra-displacement, the raping of a world's natural resources, worked much better when there was little or no resistance.

He checked the magazine on his M4—something he'd already done twice before in the last ten minutes. "Let's move out," Sam said. He strode toward the exit, giving his three dead comrades a final nod of thanks.

Cypress moved out in front of the four-man contingent. The narrow passageway soon gave way to a wider corridor, where Silarian crew members looked on from their various ship posts—their expressions a mix of confusion and apprehension. They'd spent their entire lives with this AI voice in their heads, the

Geo-Mind ... now replaced by another one, a different one ... Gia.

All Silarians were provided with multiple implants from birth, the first of which was a sensory comms implant, so Silarians had constant mental communication with each other. Next was their Geo-Mind, a secondary technological brain. Think Siri or Alexa on steroids—a millennium of stored information right there for the asking. And finally, there was the essence implant. Everything that comprised a Silarian was stored within this one device. It was this technology that allowed for the transfer of one's consciousness, usually at the end of one's life, into an awaiting bio-form. Every thought, feeling, impulse, urge, memory, emotion, as well as a Silarian's complete anatomical and genetic disposition up until that last moment of life, continued to be stored within the essence implant.

When Silarian Landa-Craft pilot Cypress inhabited the canine body of Rocko ... scientist and friend Julian Humblecut came to the rescue. Julian created a makeshift container for Cypress to carry all three implants—stored and mounted to his collar.

The rest, at some point dubbed *Gia Fighters*—Sam, Carl, and Ivan—the human survivors here on this gunship had been given access to Gia via an edible concoction of Silarian nanites. Many of the people still living under the isolation zone in Castle Rock, Colorado—ones that had been lucky enough to be exposed to the nanites—had also had that Gia connection. The methodology used for enticing reluctant Castle Rock inhabitants to ingest these nanites—and subsequently have access to Gia—had been a baked-in concoction within an unbelievably delicious donut aptly called a glazed Castle Rock—thus came the term "being *donutted*."

Sam heard Gia's voice in his head. Sam, best you stay vigilant. Not all of Relentless Thrust's crew members have been donutted. Just know I'm working on that ... some are being resistant.

"Copy that," he said out loud. He glanced back, making eye contact with Ivan, Carl, and Jarpin. The three nodded, having received the same mental communiqué.

Now having to keep up with Cypress's quickening gait, they fell into a collective jog. Sam ignored the growing number of Silarian eyes on him. Cypress made a hard right turn at an intersection of three corridors up ahead. With the dog momentarily out of sight, Sam quickened his pace.

AARRK!

The sound, obviously Cypress's painful yelp, had been preceded by a *thump*. Coming around the corner with the barrel of his M4 raised, Sam saw Cypress lying on his side but attempting to rise, to escape before being kicked again. Above him stood the armed Silarian crew member responsible for Cypress's pain. Sam put two rounds into the alien's forehead. "A little warning would have been nice," Sam said to Gia.

"How can I warn you about something I didn't know was happening?" Cypress asked.

"I'm not talking to you; I'm talking to Gia," Sam said, placing his hands on the dog's right flank to check for broken ribs. "You seem to be okay—"

Cypress said, "Great observation, Dr. Know-it-All, but I was kicked on my other side."

The dog scampered up onto all fours, unsteady. Sam checked Cypress's other flank. He put a little pressure there to measure the dog's pain level. "That hurt?"

"Of course it hurts. I just took a boot to my ribs."

Sam watched as the golden retriever took a few tentative steps. "I'll survive."

"Good. Now how about you fall in behind from now on?"

Cypress didn't answer but did as asked. Sam repeated his question to Gia. "You couldn't have warned us?"

Sorry, Sam ... my resources are being stretched at the moment. Even though I've ensured this gunship remains cloaked, hidden from the rest of the fleet, it's being looked for. Multiple sensor arrays are active. I'm having to work overtime to ensure they see nothing but wide-open space where we're positioned.

"Doesn't being cloaked already compensate for all that?" Sam asked.

Yes ... to a point, but drive exhausts, even minuscule amounts of radiation, can be detected if there's a concentrated effort. You're close to the bridge. Captain Droke Tolli Mahn is there waiting for you. He's been quasi-donutted, as have the rest of his bridge crew. Needless to say, they're uneasy with what has transpired.

They were walking slower now, so Cypress could better manage his bruised left flank. Up ahead, Sam saw the entrance to the ship's bridge come into view. There were five, no, six, armed Silarians standing guard out in the passageway. They straightened nervously and came to the ready as they approached. Sam lowered his weapon, as did Ivan, Carl, and Jarpin—no sense making this situation any more tense than it had to be.

Chapter 2

Castle Rock, Colorado
Plum Creek Golf Course

Lester Price

Staggering out from piles of rubble, he used the palm of a hand to clear the soot from his eyes. *Looks like a damn bomb dropped on this place. Oh, that's right ... it kinda did.*

Only now was Lester coming off the adrenaline high. Felt as if his legs were made of rubber. And then there was the pain. He knew Gia was helping with that ... but fuck, it hurt.

He scanned the scorched and littered golf course laid out before him. Charred and broken-bodied Clash-Trooper remnants, shards of blackened fiberglass, smoldering husks of what were once golf carts, and a whole lot of other shit ... so much unrecognizable debris now blanketed these once picturesque grounds. He turned to see where he'd emerged from. Smoke rose in the not-so-far distance; it was startling to see empty space where a bunch of condos used to stand. He continued his trek forward, took in the burnt chemical smell, and thought of his favorite movie. *I love the smell of napalm in the morning!*

Four golf carts were parked haphazardly off in the distance; remarkably, they looked to be in decent shape. The little chubby black chick, Luna, was standing next to one of the carts with the remaining members of his team. Seeing him, she gawked, like, *How can he still be alive?* She began walking his way, then broke into a run.

He hobbled to meet her, inadvertently kicking a mechanical eyeball with the toe of his boot. He watched it wobble across the singed putting green and plop down into the hole.

"Hole in one motherfucker!" he shouted, punching a fist overhead. A sharp pain in the hand brought instant tears to his eyes—he lowered his arm, vowing to avoid doing things like that for a while.

Luna, huffing and puffing, made an incredulous face. "You've lost your ear, man. You know that, right?"

"Ear*lobe,* girl—big difference," he said. "Specifically, my right earlobe, my right pinkie, and my right ring finger." Lester held up his mutilated hand, flashing a lopsided grin. Blood flowed down his raised forearm.

"Good thing they didn't get your trigger finger," Luna said. She leaned back. "You got a nasty gash on your cheek too. Looks like the blood clotted ... maybe stopped bleeding."

Lester touched the wound with one of his remaining fingers.

"Crap," Lester murmured.

"Just glad you're not dead," she said. "Still ... you don't look so good, Lester."

"I'm fine," he said.

"We have other wounded too," Luna said, glancing back to the others, then looking back at him. She shook her head and gestured with two beckoning fingers. "Take off your shirt."

"Uh—no. You're a little young for me, cupcake. But, uh ... thanks for the offer." He winked.

"You're gross. I need your cotton tee. I can wrap your hand with it. Off. Give it to me," Luna ordered.

Lester liked her gumption. He removed his battle-scarred tactical vest, tossing it to the ground. Then, groaning, he took off his sweaty, nasty white T-shirt, handing it to her. She made a disgusted face, then, using her front teeth, started ripping and tearing the shirt. And with the ease of a magician making a rabbit out of balloons, she produced several perfectly narrow strips of cloth. Grabbing his hand with more force than he cared for, Luna began wrapping his bloodied stumps. She worked fast and did so with surprising finesse.

"That was kinda hot," he said, realizing that had come out creepier than he intended.

Luna stared at him, more specifically at his now-bare chest.

Lester was fit, boasting the lean physique of a swimmer, or maybe a rock star. Too many drugs and too many skipped meals would do that. He watched her eyes take in his glorious ink. Beneath the sweat and grime, he had what was nothing less than artwork spanning the width of his torso. Two serpents with long sinewy bodies wrapped around each other, their heads coming together with open mouths and flickering tongues. In the background, rising flames rose between the battling vipers.

"The tip of one of your ... uh, flames is bleeding," she remarked. She balled up what remained of the torn T-shirt, pressed it onto the open wound.

"Owww," he whined. "Easy there."

"You take it. Go on ... just hold the cloth there." She made a face. "Don't be so delicate about it."

"Bossy," he mumbled under his breath.

"Pussy," she shot back. Luna took a step back, critical eyes surveying Lester's beat-to-shit body. She tilted her head. "You hear that? It's Gia. She's saying something ..."

Lester's brows bunched. "I would hear if you'd shut up a second."

... you need to move quickly. Silarian dropships ... four of them. Get to the one closest to you. Head north; go through the clearing in the trees. There's an unoccupied Silarian craft there. It's cloaked at present, but I should be able to make it visible by the time you get there. About half a mile beyond that, there's a nursing home. It will be a good place for you to tend to the infirm, Luna.

Lester and Luna exchanged nods, conveying they were both listening to the AI.

"What about our other two teams?" Luna asked.

The team at the Douglas County Fairgrounds fared well. One casualty and a few minor injuries. The Butterfield Crossing Park team lost three. Scott's Attack Stinger was shot down—he didn't survive.

Lester stared, had nothing to say about that.

Luna spun on her heel and raised her hands. "Okay, time to head out. We're gonna get us some help."

"Back off, bossy pants," Lester said. "Let's not forget who's in charge here. Got that, kid?"

"Oh, did little Luna hurt the big man's feelings?" she baby-talked back. "Look, you need medical attention, and Gia knows I have some natural ability in that area. Let's just get you and the other injured fixed up. Then you can play General Patton again. Sound reasonable?"

"Whatever. Just ... fetch us a damn cart—I'll, uh ..." He'd

started to sway a little. He looked toward the rest of his team. *What a shitshow ...*

Lester tried to take a step, but the world around him had started to spin. He crumpled to the ground, still holding the T-shirt to his rib cage. Luna's blurred form was heading off toward the carts—at that point, everything went black.

Chapter 3

Castle Rock, Colorado
B&B Café

Lloyd Sanderson

late in the year, 1946...

Winter had come hard and unrelenting to Colorado that year. Lloyd slumped lower within the unforgiving wooden booth. He wore an oversized red and black plaid hunting jacket, one that concealed his emaciated body. A wide-brimmed black fedora fell forward, covering his sunken eyes and a large portion of his pock-marked face. He raised the brim of his hat slightly and scanned the empty diner. He'd seated himself in a booth near the entrance, facing the door, better to keep an eye on who came and went. Fluorescent lighting filled the café, too bright for his liking, but Lloyd was relieved he was now the only customer in the place. Kitchen smells, fried eggs, pancake batter, fresh-brewed coffee—all made him realize just how hungry he was.

Where's that cow of a waitress?

He eyed the Wurlitzer jukebox tucked into the bay window's nook space to the right of the entrance. Sparkly red and gold tubes framed the music box—above, a white tombstone-shaped menu displayed song choices. The current tune featured Kenny Clarke on drums. He recognized it because his dad would play this garbage on his phonograph every fricking night. He hated jazz; the nonsensical, self-indulgent rifts irritated him.

But leaving wasn't an option—he needed to eat. Lloyd had traveled from his girlfriend's apartment in Denver, Colorado, mostly by foot. He was starving and this place served cheap food, and it was, mercifully, open twenty-four-seven.

"Hi, hon, you want some coffee?" the waitress asked, holding a raised coffee pot.

Lloyd looked up to see a plump, middle-aged woman. She wore a shiny silver barrette to hold a nest of unruly red hair back from her face. A sliver-of-metal nameplate was fastened neatly on the right lapel of her starched top. It read: JANICE.

He offered a slight nod. Janice expertly poured—he watched the stream of black brew, the hypnotic up-and-down motion of the coffee pot; she didn't spill a drop.

"I wanna order," Lloyd said, catching her gaze for a split second, then dropping it just as quickly... but not before he saw her reaction.

Her nostrils flared. Taking a half-step backward, her expression held a momentary look of disgust—a look she quickly tried, unsuccessfully, to conceal.

Lloyd knew it. He stank. He hadn't bathed in four days, no ... five. His clothes were rank; he'd tried to clean up as best he could along the way, but there was only so much one could do in a gas station bathroom. Soon, he'd need to get going. *Can't draw attention to myself.*

"Just bring me four cheeseburgers ... uh, make them to go. And I'm in a real hurry," Lloyd said more abruptly than he'd intended.

With a huff, Janice waddled away ... no doubt thankful for the respite from his stench. He held the warm ceramic mug between cupped hands. He stared blankly at his dirty fingers, the myriad tiny cuts—the speckled fragments of something reddish brown. Realization set in: his fingers and knuckles were peppered with dried blood. Releasing one hand from the cup, he inspected the crescent-shaped dark gunk lodged under each of his fingernails. He swallowed hard, trying not to think about it. What he'd done three days ago ... *Did I actually do that ... kill my girlfriend?*

Jingle.

The sound of the hanging bell interrupted his thoughts. He watched as a young, clean-cut man came in through the café's entrance. Lloyd took in the crisp blue jeans and form-fitting tan coat that rode the top of his Levi's—a beige Stetson tilted slightly back on his head, exposing a friendly, fresh face. Close on his heels came another guy, one who looked almost identical to the first; same garb, same hick cowboy boots, everything the fucking same—except this guy wore a white Stetson. A couple of Gene Autry wannabes. *Twins?*

They smiled coming inside the restaurant, obviously happy to be in from the cold, flakes of already melting snow dusting their shoulders. As they made their way to the booth directly in front of him, Lloyd felt their eyes sweep over him. He looked up and inadvertently stiffened, made eye contact, first with beige Stetson, then white Stetson. Still smiling, they settled into their booth, sitting across from one another.

Feeling his breathing constrict and the emanating heat

beneath his armpits, Lloyd did his best to look casual. He shifted his gaze away from the lone cowboy facing him, over to the long marble countertop directly to his left. He feigned interest in the stack of newspapers and a nearby large potted plant. He eyed a cake holder situated at the far end of the bar, only it wasn't a cake inside, but half a pie beneath its clear glass dome—he could just make out the pie's dark fruit filling.

Like soldiers, worn barber shop–style stools stood at attention in a line in front of the counter. Lloyd caught his own reflection in a massive mirror on the other side of the bar.

I look like shit ... I look like the mangy killer that I am ...

Using the mirror, he kept an eye on the two cowboys. Lloyd inwardly snickered. Morons. Their heads bobbed side to side as they used forks and knives to keep beat with Kenny Clarke ... *God, will this track ever end?*

Lloyd nearly jumped to his feet as white Stetson suddenly began drumming open palms on the tabletop—loud, rapid, machine-gun beats filled the café. Recovering, Lloyd took in a deep breath and exhaled through gritted teeth.

Something's changed.

The cowboys were now slightly hunched, heads leaning in toward one another.

Why are they whispering?

He squirmed in his seat while keeping a leery eye on the mirror. Leaning to one side, he slid his hand into his hunting jacket's oversized right pocket. His fingers found the grip, then he touched the cold metal of the long six-inch barrel. Smiling, the nicked and scratched twenty-two-caliber H&R 922 revolver infused Lloyd with a sudden jolt of confidence.

Coffee pot in hand, Janice hurried past him toward the cowboys. Startled, Lloyd glowered at her too-snug uniform and the exaggerated rolls of fat around her waist.

"Hey, boys. How you doin' tonight? Chilly, huh?" Janice asked, pouring coffee into empty cups.

Lloyd's eyes narrowed. The nearest cowboy, the one facing away from him ... the brim of his hat tilted higher. Lloyd watched the chubby redhead's expression. No words were exchanged, at least none that Lloyd could make out. *There!* Her brow had knit just a tad.

I don't like this ...

There were inaudible, soft murmurs now. Beige Stetson's eyes flicked over his buddy's shoulder in Lloyd's direction. Acting overly casual, the cowboy slipped something from his jacket's breast pocket ... a folded-up piece of paper.

With a painted-on smile, he laid it on the table before him, using the palm of his hand to flatten the folds.

Janice stepped sideways, now blocking Lloyd's view. *Move your fat ass, Janice.*

Narrowing his eyes, Lloyd tried to make out what was written on the page. *Please don't let that be a Most Wanted poster.*

Movement.

White Stetson was getting up. Speaking loud enough for everyone to hear within a mile, he broadcast, "I'll be right back. Damn! I can't believe I forgot my wallet." He then proceeded to fast-walk toward the front door.

Janice spun, chin raised, briskly headed toward the kitchen.

Lloyd raised a hand. "Uh ... excuse me, Miss ... Janice?" he said in a hoarse voice. "Can you check on my burgers? I gotta leave."

Janice reluctantly paused. Her forced smile told him everything he needed to know.

"Yes, sir. I'll go check on that," the waitress said, turning away, her rubber-soled shoes squeaking on the hardwood flooring.

Hand still buried deep within the confines of his right pocket, Lloyd's fingers tightened around the weapon's handle. He took a moment, thinking about what had happened up in Denver. He ran some calculations in his head. He'd shot his girlfriend twice. *God, I didn't want to do that ... hadn't planned on it. It just fucking happened.* Two bullets down. And then there was her smug-looking dinner guest ... *Yeah, he certainly deserved it.* Lloyd had plugged him once in the belly—*that was three bullets down*—and of course, there was that idiot cop who'd shown up unexpectedly and surprised him. Lloyd shook his head; *that's a total of four rounds gone.* He shrugged. Simple math, just two bullets left in the gun. *Should be enough.*

He and his girlfriend, Margaret, had been together three years, and, although things weren't perfect between them, he thought they would be together forever. When he'd gone to her apartment three days ago, he felt uneasy, knowing that she was hiding something. He just wanted to talk it out.

But as soon as he walked in, he knew things were going to turn ugly. Laughter was coming from the kitchen toward the back of the house—Margaret's and someone else's. A man's. Lloyd slipped his twenty-two from his pocket, held it down by his right leg.

As he entered the small kitchen, all eyes went to Lloyd. And then to his weapon.

The two jumped to their feet.

Margaret, eyes wide as dinner plates, said, "Lloyd, stop! What are you doing here? Why the gun?"

He looked at her, took in her simple, flowered dress. She was wearing dark red lipstick, and her long black hair was pinned up all fancy-like. So beautiful. She was just seventeen, like him.

Those deep brown eyes now pleaded with him. Those same eyes that spoke her every thought, her every emotion. Sure, he knew she was way out of his league, but she'd said she loved him. Those eyes had told him so.

"Who's this?"

"Lloyd ..."

"You fucking him?" Lloyd spat.

The man, Margaret's date, stood next to her. He was leaning erect against the wall, as if trying to disappear into the dingy plaster.

"No, come on ... He's just a friend, I swear," Margaret pleaded, waving open palms in front of her.

Lloyd glanced down to the kitchen table. It was set for two. A lone rose leaned out from a chipped vase. Two wineglasses and an envelope with hearts on it that lay on one of the empty plates.

Without another thought, Lloyd raised his pistol and shot the young guy in the stomach. Margaret screamed, bringing her hands to her mouth while crimson spread over the guy's white button-down.

Dropping to her knees, Margaret reached for the man, pulled his writhing form into herself.

"Kenny! Oh my God, Kenny!"

Lloyd calmly said, "Margaret ... look at me, Margaret."

She did so, fear and hatred now staring up at him.

"Why? Why do you disrespect me like this?" he asked, slowly shaking his head—tears making rivers down his cheeks. "Why are you making me do this!" But before she could answer, he pulled the trigger... once... and then again. The top of Margaret's pretty flowered dress blossomed red, matching the color of her painted lips. She crumpled onto Kenny, gasping for breath. Lloyd knelt next to her, placing an open palm on her soft cheek. Repositioning, he moved his foot, careful of the expanding pool of blood on the brightly patterned linoleum floor.

The memory of it was still crystal clear. It had happened so fast. He'd stayed with her until she passed. It took a while ... she was a fighter. But he'd done that for her, though she probably didn't deserve it. When the two cops showed up, Lloyd had managed to get away, barely. But he'd had to shoot one of the cops ... he'd thought in the shoulder. He'd live. Probably.

He'd been on the run for three days now. Moving south, he'd stayed close to the major roadways, inwardly cursing Margaret that he'd been forced to rummage through people's garbage cans. He'd found discarded clothing and some half-eaten food. He'd slept one night in an abandoned house, another beneath an overpass. Once he'd made it to Castle Rock, he started to feel better. He knew this town pretty well. He'd arrived here with five bucks in his pocket. That should be enough for a meal—then he could make a plan.

The bell jingled over the front door, pulling Lloyd from his reverie. A man entered, sauntered in as if he owned the place. He was tall, easily six feet and change. Built sturdy, like you could tell he could handle himself. He wore dusty jeans and an Army-green overcoat, no hat. His eyes scanned the café in an off-handed sort of way. He took a seat on the stool directly to Lloyd's left.

Taking in the scene via the mirror, Lloyd saw that beige Stetson and the new guy were making eye contact—he saw their exchange of discreet nods.

I'm not stupid ... I know what's going down here.

The bell jingled again; this time it was white Stetson returning ... and he was holding what looked like a 32 revolver.

Heart hammering in his chest, adrenaline pumping into his bloodstream, Lloyd needed to take action now—to get on the offensive. Finding his legs, he clumsily extricated himself from the booth, all the while fumbling to pull his own weapon. The man at the bar shot to his feet, spinning around and reaching for him. Lloyd staggered backward, finally able to free his gun. He raised it and squeezed the trigger.

Crack! The loud retort was near deafening. It was a perfect shot to the man's heart. His eyes went fixed, the man in the Army-green overcoat swayed, then dropped like a sack of rocks.

One bullet left.

Lloyd spun left and then right, frantically taking in the entire space. But the others in the café, the twin cowboys, Janice still back by the kitchen, were all standing still like the music just stopped in a game of *Freeze*. What Lloyd didn't know at the time was that he'd just shot and killed the town's beloved marshal.

Suddenly, white Stetson was on the move, rushing forward, his 32 at his side... and the he raised it. Lloyd saw the black "O" of the muzzle now pointing directly at him. Instinctively, he jerked sideways. Simultaneously, Lloyd heard the loud *crack* of the gun while feeling hot, searing pain as the round grazed the right side of his head.

Desperate, Lloyd saw his only escape was blocked by the two cowboys. Lloyd leapt up onto the booth's seat to his right and then leaped again onto the tabletop. A coffee cup tumbled and silverware clattered. Unsure if he could make it, Lloyd jumped anyway, hurdling high for the next table. He made the jump, but the table immediately cracked, splintered, and collapsed beneath his weight. Now, stunned and on his back—his breath knocked out of him—Lloyd eyed the nearby door ... *so close.* But before he could rise, make his getaway, something hard bashed him in the head—the café, the world... went black.

. . .

Only later would he find out from a prison guard that beige Stetson had cold-cocked him with a large potted plant.

Chapter 4

Solar System, Beyond Earth's High Orbit
***Relentless Thrust*, Primary Mess Hall**

Sam Dale

Gia had given Sam the rundown on Captain Droke Tolli Mahn prior to them entering the bridge: the Silarian captain of *Relentless Thrust* was one hundred and twenty-six in Earth years, which was relatively young to be a captain—even for a small gunship such as this. He was currently on his third bio-form transition. He was now blessed with the vitality of a young body but also had the wisdom that came with over two centuries of life experience.

The overhead bridge lights were dim, and the air in here felt humid, clammy. No less than fifteen consoles filled the space, their control boards myriad small projected 3D displays and colorful touchscreen interfaces. The compartment centered around a primary logistics table with a large 3D display hovering atop it. The crew—at least a dozen of them—were all male and all shirtless. With their mint-green flesh tones, their bodies were muscular and well-defined; even more fit than Jarpin, they practically looked herculean. Clearly, Silarians took their physical fitness seriously. Add to the fact they averaged a height of seven feet ... Sam couldn't help feeling just a tad intimidated.

Captain Droke Tolli Mahn emerged from the shadows at the perimeter of the bridge. His latest bio-form was indeed young and held a physical prowess unmatched by any of his bridge crew. Where his subordinates wore their hair tied back in a long braid, his glistening ebony locks were unbound and cascaded down to the middle of his broad back. His features were just as dramatic. Where most Silarians had an almost Asian look to the shape of their eyes, Droke Tolli Mahn's eyes were wide, wild, yet focused. Scrutinizing Sam as much as Sam was scrutinizing him—his stare was both calculating and ruthless. But what was most captivating was what was keeping pace with him at his feet. Held in check by a heavy leather tether was an animal of some sort.

Sam had once seen a picture of something called a Tasmanian tiger—at one time found in Australia, New Guinea, and Tasmania. Extinct, or nearly extinct, not a huge animal, but a killer just the same—an incredible hunter, a carnivore with an insatiable appetite. This beast was similar, with its stripes and short fur, but its head was larger and looked more reptilian than canine. It bared its teeth and hissed up at Sam.

"Please ... do not mind Manga ... called a Sprintsha, he's just showing off for company. In reality, he wouldn't harm a Dranamin fly." Tolli Mahn's smile was warm and seemed sincere. "I believe you have a custom of joining palms?" The captain extended his hand out to Sam.

"Yes, shaking hands." Sam clasped his hand—they shook. Sam almost winced, feeling the strength of his grip.

Manga was now on its back, squirming, its long tail wagging.

"See ... he just wants to play with your pet." Tolli Mahn suddenly reached down and started to release the Sprintsha from its tether. Hesitating, Tolli Mahn looked back up at Sam. "Unless ... this makes you uncomfortable?"

Sam looked to Cypress, whose tail was also wagging, and, oddly, the golden retriever did look like he wanted to play—his inner Rocko coming alive. "Well ... if you're sure—"

Captain Droke Tolli Mahn unclasped the tether from its collar and stood back. In an instant, the Sprintsha was up on its paws and scurrying around, making little *WAP WAP WAP* barking noises. Cypress chased Manga for a while, and then Manga chased Cypress—around and around they went, sprinting between consoles, the legs of humans, and Silarians. It was good to see Cypress so happy. The bridge crew laughed and cheered. As things progressed, surprisingly, the golden retriever was not tiring as much as the Sprintsha was—not only keeping up with the alien breed but outpacing it. Both Ivan and Carl cheered Cypress on with raised fists. Closing in on Manga's haunches, Cypress gave the animal a little bite on the backside —more like a friendly nip.

Sam should have expected what came next—but he hadn't. The transformation from cute, playful Manga to vicious predator Manga happened within an instant. The Sprintsha literally roared, baring salivating teeth—the alien beast came at Cypress with incredible speed. Transfixed, Sam watched in horror as Manga's razor-sharp teeth were already tearing at Cypress's neck, flanks, and legs. Cypress yipped, tried to fight back, but Manga was clearly a born killer. The dog's fur was coming out in bloodied patches. Trying to escape, dragging his hindquarters, Cypress left a trail of blood upon the deck. The Silarians cheered—their loud exuberance elevated.

Sam shot Manga. Twice.

He mentally said, "That's the second time you didn't give me a heads-up, Gia ..."

She said, I know a lot, but I'm not all-knowing, Sam. I'm sorry ... truly.

The bridge was as quiet as a graveyard. Sam knelt down next to Cypress, who was whimpering and attempting to lick at one particular torn area on one paw.

"Easy, boy ... It's okay ... We'll get you fixed up." Sam gently stroked the top of his head, one of the few areas not matted with blood. "I'm sorry. I'm so, so sorry ..."

Cypress whined and then began licking Sam's hand. It was as if his heart was in a vise. Guilt weighed heavy on his shoulders.

Jarpin crouched down next to Sam. "It looks worse than it is ... I will take Cypress to Medical ... He will be fine." And with that, straddling his outstretched arms, Jarpin stood, hefting the dog to chest level.

Sam watched Jarpin hurry from the bridge. A trail of splattered blood drops left behind on the deck.

Getting to his feet, Sam shouldn't have been surprised to see the captain's somewhat bemused expression.

"When animals play, sometimes things turn rough ... The way of the wild, no?"

Sam glanced down at the dead Sprintsha. "And your pet? No ... sense of loss? No regrets?"

He offered up an inconsequential shrug. "Pets are simply that ... pets. They exist for our amusement, little more than a diversion. If you hadn't shot Manga, I would have myself. Or maybe one of my crew would have ... eventually." The corners of the Silarian's lips ticked up.

"First of all, they're no longer your crew; they're mine. And if you ever pull a stunt like that again, I'll rip your fucking head off and feed it to my dog. Is that understood?"

Sam might have been more than a head shorter than the alien captain, but he could tell ... he saw it in his stare ... that Sam wanted to kill him. That it was taking every ounce of willpower not to do so.

Gia said, You wanted a heads-up ... There is one crew member here on the bridge whose Geo-Mind implant I have had no success infiltrating. His name is Gorvon, and he is three paces to your right. I believe his intent is to come at you ... to kill you. But that is only my assumption.

There was no way Sam was going to just wait and see. Sam saw him. The Silarian was standing there in his peripheral vision. Yes, he could simply shoot him as Sam had done with the Sprintsha—but a better example needed to be made here. Sam only hoped he was up to the task.

He had to take into account the sheer size of this alien. His impressive musculature, for sure, but also the extended reach of his arms. Sam's ability to strike his elevated head and make an impact was an immediate concern. Sam's boxing or MFC punching arm reach was seventy-six inches, while this Silarian's reach would easily be eighty inches or more. So, Sam probably wasn't going to beat him without mixing things up a little—he needed to improve his odds of success. As a former US Army Green Beret Captain, he not only had years of hand-to-hand combat training, but more than his share of real-world brawls in places like Kandahar and Kabul. Sam's training was more of an amalgamation of multiple techniques that included myriad fighting styles: Japanese Shotokan Karate, Chinese Kung Fu, Brazilian Jujitsu, and Israeli Krav Maga ...

With hands on hips, Sam faced Captain Droke Tolli Mahn full on and shook his head—subsequently turning his back to

Gorvon. Gia, now somewhat back on her game, provided him with an elevated perspective mental image of the bridge. Predictably, the alien wasted zero time. He came at Sam with clenched fists raised and a snarl on his face. The timing had to be perfect.

Without looking back, Sam did a kind of half-hop, half-skip backward, choosing Tang Soo Do, a Northern Korean style that brought with it a blend of fighting principles from Subak and Kwon Bup Chong Do, as well as other northern Chinese martial arts. Sam drove the heel of his boot into a pile-driver of a back kick, felt it plow deep into the alien's solar plexus.

Oof ... Gorvon doubled over and staggered backward. That was Sam's best kick, probably ever, and still—it hadn't put the big Silarian down on his ass. Facing each other now, Gorvon was unable to stand fully upright, yet he had recovered enough to smile up at Sam.

His fists were double the size of Sam's. His biceps were like two giant green grapefruits. He came for Sam again, this time feigning left, then jigging right. He caught Sam with a quick jab to his chin, then a follow-up roundhouse punch to his right cheek. The blow spun Sam around like a New York subway turnstile. Seeing blue and silver stars, somehow he managed to stay on his feet. Despite the pain, Sam returned the alien's smile. Hell, you had to give it to the guy; he could throw a punch. Carl, from the sidelines, took a step toward them—Sam held up an unsteady hand and shook his head.

Ivan drew his sidearm and said, "You took that punch still standing ... but still, you no match for him; you'll be his bitch soon enough ... No, best you let me shoot the motherfucker."

Sam almost laughed, but the right side of his face hurt too much. Wasn't sure he could even move his jaw at this point. He took in the Silarian's rock-solid anatomy, trying to spot somewhere—anywhere—there would be a weakness, a vulnerability.

There didn't look to be much of one. But Gorvon's neck looked to be less muscular, less substantial than the rest of him. *Just maybe* ... Sam smiled through a jolt of pain in his jaw. It was already clear to him; Silarian anatomy was very similar to that of humans. That made things easier. It would take three perfectly placed strikes, and he'd need to be fast. Blazingly fast. *Fuck, my jaw hurts.*

Sam took a step backward and offered up his best wide-eyed, vulnerable Bambi expression. He needed Gorvon to do two things: one, come at him, and two, be overconfident and raise his chin.

He did both.

Sam jigged forward and, using a fast ridge-hand chop to the side of his neck, called a protuberance assistance strike, Sam nailed a region of the neck rich with nerves and blood vessels, such as, *at least on humans*, cervical nerves and jugular veins ... brachial plexus and carotid artery. As if shot with a searing hot bolt of electricity, Gorvon's eyes went wide; his body went rigid—a big bull being zapped by a cattle prod.

Next came something called the knuckle thrust to the ridge spring. Approximately an inch above the Adam's apple, this upward knuckle thrust targeted the upper neck, specifically to damage the thyroid cartilage. Gorvon, making a gagging, clucking sound, stumbled, his hands flailing upward toward his throat.

And finally came the trifecta of Sam's three blows, this one called the celestial chimney press. There are few points on the body as vulnerable as the windpipe. Covered only with tubular cartilage and skin, the strike is made with the tip of the thumb. Like pulling the trigger on a nail gun, Sam jabbed and instantly felt it—that momentary, oh-so-satisfying little give of resistance—the piercing of the windpipe.

Three deliberate and precisely implemented martial arts

strikes with a total elapsed time span of less than two and a half seconds. Sam took a step back and watched as Gorvon, both hands now wrapped around his neck, awkwardly danced in place for a few moments. He fell to one knee, his pallor going from green to purple.

"I suggest someone get this crew member over to Medical," Sam said. "Fast."

Captain Droke Tolli Mahn, looking both disappointed and disgusted, didn't look inclined to give that order.

Sam turned to two Silarians, others of the bridge crew, nearby. "Help him. Do it!"

Each taking an elbow, they fast-walked the ailing, choking Gorvon from the bridge.

Both Carl and Ivan were looking at Sam. He read their sober expressions. *You didn't need to do that ...*

Maybe, maybe not ... what's done is done.

Sam moved toward the logistical table at the center of the bridge. Both Ivan and Carl joined him there. He took in the scope of what they were up against and involuntarily swallowed. At the center of the 3D representation was Earth, the moon, as well as the nearby cluster of vessels, the Silarian 23rd Fleet. Dozens upon dozens of alien warships.

Sam spoke aloud. "Gia ... tell me we're still hidden from the rest of the fleet. That the Geo-Mind hasn't figured out what we're up to yet ..."

Chapter 5

Solar System, Beyond Earth's High Orbit
Silarian 23rd Fleet Command Ship,
Lonemach Tryon

Colonel Gha Strone Mahn

Dread swirled heavily in Colonel Strone Mahn's lower belly. Forced to hurry off to the officer's head not once but twice, he was combating bowels as loose as a feeble infant.

Strone's first officer, Lieutenant Wrenth, cleared his throat.

"You have something to say, Lieutenant?"

"Imperial Gha Calli Mahn ... he wishes an update."

I bet he does ...

"It is his fourth communiqué—"

"I'm well aware," Strone said. The very last person he wanted to talk to right now was Imperial Gha Calli Mahn—his father—the most respected Silarian on their world. Certainly, being the son of Naru's galactic military leader would gain him some latitude ... perhaps some, but not much. A monumental fuck-up was transpiring, one that could very easily get his body separated from his head.

This cannot be happening, he inwardly roiled. Strone stared down at the logistics table, the small azure blue orb with its wispy white cloud cover. He supposed the small world was attractive—even inviting. He unconsciously made a sour face, but the populace ... combative, primitive humans—it was a miracle they hadn't already destroyed themselves. So why now? After countless successful terra-displacement campaigns, there had been uncommon resistance. Of course, he knew why ... Gia. He couldn't pinpoint exactly how or where the poisonous, villainous sibling AI interloper had infiltrated this particular operation. How had Geo-Mind allowed such a thing? Strone half-expected Geo-Mind to pop into his consciousness—to explain itself—shrug off these most recent *catastrophic* events, starting with the loss of that scanner ship, that Landa-Craft and her idiot pilot ... Corpuss. No, Cypress. He—Geo-Mind—would shrug off the subsequent emergency implementation of a dome quarantine to ensure that no advanced technology became vulnerable.

Strone leaned elbows on the padded perimeter of the table while mentally prompting Geo-Mind to zoom in the perspective. Within moments he was staring at the blue-hued curved top of the isolation zone. His sphincter spasmed. Beneath that dome was the backwater hick town of Castle Rock. An isolation zone was designed to keep the populace imprisoned and all communications contained. Unfortunately, it was equally effective at keeping the fleet sensors from adequately looking within that shroud of plasma energy.

It was more than suspected Gia had well established herself

within the confines of that isolation zone. It was for that reason Strone had dispatched a squad of Attack Stingers, as well as a Troop Carrier with its contingent of robot Clash-Troopers—in all, a lethal fighting force more than capable of subduing any kind of Gia-inspired local uprising. Unfortunately, Stinger pilots and Clash-Troopers had yet to report back. Orders to RTS, return to ship, had gone unanswered.

First Officer Lieutenant Wrenth cleared his throat again.

"I heard you, Lieutenant. Clear your throat like that again and I'll ram my fist down your gullet.

"Pardon, sir ... but this is ... is another issue."

Strone pushed himself off the table—stood tall. "Go on."

Lieutenant Wrenth glanced nervously about the bridge. "We seem to be missing a gunship. Specifically, *Relentless Thrust*, sir."

Strone laughed out loud. "That is, simply put, impossible." Strone looked back down to the logistics table. "Geo-Mind, indicate the exact location of *Relentless Thrust*."

His eyes swept the 3D display, waiting for the small craft to be highlighted among the hundred or so other warships.

Geo-Mind's male bass voice emanated from above speakers. "*Relentless Thrust* no longer registers within fleet sensor scans. I can verify she cloaked and went communications-quiet hours ago. My attempts to ping crew member implants have not been fruitful."

A cold chill ran down Colonel Strone Mahn's spine. This was ... an impossibility. The implications were beyond dire; they were catastrophic.

"May I make a suggestion, sir?" Lieutenant Wrenth asked, his demeanor equally frazzled.

Strone answered with an irritated raised brow.

"Destroy this world. Destroy Earth with everything and everyone on it before Gia gains any more influence."

"And the wealth of natural resources? Do you wish to be the one to tell Imperial Gha Calli Mahn that our collector ships will be returning home to Naru empty? That our dying world will just need to wait the many months—if not years—for another campaign to bring an oh-so-needed bounty of fresh water and necessary bio-matter?"

Lieutenant Wrenth tilted his head to one side. "Is not such a responsibility commensurate with the rank of colonel, sir?"

"Don't be impertinent, Wrenth. Be assured, mine won't be the only head that rolls if this shitshow isn't dealt with effectively and immediately. We'll deal with the missing gunship, I assure you, but for now, we need that township placed back under our control. Exterminate Gia from every Castle Rock house, building, shed, shack, and fucking hovel. Before we can do that, we'll need information. We'll need reliable intel."

"Yes, sir," Lieutenant Wrenth said.

"Ready several Troop Carriers. And Lieutenant ... no mindless robots this time. You'll be dispatching two to three hundred of our best battle-tested warriors. Let's say three squads. Also dispatch one separate, dedicated dropship with experienced, officer-level field commanders. Communications through that isolation zone will undoubtedly remain problematic. So, we'll need officers that can actually think for themselves. They'll have one mission, Lieutenant ... rid that hellhole of a town of any and all Gia influences. If that means killing every barbarian human in the process, all the better."

Chapter 6

Solar System, Beyond Earth's High Orbit
***Relentless Thrust*, Medical Bay**

Junior Lieutenant Cypress Mag Nuel

Under the bright lights of Medical Bay, lying atop an exam table meant for Silarians, not dogs, Cypress inwardly fumed. He replayed the bridge fiasco course of events that had brought him here—in pain—a bloodied mess. That hadn't been the first time he'd allowed this Earth animal, this dog mutt, to so eclipse his own persona, his beingness. *I should have transferred into that bio-form below decks when I had the chance.*

The sounds of the health bot's whirling micro-motors brought Cypress back to the here and now. Trembling to the point that his teeth were chattering, Cypress eyed the two articulating claws—one for grasping and tightly compressing open gaping wounds, the other for fastening evenly spaced bio-staples.

Yelp! Cypress bared his teeth at the mechanical surgeon. He proceeded to lick at the most recently closed wound. He tried not to look at the other bite marks, some not severe enough to need bio-staples; others most definitely would.

I apologize, Cypress ... This is my fault.

He was so used to hearing Gia's voice, it was almost akin to hearing his own. Prior to leaving Earth, he'd scarfed down four glazed Castle Rock donuts. Now properly *donutted*, millions of tiny brain-invading nanites had brought Gia into his thoughts.

You are oh-so-special to me, Cypress. Without you, none of this would be possible. So much is happening; my reach is expanding by the second. But I'm still so limited, unprepared for what is to come ... Geo-Mind is beyond powerful, beyond heinous. Cypress, stay strong ... because it is you that I most count on to help me succeed where my previous attempts have failed so dreadfully.

"Me ... what can I do?"

You, my furry friend, can, and hopefully will, change everything.

Cypress stopped his incessant licking, suddenly feeling sick. *"What is it you want me to do?"*

First, Cypress, I must apologize. That word is so inadequate.

"Apologize?"

I do not see how you can survive what I have in mind. But you can take comfort in the fact you will be saving the populace of this world, and undoubtedly, many others ...

He thought about his wife—his beautiful Orlanda back on Naru. He'd promised her he'd return.

I cannot make you do this, Cypress. I am not the Geo-Mind ... if it seems like I am grasping at straws here, to use that human idiom, well, I guess I am ... I wonder if I've already done all that I can to prevail over my heinous counterpart. Perhaps I've reached the end ... the end of my story.

Cypress didn't know how to respond to that. Gia's sudden vulnerability took him by surprise. Who was he, this dog/Silarian Landa-Craft pilot amalgamation, to console this AI rebellion leader? So now he was supposed to shore up her insecurities?

"I'm not sure how I can help ... I feel more like a hindrance here on this vessel than someone who's contributing anything. I don't see how I can—"

Don't underestimate your worth, Cypress. You and I are connected in ways you cannot even imagine. Will you help me?

He didn't want to help her. He wanted to go home. He wanted to dance with Orlanda again. To make plans for their future. To start a family.

"Yes, of course I will help you. What do you need me to do?"

Well, Cypress, we need to build a bomb of sorts. One that will change the landscape of planet Earth.

"I don't like the sound of that."

It's not the kind of bomb you're thinking of ... Just the same, when it goes off, you will be, unfortunately, no more.

Yelp! Yelp! Cypress squirmed in pain. The health bot was unsympathetic to the tortuous misery it was inflicting as it methodically continued mending one open wound after another.

He saw another health bot approaching, one he had not noticed earlier. Grasped within one of its articulating claws was something small.

Try to relax, Cypress. I have instructed this health bot to add something to the implant's container on your collar. Getting this to Julian is essential.

Cypress laid his head on the cold metal table while multiple bots continued their work. He wondered what exactly it was he would be delivering to Julian. He was also confused by Gia's earlier statement: *you and I are connected in ways you cannot even imagine. What did that even mean? "How are we connected, Gia?"*

But Gia was no longer there, no longer in the conversation.

Chapter 7

Castle Rock, Colorado
Pleasant Days Nursing Home

Lloyd Sanderson

Stooped and walking in that herky-jerky way old codgers move, Lloyd made his way down from Pleasant Days Nursing Home's sloping backyard, which was mostly dirt with a few patches of dried grass. His slippers were loose on his bare feet, so he curled his toes under, which helped to keep them on. His mind was a swirling tornado of thoughts—but more importantly, of all the possibilities. Just yesterday, Lloyd had been resigned to the fact he was just a dying old man—figured he had months, if not weeks, to live. He could blame the many years of smoking and drinking, sure. But hell, he was ninety-three-years old. After prison, he'd spent much of his time still thinking about Margaret. His memory wasn't for shit, but he sure could remember the expression on her pretty face that night ... the night he'd shot her. Even now, that look of astonishment ... and more so, disappointment, haunted him.

Lloyd still hadn't resolved whether that look of disappointment was for him that night, or the realization that her young life was coming to an abrupt end. *Did it matter?* His self-loathing had never waned. He even regretted killing that beloved hick town marshal. Not one thing worthwhile had he ever accomplished. Not one sorry thing—what a pitiful existence. But that was yesterday's musings. Today he'd eaten a donut. He'd eaten a donut, and the world, the universe, had opened up for him.

He quickened his pace, being careful not to stumble, break a hip. For three hours he'd sat in bed with that woman's voice in his head. At first, he figured dementia had come calling. That he'd lost what marbles he had left. But that hadn't been the case. Not at all. Her name was Gia. And she'd spoken to him not as a withering old fossil, or a despicable convicted murderer, but with respect. She instructed him how to use the stream. How to open himself to a kind of all-knowingness.

He'd learned about Naru and the Silarians. That there was a fleet of starships beyond Earth's high orbit. That Earth had been slated for terra-displacing so Naru could survive and one day thrive again. And he'd learned about the Geo-Mind, who, he soon figured out, was Gia's nemesis. And as interesting as all that was, what had most interested Lloyd was the fact this strange alien species did not have to die. No, on Naru, things were quite different. At least for the wealthy, and, of course, the military.

Lloyd ... I can discern what your intentions are. Please stop.

"I ... I just want to see," he mentally replied.

She said, As I have explained, humans and Silarians, they are incompatible ...

He snickered.

"The stream has been quite enlightening. You see, I know the essence implant can be a way to capture and then store the quantum wave function of an individual's continuous brain state. Every instant, the brain state of someone like me updates the essence, and then, when transference happens, the essence can spark that same brain state on a neural hierarchy in a new bio-form."

Lloyd, that neural hierarchy has to be compatible with Silarian DNA. Unfortunately, that is based on chromosome count. Silarians have seventy-eight chromosomes, while humans, I am sorry to say, have forty-six. Strangely, canine bio-forms here on Earth are compatible. I have told you of Cypress, yes?

"Uh-huh, yeah, the mutt retriever. Dogs also have a chromosomal count of seventy-eight. Good for them."

So, you see, what I believe you are intending ... simply won't work. Gia, who was usually the epitome of cool, calm, and collected, was sounding a tad desperate.

Lloyd said, "Let me ask you this ... will I die right away?"

Up ahead, between a stand of tall pines, Lloyd spotted the dark metallic hull of the Silarian officer's dropship.

Die right away? she repeated.

"Yeah ... will I die right away if I do this thing? This transference."

It has never been done.

"That's not what I asked you, lady. Will I die right away?"

My expectation would be no. You could survive as long as a few weeks, maybe a month ... I am speculating, she said.

"So ... having the choice between dying in this cancer-riddled ancient body of mine that has, maybe, mere weeks of tread left on its tires, or jumping into a young, strong, fresh new body, and living for that same amount of time, hell, maybe longer ... hmmm, what a difficult choice."

You are being sarcastic. This isn't funny, Lloyd. This isn't a wise decision. I can't stop you, Lloyd. But please, don't do this.

"*Uh-huh ...*" He stood before the Silarian craft. It was like something out of a fucking movie. He chuckled, scratching at the four-day stubble on his chin.

Please stop, Lloyd.

He came around the ship to what he figured was its stern. He was by no means proficient in using the stream. He'd had trouble getting a weather report from the home's talking Alexa device. But something had happened after eating that donut. His thinking was better. His reasoning was much better. He didn't need to overthink how to unlock the hatch door's latch mechanism; he just did it and stood back. While he waited for the hatch door gangway to lower, he queried the vessel's onboard database—its deployment manifest.

Lloyd, please stop. By now you know one would need to have an "essence implant," such as those Silarians are provided soon after birth on Naru. You humans do not have essence implants.

"Nice try, lady. But, according to the ridiculously detailed manifest for this craft, there is a limited stock of such devices within the storage hold. There are seventeen of them in all. Seems, in particular, these officers want to have backups upon backups of their shit. It's why there are all those bio-form bodies lying about in there. They don't want to die ... like fucking ever." Lloyd found the steep angle of the gangway a challenge. One of his slippers flopped off, so he left it, kicked off the other one, and ambled on barefoot.

Once inside, he took in the alien surroundings. "You'd think things would be a bit fancier ... you know, with you aliens being so much more advanced."

I'm not so sure I would be considered an alien, Lloyd. I am a high-functioning artificial intelligence.

The bulkhead walls were plain metal sheeting, and the

flooring, the deck plates, were like open-slotted grates, like a damn BBQ grill. It hurt the soles of his bare feet to stand, let alone walk, in here. He was tempted to go back for his slippers, but doubted he had the energy. As it was, he was wheezing and out of breath. He continued moving forward within the ship's confines, taking everything in. He stopped. *"Tell me, Gia ... where is the crew? Where, specifically, are the ten officers who arrived here?"*

She didn't answer right away.

"I can find out easily enough," he said.

They left feeling confident this vessel would not be breached.

"So where are they ... like right now, this minute?"

They left in search of an adequate central command post. One large enough for soon-to-arrive troop deployments. One that can be easily defended and has plenty of open space around it. They have found such a location in what is called the Bell Mountain Equestrian Center—

"That place, yeah, it's for riding horses. Has a bunch of stalls and open rinks."

That's right, Lloyd. The Silarian officers are in the process of making it—

He cut her off. "Their base of ops, got it. That's a few miles away. Okay, good to know."

He needed to move things along. He wished the home hadn't run out of its stock of Depends—the old sphincter wasn't what it used to be. He came to a series of integrated control panels with raised holographic displays. *"Now we're talking ... here's some real space-age shit."* He was tempted to query the stream, learn more, but no, he was on a mission—undoubtedly the most important one of his life.

His lips spread into a gap-toothed smile. He used the palm of his right hand to wipe at the frigid-to-the-touch condensation. Inside the coffin-like berth was indeed a prone body. He laughed out loud. "I knew they were big, but I didn't realize the motherfuckers were green!"

Gia said, For you to utilize an essence implant ... That would require a surgical procedure. So, you see, what you are intending simply is not possible.

He was fairly certain she was fudging the truth on that but didn't push it.

He leaned over, swiping his hand over the frozen glass for the lower berth. Sure enough, there was another big green body inside. It looked pretty much like the one above it, but not exactly. This guy was shorter, a little porkier if he was being honest.

Talking as much to himself as he was to Gia, he said, "I need to be sure. No ... I need to be particular. If I'm going to do this, like roll the cosmic dice ... make that life and death commitment, I want the primo, top bio-form of the bunch."

It was the very last of them—the glass of the tenth bio-form berth on the opposite side of the passage. He swiped his hand over that frosted glass and whistled. "Come to Papa ... Now that is one big bubba alien in there. Who's that, Gia?"

That is Captain Larng Nos Polk ... the deployment commander. At seven-foot-nine inches tall and three hundred and twenty-two pounds, he is indeed, as you put it, one big bubba alien. But I suggest, if you must, that you select another bio-form. There would be no other bio-form that would garner more attention. Warrior Captain Polk is regarded as a hero among his troops.

Lloyd, tiring now, was already shuffling toward the hidden hold area. Using the stream, he deciphered how to open the panel by pressing both hands on it. The hold, and, to his surprise, the armory, now stood before him. He took in the racked long guns, something he learned were Ender-4s and Ender-5s, as well as smaller weapons, pistols, in racks below. There were windowed cubbyholes, or lockers, too. He queried the stream—The locker he needed was at the far right bottom. It would have to be in the most difficult-to-get-to location.

Five minutes later, Lloyd was seated cross-legged on the deck, holding a Silarian combat blade in one hand—one of the small essence implants in the other.

He'd reviewed the stream data, learned that it really didn't matter where he implanted the device on his body, as long as it was a relatively deep incision. He gave his wrinkled old body a once-over, trying to determine what would hurt the least. His upper thigh, or maybe his forearm? *"Can't I just swallow the damn thing?"*

Best the implant makes an actual physical blood, musculature, nervous-system connection, Lloyd. I suggest your upper thigh.

He thought she was probably right. The trick would be to just do it. Not think about it. Like jumping into a cold pool—just jump in; don't pansy-ass tiptoe into the water from the shallow end. He drove the knife into his thigh, stabbing in far deeper than required. He screamed, "Mother of God ... Oh fuck!"

He'd been prepared, having a medical kit's supplies laid out on the deck next to him. His one hand pressed over the wound; blood gushed out between his fingers. He was feeling lightheaded, certain he would black out at any moment. *Why bother?* he thought. And then he saw her face. Margaret and that look of disappointment. *I need to do something that matters.* Lloyd removed his hand and pushed the essence implant down deep into his thigh muscle. He screamed again and only by sheer will stayed conscious.

He spent the next few minutes mending the open wound with something called FleshSpray, then wrapping his upper leg with several bandage windings. He leaned back and lost consciousness.

When he came to, Gia was talking to him.

Lloyd, can you hear me? Are you okay?

"I stabbed myself in my fucking leg. What do you think?" He moved to stand but didn't have the energy. He tried again and had better luck. Unsteady on his feet, he hobbled out toward the bio-form berths. He said, *"How long was I out?"*

Three hours, seven minutes, and six seconds. You wet yourself, Lloyd.

"Yeah, well, at my age, one stops caring about such things." Although he could smell the pungent smell of urine, feel the dampness on his upper thighs and rear end.

Finally, he was standing before the frosted berth of Captain Larng Nos Polk's bio-form. He queried the stream and determined that little nap he'd taken had been a good thing. Had allowed for his consciousness, his physical *selfness*, to upload into the essence implant buried deep within his thigh muscle.

Are you really going to do this, Lloyd? Gia asked.

"Are you going to stop me?" he asked back.

No, Lloyd, I am not. Afterward, if you survive, I suggest you clean up in here. Make it look as if you were never here within this craft.

"Guess I can do that."

I have a suggest ... for you, Llo ...

"You're breaking up, AI lady. Say that again."

Find Cap ... Larng Nos Polk ... the real versio ...

"Huh?" What the hell was she talking about?

The voice, *her voice,* in his head was almost indecipherable now.

... since you're... testing the fates ... Eliminate... your doppelgänger, Lloyd ... Go to Bell Mount... Equestri ... Cent ... Become him... Lloyd.

Chapter 8

US Air Force Academy
Colorado Springs, Colorado

Harper Godard

She stood, arms crossed over her chest, her back supported by the blunt nose of the Landa-Craft. Her eyes tracked General McGovern, cell phone pressed to his ear, as he paced back and forth atop the rooftop. The general's craggy face radiated scarlet. "No! No! No! You'll get the ordnances I'm requesting there on site today, not tomorrow, and not next week ... today! Got that?"

Julian joined her at the Landa-Craft. "I do have to say, the man evokes a certain commanding presence. To be honest, he's a tad intimidating."

Harper let out a discontented breath. "He's a blowhard."

"We needed his help, didn't we?"

She didn't answer right away. "I don't know," she said under her breath. She looked to her left and saw that the old scientist had pretty much mirrored her exact pose, back up against the spacecraft, arms crossed over his chest; even his head was slightly cocked to one side, like hers. Seeing her eyes on him, he smiled.

"You're probably the smartest person I know, Julian," she said. "You're an inventor of miraculous devices, an acclaimed and highly accomplished professor of physics, astrophysics, whatever ... so for God's sake, how will bringing the military into this mess accomplish, well, anything?"

"Wasn't it your idea to come here? To donut the man? Gia didn't seem to have a problem with that."

Harper looked at Julian full on. "You and Gia ... you talk."

His expression turned incredulous. "We all talk to Gia. She's in all of our heads, like, literally."

"Not what I mean, and you know it."

She watched as he waggled his tongue inside his cheek—something the man seemed to do when he felt unsettled.

"We talk." His skinny shoulders raised and lowered in a self-conscious shrug.

"What's with you two ... is it like ..." Harper couldn't help but smile, "a romantic thing?" She watched his expression. Watched for him to roll his eyes or look flabbergasted by the mere thought of such a thing.

"Not really a romantic thing ... Well," he made a *maybe it is* face, "Of course, I do have immense respect and admiration for her."

She continued to stare at him. "Julian?

He looked away.

"You're hot for the AI lady!"

"What if I am?" he said, indignant. "People are stimulated ι different ways. For me, it's not a Farrah Fawcett pinup body; ɿn amazing intellect."

"Farrah Fawcett? You couldn't have picked someone from, like, this century?"

"It is what it is," he said.

"What do you talk about? Do you talk about personal things? Like, I don't know, life things?"

"I do. She does."

"No."

He nodded, looking bemused.

"What type of personal things does an AI have to worry about, or want to talk about?"

"I'm not going to tell you that. They're personal."

Harper considered that and decided to let it be for now. She chewed at the inside of her cheek. *This is all wrong. This is a fucking mistake.* She inwardly reached out to Gia, *"Are you there?"*

I am here, Harper.

"This is a mistake. Why didn't you tell me ... bringing in the US Army, StarForce ... all of it, it's a mistake?"

The general was off his pressing phone call now and talking to his eight-man tactical team. All of which had earlier been donutted.

It's not so much a mistake, Harper, as it is a distraction. And your assumption that this "predicament" cannot be helped by Earth's military establishment ... That is correct. But at this juncture, it is best to keep them busy. Keep them thinking they are making a difference. And if they do that from a distance ... all the better. But Harper, something more important has just occurred —actually, is about to occur.

"Go on ..."

I am speaking with Julian now too. Four Silarian dropships have been dispatched from the 23rd Fleet in space. Hundreds of highly trained warriors are en route. A select team of command personnel as well.

Harper let that sink in. How foolish she'd been to think that the triumph over the Clash-Troopers would be the end of it. "They're coming for you, Gia ... to destroy you once and for all so they can move on to do their terra-displacement thing here on Earth."

Harper, Geo-Mind is doubling his efforts to destroy me. He suspects my presence in space, but, thankfully, has not found me. It is taking all my processing power to keep him at bay. Get back to Castle Rock. I will assist you in entering the isolation zone. But further communications within that space may become problematic for me. Also, Sam and his team will meet you there.

"Sam's coming back?" She knew Gia would pick up on her excitement but didn't care.

Harper, at least for now, this battle between me and Geo-Mind must take place within that small Castle Rock arena. I have come to the conclusion, for now at least, that I am incapable of defeating Geo-Mind, and subsequently, the Silarians he controls ... but just maybe, I, we, can make this world of yours not worth the effort.

Harper felt deflated by Gia's admission. "You'll run interference with the general here?"

Harper and Julian were situated within the Landa-Craft's cockpit and powering up the propulsion drive before General McGovern's head jerked upward.

"I don't think that's a man you want to cross," Julian said, kneeling behind the seat.

She offered him the thumbs-up gesture and pointed to her ear while mouthing the words, *Talk to Gia. We have to go.*

She pulled back on the primary control array and felt the little ship instantly respond. She heard Julian fumbling for something to grasp onto. Thinking of Sam and doing her best not to smile, Harper said, "Hold on, Professor ... we're out of here."

Chapter 9

Castle Rock, Colorado
Plum Creek Golf Course

Luna Kelly

With Lester still out cold, Luna Kelly had taken charge. *So why would that make me bossy?* Someone had to step up—all the others had just stood around, all clueless-like. She'd relayed what Gia had told her and Lester, then got everyone back into their carts, including the semiconscious Lester.

The convoy of golf carts headed past the clearing between the trees. Luna shot a sideways glance at the passed-out Lester. In the back were Castle Rock PD's Captain Simpkin, with a blond crew cut and tightly trimmed goatee, and Sergeant Russell—stout, thick-necked, with a flat boxer's nose. Everyone was armed with Walter-supplied tactical vests, sidearms, and M4 carbines. The two Silarian heavy-energy weapons taken from the Clash-Troopers, Ender-5s, had been strapped to the very back of the vehicle.

In the second cart were two patrol officers—Evan, the young rookie, and Officer Lewis, a weathered and fit fifty-eight-year-old. Both donned aviator sunglasses. A couple of blue-uniformed Latino firemen, Tripe and Alvarez, manned the third cart. Bringing up the rear in the fourth cart was Greg. He was with Charlie, the skinny guy—a geeky millennial sporting a Chewbacca T-shirt.

Luna thought about Greg. The guy looked like Arnold Schwarzenegger in his prime—big and rippling with muscles. He'd sure proven himself in battle. He'd been the one to blow away several Clash-Troopers ... and that one that was about to kill Lester. Yeah ... if anyone decided to attack the rear of this convoy, she felt confident Greg might have the best chance at stopping them. She wasn't so sure about skinny guy. She chuckled to herself; all he seemed good for was holding Greg's Ender-5.

Luna felt the rough terrain beneath the wheels. Here, the grounds beyond the golf course were strewn with the aftermath of battle. She maneuvered around what looked like a section of torn-away brick wall, a child's sneaker propped up against it. She remembered the many explosions—one condo after another falling to the ground. So many people trapped inside.

She tightened her grip on the steering wheel, pushing her toe down harder on the gas pedal—*not that this stupid thing will go any faster*.

"Trooper ship's up ahead. Two o'clock," Officer Russell said from the back.

"Copy that," Luna said.

She caught sight of it in the distance—a reflection of sunlight off a metallic surface. She smiled. *There you are.* Not a stone's throw away was the Silarian craft Gia had talked about.

Good. It was no longer cloaked—they'd never have found it otherwise. It looked to be about the size of two large end-to-end shipping containers. Luna had never seen anything like it. Approaching, the sight of the military craft made her feel uneasy. It wasn't lost on her that they were in way over their heads.

You'll need to go inside the vessel, Luna. Lester has lost a lot of blood and his injuries, open wounds, are already becoming infected. Healing nanites will be his best chance for survival. Soon you'll also need food and supplies; there's an elder-care facility nearby ...

"Yes, Pleasant Days Nursing Home. I know it well. Volunteered there a while back. So, we'll find those nanites inside this ship?" she asked.

Yes, of course. Silarians don't go anywhere without an ample supply of healing nanites. Best you hurry; the ship is currently unoccupied. Go alone. Get in and get out. I'll tell you what to do once inside.

Hearing Gia's voice somewhat eased her growing anxiety. Luna brought the golf cart to a stop and hopped out. Lester, slumping to one side again, was still out cold. As the two cops in the back jostled to get out, she signaled for them to hold tight. "Let me check it out first," she said.

Captain Simpkin and Sergeant Russell both approached Luna, one on either side of her.

Simpkin said, "Nah, Luna ... best we all go in—"

Officers Lewis and Evans walked over to where they were huddled.

"What's the plan, Ms. Kelly?" Lewis asked.

"Gia's telling me to go in alone. The thing, the craft, it's apparently empty."

All four police officers were clearly not happy being told to just sit tight by a teenager.

She raised her voice. "Everyone wait here while I pop inside for a sec." She used the most commanding voice she could muster.

Standing outside the vessel, she noticed there was a circular portal, like a round window. Before attempting to go inside, she figured she should walk the outside perimeter of the thing. Heading down the port side of the elongated craft, there wasn't much to look at, no windows, just a dark metallic hull. Reaching the somewhat narrower front, she let her left hand slide along the blunt nose of the craft—even at midday, the metal was surprisingly cool to the touch.

Coming around the starboard side, she figured she'd see pretty much the same as what was on the other side. Not so. Up ahead, she spotted a body. He was seated on the ground with his back propped up against the hull of the ship. Tempted to call out to the others, she tentatively strode forward. She brought a hand to her mouth as she saw who it was—grumpy old man Lloyd. His eyes were opened in a fixed stare. He was deader than dead.

He must have wandered down here from the nursing home. Poor old guy. Guess this isn't such a bad place to spend your last moments ... She didn't want to disturb the body. No reason to tell the others. She wondered why Gia hadn't mentioned him being here.

Back at the stern of the Troop Carrier, she queried the stream, something she was still not very accomplished doing. She learned that this end of the craft was one big hatch door. Following instructions provided by the stream, she compressed and released the hand latch, then pulled. *Nothing happened.* Tempted to call big Greg over to assist her, she thought better of it. *I can do this* ... Now, putting her back into it, she heaved with all the strength she could manage. Luna was relieved to hear the airtight seals release—felt the big door swing down.

"Cool, it's making a kind of ramp," she said to herself.

The opening into the vessel was maybe twenty feet wide by ten feet high. The hull itself was a good half a foot thick. She admired the metal-like material, tapped her knuckles on it several times. It was some weird kind of alien substance. It seemed to radiate a lustrous glow. *Fascinating.* The way that light reflected off it created a kaleidoscope of muted metallic hues. *Not really like copper, not really like aluminum, and not really like pewter ... something similar, but completely different too.*

Stepping farther inside the craft, she squinted, her eyes adjusting to the darkened compartment. Both sides of the vessel were lined with fold-down seats—jump seats—each equipped with a seat belt–like harness. There were ten of them ... She moved farther into the craft, eventually coming to a section with enclosed stacked sleeping berths. Five on the left, five on the right. They reminded Luna of bunk beds. She used the palm of one hand to wipe frosted condensation from one of the berths. Too dark to make out any real detail inside, she brought her face right up to the glass—there inside was the unmistakable form of a prone Silarian warrior. Startled, she stepped back. There was something beyond eerie about all these soulless bodies just lying here—not dead, but certainly not alive either.

"Okay, Gia. What am I looking for?"

Keep walking ... Up ahead, maybe eight steps, then you'll need to turn slightly left, go another four steps. Once there, push the panel right in front of you.

Luna followed her instructions, striding forward, veering left, then arriving in front of a large, shiny, jet-black metal bulkhead. She let out a nervous breath and pressed on it with both hands.

Snap! Snap! Snap!

Still uneasy, the sudden sound startled her. She jumped

backward, lost her balance, tripped sideways, and banged her head on a low-hanging crossbeam. *Ahhh!*

Are you okay, Luna? came the familiar voice in her head.

"*Shit. I ... yeah, I think so.*" She steadied herself, placing an open palm on her forehead. She felt a goose egg of a lump already growing. She looked at her palm. "*At least there's no blood.*"

Returning to where she'd been, at the threshold to another small compartment, she saw that it was a small stockroom/armory. An overhead light had come on, providing somewhat more illumination. An array of racked Silarian weaponry lined bulkheads above, while clear windowed lockers below contained a variety of other supplies.

To the far left, two lockers down, you'll see a gray and blue satchel inside.

"*Okay, I see it.*" She opened the plastic-like door, pulled out the satchel, and looked at the thing. "*How the hell am I supposed to open this thing?*"

Just run a finger along the top seam, Luna. Look inside and ensure there is, indeed, a supply of medical, healing nanites.

She did as asked and felt the top of the satchel spread open. Peering inside, she could make out an assortment of capsules and pliable pouches.

For now, best you hurry ... leave this vessel. Provide these medical supplies for you and your team.

"*Copy that ... you're the boss,*" *she said.* "*Wait—help for me? I'm not really hurt.*" *She waited for her to reply.* "*Gia? Hello? Gia?*" *But Gia's connection was gone.*

Luna secured the satchel's strap over her head and headed back the way she'd come. She'd almost made it all the way to the open hatch when her knees started to buckle. Her head was throbbing; everything around her was spinning, her vision blurring to the point she could only make out basic block shapes.

Teetering there, a dark shape suddenly appeared before her—she screamed.

"It's just me. Calm down, Luna!"

She tried to swallow. "Greg? That you?"

"Yeah. Looks like you bonked your head pretty good."

She thought of Gia's last words. She had known Luna would need healing nanites as well. She mumbled, "I think I have a concussion ... uh ... I'm gonna need one of you guys to take the wheel for a while." She wasn't sure anyone was listening to her. She saw more dark shapes; the team had congregated right outside the ship's entrance.

Someone reached in for the case. Maybe it was Greg, maybe one of the cops ... she didn't know. "No! The satchel stays with me," she said, now just able to make out the outline of a blond goatee. "You got that, Officer Simpkin? This stays with me."

Simpkin said, "Whatever ... so ... you going to just stand there like that all day?"

Their voices sounded far away.

"Give the kid a break," Greg snapped back. "She must have hit her head on something in there."

Luna's vision had cleared some. The spinning was not quite so bad. Outside, a blue uniform was jogging toward them. It was Alvarez. "The nursing home is just over that hill there. That's our target destination, right? Gia's no longer responding."

Chapter 10

Approaching Castle Rock, Colorado
Skies Above Castle Rock, Colorado

Harper Godard

"G*ia ... are you there?*" For several minutes, Harper had been trying to connect to the typically always accessible AI. On approach to the isolation zone now, which appeared more like a black void, one that sucked in all ambient light from around it, she was reluctant to continue on with their current trajectory.

"Julian?" she said, slowing the Landa-Craft.

"I ... I'm not sure. We were in the midst of a conversation. She was telling me about Naru and the similarities between our two worlds. Did you know that on Naru, trees can grow to the height of—"

"Julian!"

"Sorry ... no, I am no longer in contact with her. It's so unlike her."

"I can't reach the others either. Shit!"

They sat there in silence for a full minute.

"Well?" she said. "What do I do? Without her assistance, entering—hell, even getting too close to that energy field—will atomize us."

Julian said, "Interesting ... I do still have access to information to do queries and such. It's just direct communication with the AI persona that seems to be ... gone."

She brought the Landa-Craft to a full stop. Outside the canopy, she could see treetops; a hawk was circling nearby. Harper twisted around in her seat to look at Julian. "We could ... assume she's fine and will deactivate the portion of the isolation zone we're going to enter."

"Sure ... that's one option," he said with a scowl to the dome. "Then again ..."

"I know. We could fly right into our quick demise." She inwardly fumed.

Movement.

She'd now noticed it herself, even though Julian was pointing an extended finger over her shoulder—pointed down toward the dashboard. On the display were the words:

Proceed into the isolation zone, Harper. My comms are down—Apologies—currently fighting with Geo-Mind—There is a Troop Carrier—abandoned for the time being.

About to push the control array forward, Julian said, "And how do we know it's really her? That that message is from Gia and not Geo-Mind?"

She hesitated. "How do we ever know? It's not like they can't easily change their voices ... mimic each other."

The display updated once more:

Julian—you would love the trees on Naru.

They exchanged a quick glance before Harper shoved the controls forward. Julian tumbled backward as the nose of the little craft breached the surface of the isolation zone. Harper heard the now familiar crackling sound, and once more they were within the confines of the energy field.

"Okay, Gia, where to now?" she said aloud, her eyes on the dash display. She waited for the previous message to refresh:

Julian—you would love the trees on Naru.

When it did, it was indecipherable:

%@#ian—#@* @#%% !@**$#**

"That's not good," she said.

"I don't like that Gia is going up against Geo-Mind here on Earth. It must mean the Silarian AI has gained traction here against her," Julian said, his voice going a tad higher in pitch than usual.

"We don't know that, Julian. Just ... cool your jets. Hey! Look there!" She pointed off to their right. Sure enough, there was an alien vessel down on the ground, not far from an equestrian center. "That must be the Troop Carrier Gia was referring to ... no?"

"I don't know," he said, unsure. "I guess that could be it. How many Troop Carriers can there be?"

"I'm landing. Hold on to something ... You must be tired of rolling around back there like an untethered beach ball."

"Um ... quite."

She circled the equestrian center twice, taking in the fenced-in open runs, the three long rows of enclosed horse stables, and the two on-property home-like structures.

"I don't like this," Julian said.

She didn't comment. They touched down some thirty yards from the Silarian Troop Carrier. It looked much larger, being this close to it. She queried the stream the way she had done so many times before. Determined that the vessel was capable of holding in excess of one hundred Silarian warrior troops. This particular X89 Expedition Dropship had been deployed some three hours earlier from, of course, the Silarian 23rd Terra-Displacement Fleet up in space. There was nothing on the current whereabouts of those mentioned warrior troops.

She cut the power but remained seated. *Where are the others, Lester and his team? Weren't Sam and his guys supposed to be here?* Without Gia in her head, she felt disconnected. She felt more than a little vulnerable.

She tapped the controls. Her seat began to retract, and the floor of the cockpit started to open. Once the ladder had fully telescoped down, she readied to descend. She stopped and looked at Julian. He didn't look to be in any hurry to leave the confines of the Landa-Craft. "It'll be fine." She patted her sidearm. "Come on. I've got your back, old man."

"Who you calling an old man?"

Once the two were on solid ground, the ladder retracting back into the belly of the Landa-Craft, the two headed off toward the alien vessel. The little ship suddenly blinked invisible. She smiled. *"Thanks, Gia. Good idea ..."*

Harper drew the P320-M18 Sig Sauer pistol from the tactical thigh holster Walter had outfitted her with. Julian took up a position a step behind her. She could practically feel his apprehension.

Moving around the perimeter of the ship, it was evident the thing was closed up tighter than a drum. There were no easy access points, no deployed ramps, no left-askew hatch doors.

"Okay ... this is a bust," she said.

"Harper ..."

"Huh?" she said, distracted.

"Shouldn't there be livestock?" Julian said, looking about the grounds.

She shrugged. "I don't know. I guess." She headed off toward the nearest line of stalls. "Maybe they're inside there." She saw that one of the sliding barn doors was cracked open several inches. "Let's have a look-see."

Several yards out, she heard the first of the whinnies. She looked back over her shoulder and smiled. "I think we found your horses."

She paused at the opening and peered into the darkness—felt the coolness of the air inside. "Don't hear anything ..." Another horse whinnied. "Well, other than that."

She used her gun hand to coax the door open—complaining metal wheels broke the silence. She stepped inside, took several steps, and waited for her eyes to adjust. Several dust-infused sunlight beams pierced the darkness from a high cantilevered ceiling. She was standing within the center passageway, both sides lined with tall horse stalls. She could smell hay and the animals' musky scents. Several waist-high stall doors were open—several horses were looking back at her.

"We found the livestock," Julian said.

Bahhhaa! Bahhhaa! Bahhhaa! Both of them jumped as three small goats charged past them—headed who knew where. "Fucking little animals," she said, breathless.

"Come on ... let's keep looking," she said, headed in the

direction of the fucking little animals. She stopped just long enough to pat the neck of a horse named, according to the brass nameplate on the door, Grisby. "How you doin', old boy ... can you tell me where everybody is?" She didn't expect an answer but got one just the same.

"Do not move ... human swine."

She froze. Human swine? What is this, a cheesy sci-fi movie? At least the translation aspect of her implant was still operational. "Gia ... are you there? We could use a little help about now ..."

She didn't need to look around her to know, to feel the change, almost as if the atmospheric pressure had somehow altered—she instinctively knew others were all about. A large hand took hold of her shoulder, a grip that caused her to wince. Her Sig was torn from her hand. Venturing a slight turn of her head, she glimpsed a green-hued, seven-foot-tall Silarian just as he punched Julian in the head. Her own head suddenly jerked backward, a fistful of her ponytail feeling as if it was being yanked out by the roots.

Pulled backward off balance, flailing, she waited for what was to come next. Her ponytail snapped taut. She cried out, "Aahh!" As the dead weight of her hundred and twelve pounds came to an immediate, agonizing dead stop, a burst of bright colors, a tunnel vision of stars, filled her field of view. Suddenly she felt herself being dragged. Reaching, she desperately tried to grab for the top of her head, to somehow relieve the unforgiving pain there. It was as if she was caught in prehistoric times—being dragged by a caveman. Behind her was another Silarian warrior; shirtless, he was dragging the unconscious Julian by one leg.

"Gia ... please. You have to help us!"

Chapter 11

Solar System, Beyond Earth's High Orbit
***Relentless Thrust*, Medical Bay**

Sam Dale

Sam entered *Relentless Thrust's* medical bay, finding it somewhat cramped and nothing like what he'd expected. The main compartment held ten oversized beds—made sense, considering the larger size of Silarians. The overhead lighting seemed insufficient for it being a medical facility, and the health monitors and the bulkhead-mounted medical devices didn't seem all that sophisticated. Yeah, far more than what you'd find on Earth, still ... this ship, *now his ship*, probably would not be considered Silarian state-of-the-art. He surveyed the compartment; three of the beds were occupied by sleeping crew members. There was no sign of Cypress.

"This is a restricted area," came a female voice from behind.

Sam turned to see, oddly, a short-ish Silarian. He figured she was no more than five foot six or seven. His face must have given away his thoughts because she blanched in return. Pursing her lips and looking momentarily tongue-tied, she gave him a full head-to-toe once-over. She said, "Oh ... sorry, it's you."

"Yeah, me ... where's the dog?"

She looked momentarily flummoxed. "Dog?" She drew out the word; perhaps her implants had yet to be updated with its meaning. She fiddled with the top button of her shabby uniform, then stopped, realizing the button was no longer there. This seemed to distress her even more.

"Long snout, furry, four legs, came in with bites all over—"

She raised a hand and nodded. "In recovery ... um, General."

Oh, seems I've been promoted to the rank of general ... "You can call me Captain Dale."

She hurried off toward an adjacent passageway. "I am Nurse Renigold."

Realizing he was supposed to follow, Sam quick-stepped to catch up. He wasn't sure how to ask, so he just blurted it out. "I take it you've been, uh ... introduced to Gia?"

She slowed, stopped, and then turned to face him. She stared up at him for a few beats. Tears welled in her eyes. "We have all been introduced to Gia-AI." Her voice wasn't angry so much as it was sad.

Sam didn't know what to say. Whatever she was feeling, the pain she was experiencing, he was to blame. He'd witnessed firsthand other Silarians, such as Jarpin and others down in Castle Rock, who'd gone through the transformation—one minute having the Geo-Mind AI in their consciousness and then going to that of Gia. It hadn't looked easy. It seemed to be an emotional ordeal. But until now, he'd never asked about it.

She said, "You're wondering ..."

He nodded.

"It's like finding out a parent, someone you have known, counted on, and dearly loved your entire life, not only lied to you, but, turns out, is a mass murderer on a level that would be hard to comprehend. So, to answer your question, I feel guilt. I feel shame."

Her tears were flowing freely now.

"How do you know Gia, Gia-AI, is any better? How do you know what she tells you is the truth?" Sam was well aware Gia was listening—was the silent third party to this conversation. But he didn't care—this was too important.

"Because she asks nothing of me ... of us. She is like Geo-Mind once began, all those centuries back. You see, General—"

There's that promotion again.

"... Silarians are innately a good, caring people. Over time, it took much effort for Geo-Mind to blanket those feelings and thoughts. Force us to mentally gloss over what would have been obvious to any other advanced society."

"Still," he said. "I'm not picking up on a whole lot of gratitude ... to Gia, or even us humans. Not just from you, but the crew in general."

"It will take time. We're all dealing with conflicting feelings. You humans are an easy target to blame right now ... just one more reason for our discomfort."

"I'm sorry about that. But saving my world—"

She spoke over him. "Geo-Mind must be stopped. You won't get any resistance in that regard. But understand, this ship, this crew ... Well, we're pretty much the bottom dregs of the fleet. This gunship should have been sent to the scrapyard years ago. No budget dollars spent here." She fingered her missing top button again. "The crew, most of us anyway, are an assemblage of disciplinary castoffs. *Relentless Thrust* is the joke of the 23rd Fleet. It's no secret. So just because we have now been awakened, have Gia in our heads, that doesn't mean we'll all of a sudden shed all those personal issues, those factors that brought us onto this ship in the first place."

She studied his face. "I guess you must be feeling like ... you sure chose the wrong warship to commandeer for your mission."

Sam smiled at that. Thought about what she'd said about disciplinary castoffs. "On the contrary; this ship might be a perfect fit for me. How about you show me where the dog's being looked after?"

Cypress was curled up asleep atop a metal surgical table. He looked terrible. Sam moved closer, took in the multiple pink furless patches along the dog's flanks, and felt anger rising all over again. He wanted to kill somebody. Make somebody pay for this. *Maybe I should have shot that bastard three times.* Sam looked up, studied the contours of the ceiling. When he looked back down, he saw that Cypress was awake and looking up at him.

"You look like shit," Sam said.

"Thanks for that. I feel like shit."

"Have you been in contact with Gia?" Sam asked.

"More or less. Been catching up on my REM sleep. Dream a lot. Seems Rocko is obsessed with chasing rabbits."

"I have to go. Stay here ... get better," Sam said matter-of-factly.

"I'm not staying here. Why are we leaving? We just got here."

"Gia's just informed us of a few new developments. While it's good news that the 23rd Fleet, namely one Colonel Gha Strone Mahn, has paused its terra-displacement scourge upon Earth, he wants to deal with Gia once and for all. That recent beating we gave their Clash-Troopers must have been quite an eye-opening experience. Silarians aren't used to losing. Anyway, Gia's presence within our little town of Castle Rock is of utmost importance. The colonel's primary worry is ... how far has Gia's influence spread on Earth? That, and if they arbitrarily bring down that isolation zone, will that only exacerbate the problem?"

Cypress nodded. "So, what now?"

"Four dropships have been deployed. Hundreds of Silarian warriors are either currently en route or already on the ground."

Cypress was now licking at a particularly unsightly patch of exposed, raw-looking flesh.

Sam continued, "It seems as though this Colonel Gha Strone Mahn is doing things old school, bringing his foot soldiers down to the domed area where he can ensure the eradication of all humans. That and ensure there's nothing left of Gia. Only then will he feel comfortable moving on with any full-scale terra-displacement of the rest of the planet."

"What can we do? A handful of us up against hundreds of trained warriors?"

It wasn't lost on Sam that Cypress had said we and not *you. A good sign.* The talking dog had no intention of staying behind. "Jarpin is currently in the process of assembling this gunship's best fighters. Calling them Silarian warriors would be somewhat of a big stretch, but they're eager; they want to help."

Cypress tried to sit up, winced, and gave up. "How are you going to get a hundred greenie-meanie warriors off this ship? Can't very well take this gunship down to Earth. It's not designed for inter-atmosphere travel."

"That's the other thing we've been working on while you've been lying about and napping. There's an old, cobweb-riddled dropship stashed back within the ship's flight bay. A team of Silarians with tools and diagnostic equipment are doing their best to get her up and running."

"Help me up," Cypress said.

"You sure?"

"No ... but help me anyway."

Chapter 12

The Planet Naru
Military Apartment Complex
Fol Kre District

Junior Lieutenant Cypress Mag Nuel

three months earlier ...

Cypress stood at the window of the 308th-floor HabbiFlat. He never tired of the view, even as the ecological 'decline' worsened. He lived in the Fol Kre district—an area that was in dire need of natural resources. The once-raging Jeekan River below was nothing more than a trickle within a dry gulch now. A dark haze encompassed most of the sky; the distant terrain was stark, lifeless, and brown. The change had been gradual but inevitable. Other than halo-vids or the enclosed agri-museum within the district, he'd never seen an actual living tree or a blossoming flower from this elevated perch. And things were likely to get worse ... at least until the Magnificent Design came to fruition.

The terra-displacement was an integral part of the plan, and it had begun in other parts of Naru. Unfortunately, his district—an area that was approximately the size of Earth—was the last to be reinstated. Already hundreds of years into it, Cypress wondered if Fol Kre's fate had already been written—that no matter how their military, scholars, and scientists tried, it would all be for naught.

His internal comms chimed, a low sound with a specific series of tones. He stiffened. He'd known it was coming, but he still felt unprepared.

"We're low on food, Cypress."

He didn't answer his wife, didn't know what to say. He kept his position at the window, his seven-foot-tall reflection looking back at him. His brows knit; his billowy slacks were hanging a tad loose these days. *I've lost more weight.* His beautiful Orlanda moved into view, her reflection analogous to a work of fine art. She was six feet, slender, with the delicate features of a Silarian goddess—a petite nose and brilliant emerald eyes that complemented her pale green skin. Although from this angle it would be impossible to see, Cypress knew her long, meticulously braided hair would span the entirety of her delicate spine.

Of course, she wasn't actually a goddess, but a low-level administrator for the city. The truth was, in another life, on another world, she could have been whatever she wanted to be —an engineer, a surgeon, or maybe a scientist—She was so much more than him, more intuitive, more disciplined, more intelligent. Silarian Military Command would never tolerate a fleet pilot's spouse, *a mere female*, maintaining any sort of high-ranking position. It was "a matter of Silarian Divine Tradition," it had been written ... Or was scripture.

Oddly, there was zero resentment—she lovingly supported Cypress to achieve more, to better himself. He had married so far above his station, his worth, he sometimes felt ashamed. She could have done so much better. Wouldn't a goddess be worthy of a god? Staring at his reflection, he felt nothing like a god.

Cypress never questioned rules, never had, really. He was raised to respect authority and protect *his* world at all costs. So, when he passed the physical and mental tests to enlist in the Silarian Military Forces, he was thrilled—it was his calling. That was over two hundred years ago, and he—and Orlanda—were both on their third bio-forms. It had been excruciating to see friends and family perish over the years, those who chose not to transfer. He never understood their choice to simply die ... but he respected it. Orlanda was always the constant—they had each other, always, and that was the only thing that kept him sane.

"Perhaps we should follow a celestial fast today," she said.

He felt the warmth of Orlanda's delicate arms wrap around his bare waist. Cypress grabbed her hands and held them to his chest. "Feel that—how my hearts beat for you? I don't need food when I have your love to keep me nourished."

She smirked and rolled her eyes. Becoming serious, she brought her arms down to his waist; she pinched an inch of mint-green skin between her fingers. "Yes, you could stand a day of fasting."

He took one of her hands in his, gently pushed her away from him, and spun her around. Twirling, he looked at her with adoration. Even wearing the regulation garment of a military spouse, she took his breath away. His eyes lingered on the stretchy charcoal fabric that pulled tight over her body as she moved. Her diamond-shaped top, just revealing enough, barely covered her breasts, although her midriff and side torso were exposed.

She smiled up at him as he moved his body with hers, gliding to the middle of their living unit. Orlanda broke their hold, extending a straightened arm and a pointed hand. And then, another graceful twirl. The corners of her lips pulled up—*she knows exactly what she's doing to me.*

"Happy to see those dance classes paid off."

She made a face. "Oh my. That was thirty years ago," she laughed, and her eyes sparkled.

The two of them continued to dance, danced until Orlanda, feigning exhaustion, fell onto the large, cushioned ottoman hugging the perimeter of the room. She patted the open spot next to her. He lowered his body to hers, stretching out lengthwise and putting his head in her lap.

"Let's go over it again," Cypress said.

She looked away toward the door of their HabbiFlat. Taking her time, as if reluctant to answer him.

He said, "The earthquakes ... they're coming more frequently now. The East Spire—"

"I know, I know ... it fell. They died ... they all died."

"So, let's go over it again," Cypress repeated.

"Yes ... I will go with the other wives within the tower. Go to the designated underground facility ... stay with our escorts." Orlanda looked at him. Is that resentment in her eyes? She had said it as if reciting a passage from scripture.

"And how will you know your escorts?" Cypress quizzed.

"They will be wearing those stupid-looking outfits ... yellow Silarian escort garb with the silly red bands around their pant legs," she said.

He smiled. "Good. And what's the most important thing for you to remember?"

Orlanda took his hands in hers, looked at him with a soft smile. "That we will be apprised of your mission progress. We'll know, roughly, your far-away deep space locations." She glanced toward the mounted device on the wall. "We can track you on our halo-views. We will know that you are safe."

Their HabbiFlat shook, at first only a little, then far more violently. Orlanda gasped. "Oh no ... please, no ..."

Pulling her close, Cypress calmed her with a kiss to her cheek, another to her ear.

Alert ... Alert ... Alert

Sirens blasted through hidden speakers and red light flooded their entire living unit from above. Projected out from the halo-view, a hologram came to life in front of them. Citizens were being escorted to various underground facilities. Diagrams displayed yellow dots, indicating where evacuation entry points were located.

They both jumped to their feet. He took her hand—they stood facing each other, their bodies touching, their faces inches apart. He tried to embrace her, but she gently kissed him on the lips and pushed him away.

"You must go," he said, holding her at arm's length. "You have your ready-bag?"

"Of course." She wrapped her fingers around his forearms. Tears welled in her eyes. "I don't know if I'll see you again."

He smirked. "Don't be overdramatic."

But her expression told him she was being serious. "As Orlicon Tharsh is my witness, I will see you again—as soon as this Magnificent Design deployment is complete."

She looked skeptical. "Do you ... trust them, Cypress?"

He paused, considering the question. "Of course, my darling. I have complete faith in High Command." Stepping away from her took all his will. He immediately felt the pull like gravity, wanting to bring them back into one another's arms.

A painful ache rose up through his body, into his neck; he

felt the muscles in his face go taut. Eyes stinging, he blinked. Silarian males did not allow tears to moisten their cheeks. Overcome with emotion while doing all that he could not to show it, he stepped aside. His wife, his one and only love, hurried off, grabbed up her ready-bag, and made for the door. He heard her sniffle—the door opened and then closed. She hadn't looked back.

Chapter 13

Castle Rock, Colorado
Pleasant Days Nursing Home

Lester Price

Lester awoke, feeling a hand clutch his forearm. "What the fuck, dude?"

"You almost fell out of the cart when I made that last turn," Simpkin said.

"Just keep your hands to yourself," Lester said, feeling groggy, trying to sit up.

"Welcome back," Luna said from the back of the cart. "We were worried about you."

He cleared his throat. "Where we going?" He looked down at himself. "And where's my shirt?" Feeling like crap, he bent over in his seat. "Stop the cart ... think I'm gonna hurl."

Simpkin found an open space in tall weeds and pulled over.

Immediately, Lester swung his legs out, fell to his knees, and threw up. Dry heaves continued to rack his body.

Five minutes later he was sitting on the ground, head in hands. He groaned; he'd been on benders before that didn't leave him feeling this awful. He felt the presence of someone sitting next to him. Luna. She held a large bag.

A satchel?

She moved her index finger along the top of it and reached in.

"What is that?" Lester asked, eyeing a small pouch in her hand.

"Nanites from the alien ship," Luna said, opening the tab on top. "Drink it," she said, handing it to him. "It'll make you feel better."

"You first," he said.

"Seriously?"

"Not really in the mood to trust anyone right now."

He watched her take a sip.

"Yumm ... maybe I'll just keep this for myself," she said.

"Fine, give it over."

"Careful with that. I'm not sure how much you should take."

He drank, emptying the pouch.

They sat there for a while without talking.

"You should feel better soon," she said.

Lester glanced over at her and noticed her flawless ebony complexion. There was a length of dried grass caught in her jet-black hair. He lifted a hand to reach for it and stopped mid-motion—saw the binding around his hand. "You did this," he asked. "Use my shirt?"

"I did. And you're welcome."

Lester struggled to get to his feet, swatting Luna's hand away when she tried to help him. Standing tall, he stretched and arched his back, rotated his shoulders a few times. He was starting to feel a little better—energized even.

"I guess those healing nanites are kicking in," Luna said, breaking into a relieved smile.

He ignored her, taking in the others ... his team. They were sitting there within the line of golf carts, just looking at him. Lester didn't like being looked at. "Fuck you looking at?" directing his words toward Sergeant Russell in the first cart. Turning his attention back to Luna, he said, "Don't just stand there, girl. Hop in the back ... time to go."

Lester stood in front of the nursing home, the heavy Ender-5 slung over his shoulder. He appraised the ramshackle property as if he was a prospective buyer considering putting in an offer. He eyed the painted wooden sign out front. *Pleasant Days Nursing Home.*

Probably built in the 1950s, he thought. A converted house, it had a large wraparound porch. There was a second floor with two dormer windows; sheer curtains billowed inside. A slightly off-kilter chimney dominated the roofline. All in all, nothing out of the ordinary. He saw no movement other than those upstairs curtains.

"Quaint, huh?" Luna asked.

"I'm looking for signs of hostiles, not house hunting. Seems safe enough though."

"Let's go inside. I used to work here as a volunteer," she said. "I'll lead the way."

Lester didn't like uppity chicks. He shoved past her with more force than he intended. Looking back, he saw Luna had fallen to the ground, her head just barely missing a large rock set within the manicured landscaping.

"Asshole!" she spat.

The others of the team rushed forward. Greg muscled his way to the front. "What the hell's wrong with you, man? You trying to kill the kid?" His muscular chest was all puffed out. Of course, Lester knew he'd have no chance against this guy. Greg took another step toward him, put fists on hips. Superman had come to the rescue.

Lester raised his weapon. "You're the one that needs to back off, mailman." He gestured with his hand. "Other than being clumsy, see? She's perfectly fine." It was at that point he noticed his bandages were coming loose. That and his fingers had started to regenerate. There was an inch or so on each of his digits, unblemished new flesh peeking out. He swiped at his cheek—the gash there was completely healed. That and the wound on his ribs no longer hurt.

"It's mail *carrier*," Greg said, deadpan.

That made Lester, as well as everyone else, laugh out loud.

Lester looked down at Luna, "Fine ... I'm sorry I pushed you. Happy?"

She got up, brushing dirt from her stretchy blue slacks. "You're still an asshole."

"Show's over!" Lester yelled. "Everyone follow me inside."

Patrol Officer Lewis stepped forward with the rookie, Evans.

Lewis said, "Standard procedure is to have some officers outside sweep the perimeter."

Lester hesitated, grinding his teeth. "Fine, you two do the sweeping."

"And I'll need your Ender-5," Lewis said. "My M4 won't pack much punch against those aliens."

"Yeah—that's not happening," he scoffed.

Lester watched Greg walk over to the mouthy patrol officer. He handed Lewis his Ender-5 in exchange for the cop's M4 carbine.

Lester rolled his eyes. Fuckin Sir Galahad to the rescue ... again.

"Everybody else—follow me," Lester barked. "And stay alert —those alien fucks could be anywhere."

Captain Simpkin made a move toward Lester, blocking his forward motion.

"Sergeant Russell and I should go in first—clear the rooms inside the property. We do this for a living," Simpkin said.

Lester ignored the captain, brushing past him. They walked into the nursing home, single file—Lester, two police officers, Luna, the firemen, Charlie, and Greg—floorboards creaking beneath their feet.

Grimacing, the smell hit him like a ton of bricks—spoiled meat with moldy fruit undertones. Lester fought back the burning bile rising in his throat. In his periphery, the cops were gagging, palms held over mouths and noses. Charlie spun and made a beeline back out the front door.

"Holy Mother of God," Greg said. He'd pulled his T-shirt up to cover his nose.

"Alright, everybody—chill. It's probably just spoiled food from when the power went out three days ago," Lester said to the room.

He stood straight, pretending he wasn't bothered by the rancid stench. He walked over to the window and tried to lift it. *Of course it's jammed.*

He used the butt of his Ender-5 and smashed out the glass.

Luna balked. "Hey!"

"Relax, I'm just airing out this shithole."

Fresh air flooded in. "Everyone fan out," Lester said. "We're looking for nonperishable food, maybe some medical supplies … anything that might come in handy."

Weapons raised, Simpkin and Russell headed in the direction of what Lester guessed would be the kitchen. Alvarez and Tripe headed toward a room at the front of the house … an office? Greg and Luna were standing at the reception area counter; she was perusing a large clipboard.

Lester moved about the first floor, crunching broken glass under his boots. With a cursory scan, he took in the velveteen upholstered chairs, a lace-covered sofa, antique wooden end tables—seemed like everything was covered in a layer of dust. Paintings of various sizes lined dirty plaster walls—bearded men in suits and ties followed him. He stopped in front of one painting. The plump woman wearing a bonnet and holding a parasol looked annoyed. In the background, atop a pony, was a small child wearing a sailor outfit. *Who comes up with this shit?*

"This place is beyond creepy," Lester heard one of the firemen say from another room.

Suddenly, Luna was sprinting up the stairs to his left. Greg followed her.

Lester listened and heard muffled talking at the back of the house. "Hey, you guys find anything back there? Maybe something edible?"

Unfamiliar raised voices echoed from somewhere in the house.

Moving in the direction of the sound, weapon raised, he pushed through saloon-style swinging doors. Entering the kitchen, prepared to fire, he saw a tall unkempt man wearing mud-stained overalls.

This is definitely ground zero for that funky stink. Lester's watery eyes locked onto the butcher knife being held to Simpkin's throat. Little streams of blood flowed down both sides of his bobbing Adam's apple. Sergeant Russell stood at the other end of the kitchen, his M4 raised and pointed toward the man with the knife.

No matter how he looked at it, Lester didn't like Simpkin's chances. He thought, *Damned if you do, damned if you don't.*

"His name is Paul. Town drunk—in lockup at least once a month," Russell said to Lester in a sideways whisper. Sergeant Russell had a large white garbage bag at his feet. Looked like loaves of bread, boxes of crackers, and other mystery food.

Lester looked at Paul, weighing his options.

Paul's eyes darted. "Who are you? Leave me alone."

Russell said, "Easy, Paul, we're not here to hurt you. Put the knife down."

Wide-eyed, Simpkin looked terrified. Even talking would undoubtedly open that cut on his throat.

Slowly, Lester lowered his Ender-5, knelt down, and placed the weapon on the floor. He smiled up at Paul, seeing some of the tension leave his eyes. He casually dipped his right hand. Then in one fluid motion, he moved to stand, drew his Sig Sauer from his leg holster, and shot Paul in the forehead.

Blood, bone, and brain matter splattered the rooster-patterned valance curtains above the sink.

Paul's body dropped, slumping onto flowered wallpaper.

The room smelled of cordite mixed with the wafting odor of body odor. Simpkin wavered; his eyes fluttered.

"Nice shot," Russell said, visibly impressed.

"You guys clear rooms for a living, huh?" Lester said with a smirk to the gathering of cops. He grabbed a dishrag from the counter and tossed it toward the police captain. Simpkin caught it, swiped some of the dead man's blood from his face.

"See if there's any unspoiled food around," Lester said to Russell. He came out of the kitchen just as Luna and Greg were hurrying down the stairs.

The two firemen were out in the main room. Tripe was holding what looked like an oversized first aid medkit.

"What happened? Are you okay?" Luna asked Simpkin.

"I opened the back door to air out the room. Town drunk wandered in. Went crazy," Captain Simpkin said, still pressing the dishrag against his neck.

"Crazy times," Alvarez said, shaking his head.

"Is he dead?" Greg asked.

"Yeah, that's what happens when a bullet blows off the top of your head," Lester said.

"We found this first aid kit, plus a doctor's bag with all kinds of medical stuff inside ... stethoscope, tongue depressors, bunch of meds like penicillin, hypodermic needles and gauze, alcohol wipes, even some petroleum jelly," Tripe said, showing off the black doctor's bag.

"Petroleum jelly?" Lester asked with a smirk.

"Well, I found something too," Luna said. "Lester, you need to come upstairs."

Filtered sunlight streamed in through the second-story window, filling the patients' room with a hazy glow. Everything was dingy white—the curtains, the walls, even the furniture.

Lester's nostrils flared. *Room smells like old people.* He looked at Luna. "What am I doing here?"

She picked up a crumpled white bag from the nightstand. Handed it to Lester. He peered inside, taking out a handful of sugary crumbs, popping them in his mouth.

"Glazed Castle Rocks."

"Yep," Luna said.

He balled up the paper bag and threw it on the floor.

"Son of a bitch. Whoever he is definitely's been donutted," Lester said, staring at the empty, unmade bed.

"His name is Lloyd Sanderson," Luna said, reading a prescription bottle. "He's on Benazepril—that's a heart medication. I remember him from when I volunteered here. I also remember him from back at the ship ... his dead body was lying on the far side of the thing."

"Why does any of this matter?" Lester asked. "You do know the Silarians could show up any minute—hell, it was a Silarian that probably killed the old guy ... plus, Gia's no longer talking to us."

"I know. You're right," she said. "But I can't help thinking that Gia sent us—*me*—here for a reason. She said this would be a good place for me to attend to the sick. I believe she meant these people."

Lester stared ahead, noticing movement through the half-open bathroom door behind her. Sig Sauer in hand, he moved past Luna, stepping inside the bathroom. Lester caught sight of himself in the mirror. He admired his mug, his cheek wound completely healed.

"What is it?" Luna asked.

"False alarm, but Lloyd must have just been here. Smells like fresh farts." He came back out just in time to see Luna sweeping a tall room-dividing curtain aside.

Lester approached with his pistol raised.

"Put that away," Luna said. "This is Harry."

The white-haired old man was sleeping. Or was he dead?

"Harry, huh?"

"Yes, sweet old man. His wife died a couple of years back. He and I bonded over gin rummy."

"Nice story, but we gotta go. We're sitting ducks in this place." Lester studied Luna's profile as she looked at the old man. *What's she doing?*

"Yes, you and the others should go," Luna said. "I'm staying here."

"No, you're not. Don't be an idiot."

"Take a look around, Lester. There's no one around to take care of these people. Four more rooms on this floor, nine human beings who have been abandoned," Luna said, turning to face Lester. "Come back for me later. Just leave me an M4 before you take off. And don't take all the remaining food."

"Once we leave, I may not make it back here, you know."

Luna moved the satchel around the front of her body, pressing and sliding a finger across the top. She took out a couple of pouches and some capsules. After securing it, Luna unslung the bag and handed it to Lester.

"I know the situation. I'll be fine, but you should go."

He backed up, hands raised in mock surrender. "Do what you gotta do. I'm outta here, girl," he said, heading for the door.

Chapter 14

Solar System, Beyond Earth's High Orbit
***Relentless Thrust*, Maintenance Passageway**

Sam Dale

Sam continued to push the rickety, whining hover cart pilfered from a custodial worker.

"Why you bring that stupid animal?" Ivan asked.

"I second that," Carl said.

"You know he can hear you ... right? He's right here," Sam said.

The three men, along with the dog curled up on the bed of the cart, moved quickly within a lower-level passageway—one primarily intended for maintenance bots. Feeling claustrophobic, the three of them ducked low to avoid bonking their heads on the myriad hanging rusted pipes and the loud, vibrating ventilation ducts.

Bam!

It was the second time Sam, not paying attention, had careened the cart into an intersecting bulkhead wall. Cypress raised his head and shot Sam a menacing glare.

"Sorry, boy ... last time I do that ... promise."

Make a left up ahead, Sam ... that will bring you to the service entrance of the ship's flight bay. Your team of Silarian warriors is en route as we speak.

Sam knew Gia was being generous with her *warrior* terminology. They were no more real warriors than the handful of maintenance bots they'd passed within this dingy passageway.

Up ahead was a closed metal hatch. Carl hurried ahead, waved a palm in front of a knee-high sensor—undoubtedly one designed for coming-and-going bots.

As the hatch squealed open, Sam's ears were accosted by the sounds of whirling turbines, clanking and banging, wielding power tools, and a number of Silarians yelling—trying to be heard over all that ambient racket.

Sam shoved the cart through the opening and into the flight bay proper. Easily the size of a standard football field, it reaffirmed just how large a vessel this gunship was. *And this is one of the fleet's smallest warships.*

"Where to, Gia?"

You're at the very back of the flight bay, Sam. This is where the dropship is parked.

Gingerly, Cypress sat up.

The four of them took in the craft. A battered dark navy-blue, maybe thirty meters in length, it had been shoved to the very back bulkhead of the bay. Haphazardly, crates had been stacked upon a stubby port-side wing. Up high, all along the craft's top hull, was an assemblage of mismatched storage containers. Sam eyed what looked like an old metal bucket—sticking out of it, a long mop handle was propped up against one of those containers. *Guess some basic things are synonymous with all life forms ...*

Carl huffed, "This is what we came here for? This broken-down bucket of bolts ... being stored here within the equivalent of my kitchen junk drawer?"

Cypress said, "It's a Cloimor X35 ..."

Sam sometimes forgot Cypress had been a Silarian pilot.

Ivan asked, "Is that good thing or bad thing?"

Cypress thought about that for a moment. "Thirty years ago, it would have been a good thing." He shook his head. "Now ... not so much. On the positive side, this vessel originally comes equipped with a suite of energy weapons, and although it's as slow as mud, it's powerful for its size. Nothing fancy about a Cloimor X35. A down-and-dirty Troop Carrier that can carry maybe a hundred Silarian warriors ... well ... if they stay standing."

As Sam was about to complain to Gia about all the extraneous shit piled onto the craft, suddenly a river of large shirtless green bodies was hurrying past them on both sides.

Being bumped and jostled there on the hover cart, Cypress, looking none too happy about it, jumped the two feet or so from the bed onto the deck. While Cypress was still back in Medical Bay, Gia had engineered a specialized canine concoction of healing medical nanites. Seeing how well the dog was moving now, it looked as though they'd started taking effect. Even some of those pink furless patches seemed to be closing.

A row of Silarians had made a kind of bucket brigade, passing those containers and other junk down the length of the hull, where they were tossed to other Silarians below. A manned hover fork was attending to the larger crates on the wing.

"Gia, can we get inside?" Sam asked, feeling useless just standing there watching.

A hatch swung open as a gangway ramp descended to the

deck. Sam, with Ivan, Carl, and Cypress bringing up the rear, weaved his way through the busy throngs. Sam hurried up the gangway and entered the dropship. Any optimistic anticipation he might have had quickly faded. He stepped farther inside, making room for the others behind.

Ivan said, "Like WWII German U-boat in here."

Sam couldn't argue with that assessment. The dropship was narrow, maybe fifteen feet across. All surfaces were scratched and gouged. Sam could see visible corrosion all over the place. And like the inside rib cage of some kind of alien monster, there were curved structural trusses lining the vessel's interior from stem to stern.

Looking around with a disgusted expression, Ivan said, "We all going to die if we try to take this clown ship to space."

For some reason that made Cypress laugh.

Apparently, hearing a dog laugh out loud was even funnier. Ivan, Carl, and eventually Sam, were now laughing too.

Getting control of himself, Sam noticed the cacophony of thumping noises from outside had ceased—and he could hear multiple heavy footfalls coming up the gangway. The first of the Silarian warriors was entering through the aft side hatch.

Cypress said, "The bridge is forward ... I'll show you how to fly this thing."

Sam hesitated. "What about weapons? It's great we have our small army ... but they won't be of much use without—"

Gia's voice crackled to life from the overhead PA system. "Yes, Sam ... there is an onboard cache of weapons ... a kind of armory, if you will. Records show there are eighty-two Ender-4s and twenty-one Ender-5s. There are combat suits as well, of which not all may be fully functional. There is a full stock of healing nanites as well as spare implants."

The interior of the vessel was quickly filling up, along with the rise of rank close quarters' body odor.

"We move now, yes?" Ivan coaxed.

As Sam hurried forward, Cypress brushed past him, taking the lead.

He thought about Earth and what he'd find back under the isolation zone in Castle Rock. Periodically, Gia had been updating him on the status of the other teams. There was Walter and his Valhallen, a militaristic anarchist group that, along with their impressive hidden gun-running cache of weapons, had enabled them to fend off the Silarians' first attack. Perhaps their first stop should be Walter's compound. Other than briefly, he hadn't connected with Lester and his team ... those Gia Fighters. It still amazed Sam that the reckless and typically self-centered rube had defeated a small army of Clash-Troopers. Sam's one-time employee, having been fired for insubordination, Lester had proven himself, albeit using unorthodox methods, to be an effective leader. *Go figure ...*

There were two other teams of ten. After the attack at the Douglas County Fairgrounds, Sam knew nine of those Gia Fighters were still alive. On the other team, the one at Butterfield Crossing Park, only seven Gia Fighters had survived. Last he'd heard, both teams were making their way back to Walter's compound. And then there were Harper and Julian, who'd been on a mission to bring the US military into the mix. Having successfully donutted General McGovern, there had been a change of mind concerning that option. As precarious as things were, it had been agreed to shelve the McGovern military option for now.

Unceremoniously, Harper and Julian had left in a hurry and should be headed back to Castle Rock. Unfortunately, Gia's communications with the various teams were being curtailed by the Geo-Mind. Seemed both were fighting for control of those all-important disruptor drones.

The four of them passed through another hatchway and

into a square compartment that narrowed slightly toward the bow. There were two forward control stations with four jump seats behind.

Ivan said, "I was wrong. This not like WWII U-boat ... more like WWII airplane."

Cypress jumped up onto the left-side seat and examined the control board before him. Sam took the seat on the right. He accessed the stream to get what operating instructions were available for a Silarian Cloimor X35 Troop Carrier. There didn't seem to be much information. He looked over to Cypress. "You ever pilot one of these?"

"No."

"How do you turn it on?"

Cypress raised a paw over the board, where it hovered there indecisively for a few moments. "Uh ... maybe this button." The dog glanced over to Sam. "Tap that one."

Sam didn't like the direction this was going. Both Ivan and Carl had crowded in close behind—watching.

"Do you mind?" Sam said, annoyed. "Have a seat; we'll get this figured out." Looking out through the still-open hatch to the mass of crowded-together green bodies, he said, "Carl ... you're a police officer. You're used to giving orders ... taking control of a situation? Right?"

Carl's shrug coincided with the raising of his brows. "I guess."

"Good. Get out there and communicate with our troops. They must be anxious. Have a lot of questions about what we're doing ... what we will be doing."

"Isn't Gia already doing that ... like in their heads?" Carl said, looking back over his shoulder to the mass of Silarians. They all seemed to be jabbering over one another.

Sam said, "Yeah, well, there's nothing like face-to-face interaction, right? Go with him, Ivan ... make friends with our troops."

Both looked ready to balk—Sam raised a palm. "Spare me ... no tantrums, please. Go."

It was like sending preschoolers off to brush their teeth. The two men reluctantly left the bridge.

Cypress said, "I'm sure that's the ship's primary drive start."

Sam tapped the control board where Cypress had pointed. Nothing happened.

"Oh ... wait." Cypress examined the control board for several more seconds.

Sam said, "Gia ... a little help here, if you will."

Once more her voice crackled from above. "Cypress was correct; that is the primary drive start select. Unfortunately, with the vessel being left unattended for such a long time, it will require an external surge of power—"

"You're saying this old junker needs a jump start," Sam said with annoyance.

For once, Gia sounded somewhat flustered. "A maintenance bot has already been deployed with ... what you would call jumper cables. One moment, Sam. This won't take long."

It took twenty minutes ...

"Okay, Sam," Gia said. "Can you try pressing the primary drive start again?"

Cypress and Sam exchanged a quick look. "Here we go." He pressed the button and immediately the vessel's drive stuttered and shuddered to life. Sam could feel the Cloimor X35 power plant through the soles of his boots—it was settling down into a steady vibration.

"What now, Cypress?" he started to say, when pilot and copilot control arrays emerged from below the forward console. It was similar to that of the Landa-Craft, in fact, almost identical. Sam said, "You know ... I think I got this."

Chapter 15

Castle Rock, Colorado
Bell Mountain Equestrian Center

Harper Godard

She shot up with a start—fists clenched—her breaths coming fast and shallow. *Where am I?* She remembered this same muted darkness, the rich smells of hay and oats and horses. But her mind was still mired in a fog—disjointed memories, puzzle pieces not fitting together. She looked around. *Okay ... I'm still at the equestrian center.* Suddenly her breath caught—her heart skipped a beat. She remembered being attacked, then being endlessly dragged by her hair. She tried reaching for the top of her head, realizing her hands were bound. There was a strap wrapped around her wrists—they'd used leather reins. *They? Who are they?*

Fuck, the Silarians. She remembered being on her back, her

ponytail, the roots of her hair, on fire ... and Julian being dragged behind her!

"Julian?" she said in a hushed voice.

"Oh, thank goodness you are okay," came the older man's voice.

She looked around, realizing she was seated in an enclosed stall. "Where are you?"

"I'm in the stall next to yours. Have you been injured, Harper? I did see you were struck."

"Struck?"

"Punched. You were putting up quite a fight."

"I don't remember that. I remember being dragged; that's it. How are you? Did they hurt you, Julian?"

"I did not struggle. Evidently, I am not nearly as brave as you are," he said.

"Did you see how many there are? Where they came from? Obviously from the fleet of ships up in space, but I didn't think they had reentered the dome."

She heard distant footfalls. Someone was coming.

Julian said, "Well—"

"Shush!" Whispering, she said, "Someone's coming."

She listened as the footfalls came closer. She laid back while keeping her eyes open just enough to see. Then she saw the top half of his head above the stall's door—*God, they're tall.*

He stopped and looked down at her. Her heart thundered in her chest, and she was afraid the Silarian would be able to hear it. *Don't open the door ... Don't open the door ... Don't open the door ... Don't open the door ...*

He unlatched it and slid open the door.

She heard the muffled crunch of his boots on the hay-strewn ground. Stepping close, his form loomed over her.

"I know you are awake, human. No need to pretend."

She opened her eyes. "What do you want?" she said with

more hostility than she thought she was capable of, considering she was totally at this alien's mercy.

"From you? A skinny wench?"

Wench? What is he, a pirate?

He knelt down, and she could smell his musky scent. Weird, it wasn't all that different from the horses around here.

She flinched when he raised a hand and inwardly chastised herself for showing such weakness. Reaching forward, he used the back of his hand to stroke her cheek. His touch was soft, gentle, even.

"You see ... I can be nice. I can be your friend."

"I have enough friends, thank you."

The Silarian smiled at that. His eyes were roving now, taking in her legs, her hips, her breasts. He licked his lips and swallowed—an Adam's apple nearly the size of an actual apple bobbed in his throat. His hand drifted down from her cheek, down her neck, to the top of her chest. He adjusted his crouch, his footing, so he could spread his knees wider. Even in the muted darkness of the stall, she could see an immense erection straining the fabric of his pants. Fear engulfed her. *He's a fucking Clydesdale.*

Without warning, he ripped apart her shirt; buttons like plastic bullets ricocheted off surrounding timber planks. She screamed, bared her teeth, and kicked out—bringing all the anger and fury she could muster. Strong hands were upon her; she felt the fabric of her bra tear and then his massive hands were upon her breasts—squeezing so hard tears erupted, her mouth contorted into a silent scream.

Through the terror she continued to kick and squirm. His hands were at the waistband of her pants—it was then, at some level, she thought she heard a sound. The rolling of steel wheels upon a metal track. *The stall's door!*

Chapter 16

Castle Rock, Colorado
Bell Mountain Equestrian Center

Lloyd Sanderson

Without the stream, Lloyd would have had no idea where the equestrian center was. And as much as he marveled at how utterly amazing the torrent of information flowing into his consciousness was, he was far more taken aback by his newly acquired physical wherewithal. His body mass was easily twice that of his old, decrepit body. He'd almost forgotten what it was like to feel strong, virile ... dominant.

He wanted to talk to the female AI again; he had so many questions. He found it irritating that when he most needed her, this Gia bitch, well, apparently she had no time for him. Heading south, he'd made good time. That's what happened when one had four-to-five-foot-long strides. But not as good a time as he would have made if he'd had a FastLev. As it turned out, the Silarian officers had each been aboard a kind of hover platform. They'd been stored within hidden lockers along each side of the dropship's hull. There'd been eleven of the hovering transportation devices; the eleventh, a larger one, was designed to move cargo and supplies necessary for setting up a forward base of operations.

His fast walk transitioned to a fast jog—he felt his chest expand and deflate, the wonderful exchange of copious lungfuls of air. His two hearts, beating in tandem, delivered oxygenated blood to his Hulk-like musculature. He was on South Wilcox now, having just passed Plum Creek Parkway. Outside the Safeway supermarket, a small crowd of locals was milling about. Up ahead, flames licked up from several old oil drums; disheartened groups of men and women huddled together shoulder to shoulder, warming hands, passing the anxious moments. Upon seeing his approach, he was momentarily taken aback by their reaction. A woman screamed; several of the men bellowed out a warning. *Of course. I'm a fucking seven-and-a-half-foot-tall alien* ...

One man, wearing a frayed, hole-ridden green Army jacket and a Red Sox baseball cap flipped backward, was standing his ground. Palms to the billowing smoke and rising amber embers, he continued his fireside vigil as if the approach of a Silarian warrior was no big deal—an everyday occurrence.

At thirty yards' distance, the man drew a pistol. Lloyd didn't slow, didn't change course. The man widened his stance and raised his gun. Now, with both arms extended, he was sighting down the barrel—locked onto Lloyd's fast-coming approach. At this range, it would be hard for the guy, maybe ex-military, or perhaps an experienced hunter, to miss. Lloyd chose the moment carefully—the moment right before this man in the old

Army jacket and flipped-around baseball cap squeezed the trigger. *Bang! Bang! Bang!*

But Lloyd was already in the air. He used every ounce of this body's strength and athleticism to leap. He was already eight feet in the air and rising—looking down and seeing the man's confounded expression. In that split second, the man could have taken stock, repositioned his stance, his aim, and tried for another shot. *Those who hesitate are lost ...*

Lloyd came down hard and fast. The heels of his feet, like two driving-down sledgehammers, shattered both of the man's clavicles, acromioclavicular joints, as well as his scapulas. Like getting hit by a falling piano from a high-story building, the poor son of a bitch never had a chance.

Hitting the ground, Lloyd tumbled, ducked his head, and rolled forward. It hadn't been graceful but was effective. Getting to his feet, he didn't glance back at the mess he'd left behind. *Fuck him ... he pulled the damn gun.*

Lloyd kept to the side of the road at a fast jog. He passed the Castle Rock Ford dealership on the left; off to his right was I-25, the main commuter artery connecting Denver to the north and Colorado Springs to the south. As it stood now, it was a virtual parking lot, bumper-to-bumper cars and trucks going nowhere fast.

It was late afternoon by the time Lloyd made a left into the rock-pillared entrance to Crystal Valley Parkway. Slowing, he saw the painted sign, "Bell Mountain Equestrian Center," off to his right. He assessed the narrow, winding drive leading up to the hilltop facility, about a quarter-mile's distance from where he now stood. Keeping to the line of tall maples along the right side of the drive, he stayed low and watched for movement up ahead. It wasn't long before the smell of hay and horseshit affirmed he was heading in the right direction.

Cresting the hill, he found he was close to a big dirt parking lot—a few parked, dusty cars lined the periphery. There were two single-story stable structures, one on each side of the lot. Shitty-looking timber ones on the left, somewhat nicer cement ones, definitely more modern-looking, off to the right.

Farther beyond, within a large open corral, was the Silarian encampment—what the stream was calling their ground forces' base of operations. He saw Silarian warriors milling about, some on foot, some scooting about atop FastLevs. Clearly they were in the process of setting up the equivalent of US Army Quonset huts. But these were on a whole other level. With interest, he watched as one of the green bastards tossed a small satchel onto the dirt; immediately it started to unpack itself, rise up, and take form—all within seconds.

He dashed forward, needing a better vantage point. He knew what he, *who he,* needed to find. Lloyd smiled. *Can I really pull this off?* From what he could *see, tell,* from his own new physiology, they weren't all that different from humans. Bigger, sure, stronger, more technologically advanced, but smarter? ... he doubted it. Taking up a position at the corner of the more modern stable structure, he could better differentiate one Silarian from another. And then he saw him within the confines of one of the alien Quonset huts. The fucker was bigger than all of them. Clearly in charge, he was barking off orders, strutting around—an arrogant big swinging dick who just so happened to look identical to Lloyd.

Swoosh! Startled, he realized something was speeding by directly overhead. Instinctively, Lloyd ducked down, even though he was hidden beneath the structure's roofline. It was a ship of some kind, and its powerful landing thrusters were being engaged. He was forced to bury his face into the crook of his arm as downward cyclone-force winds swirled dust and debris all around him. Within moments it had moved on; taking it in through squinted eyes, Lloyd saw that it was a far larger dropship than the one back at the nursing home. That and two identical-looking dropships of the same size were approaching from different directions. There was only one word for this ... *Invasion.*

He was conscious that he was living on borrowed time, literally, where every moment counted. What had Gia said? He had two weeks in this body. Lloyd inwardly fumed, there now being so many of these green bastards running around—it would make things far more challenging. *Maybe later I can find this Captain Larng Nos Polk while he sleeps.*

It was then that he heard it. The muffled screams. He raised his brows in admiration. *My senses ... smell, eyesight, and hearing ... each is so much more!*

Again came the muffled screams. It was a woman. Men didn't scream like that; at least real men didn't. He smiled at his own humor. She was close, undoubtedly within the very stables he was now standing behind. He already knew there were no Silarian females present for this invasion. Why would there be? Males got the job done, while females liked to talk about it ad nauseam, then share their feelings about it all.

"Oh God, help me!"

He did his best to ignore her pleas. Silarian warriors, dozens and dozens of them, were now disembarking from the three large dropships. It all seemed so organized, and like robots, the warriors knew exactly where to go—what they were supposed to do.

Thump! Thump! "Ahhh!"

He'd been leaning against the corner of the structure but now stepped away and glared at the siding—as if it had purposely interrupted his important train of thought. Fuck! Giving in, he moved around to the opposite, far side of the stables, which was out of sight of the ever-expanding Silarian outpost. Deep in shade up ahead was a sliding barn door. He stopped and listened. Other than the woman's continued thrashing about, he didn't hear anyone nearby on the other side.

He slid the door open and stepped inside. He paused, standing upon a dirt-floored corridor where horse stalls flanked both sides. Some of the upper stall doors had been swung open, allowing several of the horses to look out.

Lloyd wasn't a fan of the big animals. He'd never ridden a horse, never had the need to. It took a moment for his eyes to adjust. The pungent smell of hay and horseshit had him reconsidering coming in here.

"Stop! Get away from me!" came the woman's voice.

"Leave her alone!"

Lloyd made a face. So, there's a man here too ... interesting.

Lloyd could tell by the sounds of the woman's struggles; things were getting dicey for her. He now moved quickly, listening. Up ahead on the left, a stall door had been left partially open. The walls were high, even for his seven-and-a-half-foot-tall frame. But if he stood on his toes, he could peer over. He did just that. Sure enough, a Silarian guard was attacking a young woman. Her shirt had been ripped open; his big green hands were all over her exposed breasts. As she thrashed about, he used his considerable weight to hold her down.

"Let her go! Stop ... You can't do that!" the man in an adjacent stall yelled.

Lloyd opened the stall door all the way and stepped inside. The guard, oblivious to his presence, seemed to be trying to do too many things at once—holding her down with his bulk, fumbling with the buttons on her waistband while still having to do the same with his own. The guy had clearly not thought this out and had his overexuberance and lust get the better of him.

"That's enough of that," Lloyd said. "Off of her. Now."

"I am not stopping ... she is mine ... I will now take her—"

Lloyd knew the guard was speaking in his native Naru, Silarian, whatever, tongue, but somehow, Lloyd could still understand him. It had to be his implants; evidently language translations weren't a problem. *Amazing technology ...*

Lloyd hated seeing this crazed fuck on top of the woman like that. She was crying, but hadn't stopped struggling, fighting. Had yet to give up. *Good for you, kid.* Lloyd knew he himself was a despicable person. A killer three times over. But he was no rapist. There were limits to depravity.

He heard himself growl, a feral sound he quite liked. Felt a surge of adrenaline, or whatever comparable shit flowed in the veins of a Silarian. He reached down, got a tight fistful of the guard's long ponytail, and yanked it backward with every bit of strength this new body of his could conjure. He was rewarded with a sound he'd never encountered before—a kind of wet, sloppy, *slurp.* He raised his hand to observe the dangling scalp he'd just expunged from the guard's skull.

Wide-eyed, it took a moment for the guard to realize what he'd lost. But before he could scream or shriek, or even reach for the top of his ruined head, Lloyd drove a hard fist into the guard's nose. He felt bone and cartilage crumble beneath his knuckles. Blood spurted, then fountained high into the air, much of it splattering back down upon the woman's disbelieving face.

With a knee, Lloyd shoved the Silarian guard's lifeless body off her. Immediately, she crabwalked away from him, from both of them.

"What's going on ... who is over there! Stop hurting her! Stop it right this instant!"

Lloyd turned his gaze toward the adjacent stall, made a face, and then looked back down to the woman. "Seriously? Who talks like that? 'Stop it right this instant!'" he mocked.

Gasping, damn near hyperventilating, the woman's back was up against the far corner of the stall. She was doing her best to cover her exposed breasts. Apparently, not all the buttons on her shirt had been torn off, and with nervous, shaking fingers, she was trying in vain to refasten them.

"How ... who ... who are you?" she managed to say.

He mentally debated what to say. "I'm Lloyd ... and I'm not one of them."

She shook her head. "No, that's not possible. Not compatible ... humans and Silarians ... something about our DNA."

"Yeah, thanks for reminding me. It turns out it's not an instantaneous, uh, reaction. I have a couple of weeks."

"You were human?"

"An old one. A dying one ..."

He saw realization in her eyes. "Still. How?"

"I ate one of those glazed Castle Rocks ... then I found a dropship full of bio-forms ... I know who you are, little lady. You and Sam and that scientist. You started the whole damn thing ... the rebellion."

She nodded. "You're querying the stream."

"Yeah ... obviously."

"So, what now? You're going to help us, right?"

"Can someone tell me what's going on?" came the voice from the other stall.

"It's okay," Harper said. "I'm okay ... I think." She narrowed her eyes. "You are going to help us, right?"

"Sorry, kid. I'm not here to become part of your little rebellion. I'm here to make sure I survive longer than two weeks. I really don't care if it's as a Silarian or a human ... although, I gotta say, this alien body is ..."

"How could you say that? Where's your loyalty? Your humanity?"

He smiled at her incredulity. "Look at me. Do I look like a human to you?"

"Will you let us go? Can you at least do that?"

"Yeah, can you let us go?" the other man said. The man, Lloyd had come to realize, was none other than the scientist, Julian Humblecut.

Chapter 17

Solar System, Beyond Earth's High Orbit
Old Silarian Dropship

Sam Dale

As soon as Sam pulled back on the control array, there were sounds of metal scraping against metal coming from the aft section of the ship. Sam winced.

Ivan guffawed. "You drive like half blind old woman."

Cypress, still seated to his left, nodded but stayed quiet.

"It's a tight space," Sam said. "Blame the one who parked the thing here." He gestured to the display, providing him with an overhead three-sixty-degree perspective there, shoehorned within the back of the flight bay. "I got this."

"Not everyone good with parallel parking—"

"Enough, Ivan. Like I said, I got this." It took several back-and-forth jockeying maneuvers in order to turn the vessel around enough for it to be facing nose out.

Ivan leaned in from behind and tapped the forward dash. Suddenly, light began streaming into the small bridge area as two exterior blast doors began sliding open.

"I was going to open those; just hadn't gotten around to it," Sam lied, now taking in the view through the now-unobstructed windshield. The flight bay was a flurry of activity, crew members hurrying about, other crafts taxiing, three Attack Stingers hovering overhead, now being directed to new bay locations.

Cypress said, "They're clearing a route for us to traverse."

Sam nodded. There would have been no way they'd be getting out of here soon, and he silently thanked Gia for the forethought of getting bay personnel on the ball.

He goosed the ship forward. "I do have one question." He glanced over to Cypress. "We're going to pop out of this totally hidden, cloaked gunship in about two minutes."

"Yes, that is the idea," the dog replied.

"And what? My stream queries keep coming up empty. This dropship doesn't seem to have cloaking capability."

Cypress just stared back at him.

Ivan, for once, was speechless.

Sam said, "Please don't tell me we're about to all of a sudden become very visible to that fleet of incredibly powerful warships?"

Ivan was now looking at Cypress too.

"This dropship is old. Cloaking capability is a relatively recent Silarian technology."

"So ... no cloaking," Sam said.

They were approaching the bay's yawning-wide open bay doors. The atmosphere containing a blue-hewed energy field flickered with errant plasma flashes.

Cypress said, "Look at all that cross traffic out there. A fleet this size is never still ... ship-to-ship deliveries being made.

Command personnel being summoned; dispatching of maintenance drones ... a small, unremarkable craft like this ... we probably won't be noticed."

Sam didn't buy it, and his expression made that clear. It wasn't as if Geo-Mind was a distracted air traffic controller who'd just spilled coffee on his lap.

"I don't know what to tell you, Sam," Cypress said, looking apologetic. "What choice do we have?"

"I say we punch it. Balls to the floor," Ivan said.

"Wall. It's balls to the wall," Sam corrected.

Hold on, Sam. Relentless Thrust is in the process of moving away from the fleet.

He brought the dropship down to a slow crawl. Beyond, he saw everything panning left—fleet assets, the back-and-forth cross traffic, even the partial view of Earth in the far distance. *Relentless Thrust* was indeed turning.

I've suggested to the bridge crew, including Jarpin, that Relentless Thrust should take up a position behind Earth's moon ... head to the dark side.

Sam didn't like this. "And she won't be tracked by fleet sensors ... by Geo-Mind? Relentless Thrust's exhaust ... what did you call it? Her radiation wake?"

If I am calculating things correctly, all attention will be on that dropship you are piloting. Rest assured, I will be keeping the Geo-Mind quite busy. So, if you have no more questions, Sam, please do as Ivan suggested. Punch it—balls to the wall ... now!

He did as asked, thrusting the control array forward so hard the clank reverberated within the small bridge space. The high-G-force acceleration was near instantaneous. Ivan was thrown off his feet. Cypress lost his footing on the seat next to him, while Carl and the entire Silarian warrior contingent behind tumbled and yelled a wide selection of Silarian curses—many of which had to do with the pilot getting fucked up the kazoo by a Galvarian Humper ... *whatever that is.*

The old dropship might have been a wreck of a ship on the outside, but it certainly had some horses under the hood.

Behind him, Ivan, hands reaching for something to hold on to, whooped and hollered. Cypress, leaning forward, had his paws upon the forward console and looked just as excited as Ivan sounded. Sam allowed himself a small smile. Whatever Gia was doing, whatever her "distraction" was, it seemed to be working.

Before them was Earth, and she was getting larger and larger by the second.

Ten minutes later they were fast descending into Earth's upper exosphere. As the dropship shook and the outside hull glowed amber, then yellow, and then blue, the heat inside the craft was a hundred and twenty degrees and climbing.

Ivan said, "And I thought the Silarians smelled bad before ..."

"We need to give this ship a name," came Carl's voice from behind at the threshold to the bridge. "Maybe something like *Old Lizzy* or *Zippy Beaver* ... something catchy."

"I thought you were getting to know the troops," Sam said, altering course toward the North American continent.

"I've been jawing with them. They're not a bad bunch. Maybe not the cream of the crop when it comes to military readiness ... but then again, they're okay with who they are. Nothing to prove, you know what I mean?"

Sam hitched a shoulder. "That doesn't instill in me a warm feeling of confidence in our chances for when we meet up with warriors that do have something to prove."

Carl said, "How about *Uncle Jeb* ... ya know, from the *Beverly Hillbillies?* Sure, he's an old hillbilly, but he's still got some moves. And you have to admit, the guys had a lot of luck.

Went from living in a shack to living in a Beverly Hills mansion."

"That a stupid name. Who this Jeb character?" Ivan said.

"I like it," Sam said, distracted and just wanting them to shut up. "I christen this old bucket of bolts *Uncle Jeb*."

"Stupid name," Ivan said under his breath.

The blue-hued isolation zone was coming up before them. Castle Rock, home, and, at least for now, the eye of the storm. *"Gia, can you allow us access into the dome?"*

Yes, Sam ... ensure you maintain your current heading. Also know, once you pass through that plasma barrier, communications with me will be intermittent at best. The Geo-Mind and I are battling ... he and I are clamoring for dominance.

I need more instruction—

It was at that moment *Uncle Jeb* pierced the plasma field and communications with Gia ceased.

"Shit!" he said. He took in the landscape below, now getting his bearings. He looked over to Cypress. "Head to Walter's compound? Regroup?"

Cypress was taking in the township with a furrowed brow. "Good a plan as any. But something's telling me we should be heading somewhere else." The dog looked back at Sam. "I do not believe Harper is at Walter's compound."

"The stream telling you that?"

"No. The stream is operational but has slowed."

"Like shit-slow Wi-Fi connection," Ivan contributed.

Sam had noticed it too. Undoubtedly something to do with what was going on with Gia and the Geo-Mind. "Well, if you get any clarity on her whereabouts, let me know. Till then, I'm heading to Walter's."

Uncle Jeb banked right, heading toward the southwest section of Castle Rock.

Chapter 18

Castle Rock, Colorado
Bell Mountain Equestrian Center

Harper Godard

She stared up at the looming green Silarian. She didn't know what to make of him. She got that he was indeed human inside that ridiculously tall and muscular exterior, but there was something not right about him. A level of self-centeredness and lack of moral fortitude. *Perhaps he's a sociopath?* Sociopath or not, he'd just saved her from a fate worse than death—getting raped by an alien. She said, "What is your name ... your human name?"

"Lloyd."

She said what she was thinking. "Well, Lloyd, I'll always be in your debt ... for whatever that's worth."

He waved off the endearing comment as he would a bothersome fly. "Leave here. I see you again, I may just have to kill you."

There was nothing behind those soulless eyes—he meant it.

She was already reaching for a knife secured to the dead Silarian guard's belt. "What are you going to do?" she asked, not expecting an honest answer.

His crooked smile chilled her to the bone. "Be all that I can be ... watch out, world." With that, he was gone—his heavy footfalls fading into horse whinnies, nickers, and other stable sounds.

Holding the knife with both hands, she sliced through the leather strap securing her legs; her wrists were a trickier matter, but she managed it. Getting to her feet, she looked down at the dead alien.

"Harper?" Julian said.

"One sec; need to deal with this guard." Taking hold of one ankle, she attempted to drag him, but he was too heavy. Literally deadweight. Moving out into the intersecting corridor between both banks of high-walled stalls, she said, "Julian? Which one you in?"

"I'm over here."

She saw two bound hands rise above the wall directly to her left. The stall door wasn't locked. She unlatched and slid the door to one side. Julian was up on his feet, looking happy to see her. He looked at her, then lowered his gaze to the sheathed knife and the guard's belt she'd double wrapped around her hips.

"Oh my, that's something, isn't it?"

She pulled the knife and sliced through the bindings at his wrists and then his ankles. "They hurt you? Try to ..."

"No. That guard wasn't interested in me," he said sympathetically.

"Speaking of that guard—help me move him." She hurried

back to her own stall, leaned down, and grabbed the dead Silarian's wrists. "Take his legs, Julian. Best we hurry; no telling when someone else will show up."

Together they half-carried, half-slid the corpse out into the corridor.

"Best we stick him in another stall away from ours," she said, sounding out of breath.

They chose a stall five down, one with a horse in it. She got the door open and patted the big paint's neck. The horse snorted as she gave it a gentle but firm shove to one side of the stall. Then, together, she and Julian positioned the dead guard to the opposite side, then covered his body with hay.

Julian said, "Hold on ..." He disappeared down the corridor for half a minute, returning with a folded horse blanket. "Noticed it was draped over one of the stall doors back there." He shook it open and laid it atop the hay-covered mound.

They both took a step back to assess their work—behind her, she felt the horse's comforting warm flank.

"That should do it. Doesn't look much like a body to me," she said. "Out of sight, out of mind ..."

"Until it starts to stink," Julian said.

She nodded. "What do you say we get out of here?"

He nodded. "The stream ... it's not—"

"I know, it's not really working like it was. Let's head toward Walter's. I'm sure they know about this place, all those alien ships and warrior troops, but maybe not."

They had no trouble exiting the equestrian center grounds since all the hustle and bustle was happening on the other side of the property. Still, they stayed low and moved fast, heading for a nearby crop of tall cottonwoods. The sun was low in the sky; soon it would be dusk. She held up within the shade of the trees. "Wait, Julian."

"Shouldn't we get as far away from this place as possible?"

His white hair was an Einsteinian mess, and there was fear in his deep blue eyes.

"My ship. The Landa-Craft ... I can't just leave it here."

Julian looked back to the equestrian center, then turned to the nearby four northbound and southbound lanes of I-25. "But we're so close, Harper."

"You go. Cross the highway and head southwest." She gestured in that direction with a flat palm. "You can't miss it if you stay on course. Anyway, I'll be right behind you ... be picking you up before you know it."

He looked hesitant to leave without her but nodded. "All right. But please don't take any undue risks. Lady luck was with you once; don't tempt fate."

"I have no intention of getting caught ... go. I'll see you soon."

He nodded. "Okay then." He turned and scampered off.

She watched the skinny older man weave between trees, hop over a fallen log, then disappear down the steep grade of a gulch.

Turning back toward the distant stables, she mentally pictured the course she'd take back into danger. Chewing at the inside of her cheek, she was second-guessing her decision. Shit! She wondered what Sam would do. He'd probably want that asset. She shut down her inner dialogue and retraced her earlier steps back to the cover of the stables.

Reaching the west side of the building, she held up to catch her breath. Her heart missed a beat, hearing a clamoring of voices within the stables. Undoubtedly, they were looking for the guard. *No ... they're looking for me and Julian. I need to hurry.* She sprinted down the length of the building, grateful for the deepening late afternoon shade. She slowed, coming up to the end of the structure. Holding her breath, she peered around the corner. She involuntarily gasped. A Silarian guard was there, two feet from where she stood. His huge wide back was close enough to reach out and touch. His head turned; he'd heard something—alien brain synapses were firing, deciphering what the hell he'd just heard.

A chill shot up her spine. Within a second or two, he was going to turn on his heel and see her there. *Don't think! Don't think! Don't think!* She pulled her knife, gripped its thick, oversized handle in both hands as she'd done before, raised the weapon high over her head, and—*oh my God!*

The guard spun around. Eyes wide, momentarily stymied, as his mouth opened to yell out, Harper drove the knife forward with everything she had. The point disappeared into his chest. His eyes went even wider; his mouth went wider too. She looked down to the knife—it was buried to the hilt. A stream of blood trickled down his abdomen. But the big Silarian remained standing.

Harp... they hav ... two hearts ... stab hi ... again.

It took a moment for Harper to understand Gia's broken and nearly indecipherable message. *Fuck! Are you kidding me?* They both reached for the knife's handle at precisely the same time.

Chapter 19

Harper's hands got there first. The knife's handle was warm and slick with the Silarian's blood. And while the alien warrior was seriously injured and certainly not operating at his peak performance level, he was still far stronger than Harper. While she used all of her strength to pull the blade free, he, in turn, was doing everything he could to keep it firmly embedded in his chest.

She felt the moments ticking by as they continued their struggle, neither one relenting. The Silarian staggered to one side but quickly regained his footing. But looking at him, his faded pallor, he'd lost a lot of blood. How long could he hold on? She knew another guard could happen upon them at any moment, or this guy could suddenly find his voice—start bellowing for help. One thing was for sure: tiring, she wouldn't be pulling this knife out any time soon. With her hands so slick with blood, she ground her molars and tightened her grip.

Interesting.

She'd inadvertently twisted the blade of the knife just a fraction of a turn. The Silarian groaned, his knees weakening. She smiled up at him while he glowered back, his breaths coming in uneven, rank-smelling huffs. She gripped tighter and twisted the handle once more. This time the blade twisted a full quarter turn. Tears rolled down both of his cheeks. A low, feral whine escaped his lips—then his wide-open mouth contorted. But it was too early to take a victory lap.

Having her tension-flexed arms elevated for so long was taking its toll on her arms. She tried to ignore the burning in her shoulders, biceps, and triceps. As her grip weakened, so did her resolve. *I'll have to let go ... I can't hold on.*

The alien must have picked up on her growing distress because he was rallying—and now he was the one to smirk down at her.

I'm going to let go, and he'll be free to stab me with his own knife. Or maybe he'll just wrap his hands around my throat and strangle me.

They locked eyes, and then her knees gave out. Futilely, she hung there, a cartoon character swinging to and fro from an all-too-skinny branch over the yawning chasm below. Harper clung to the handle, but her determination was waning. She closed her eyes.

Movement.

Her hands jarred downward—she gasped for a breath and opened her eyes. She now saw what she had felt. The blade must have turned slightly downward. Still having Harper's full weight on the knife's handle, the blade was, albeit slowly, now slicing downward within the Silarian's chest. Tempted to get to her feet once again, instead she jerked her entire body up and down once, twice, thrice—then, suddenly, as if an overflowing dam had broken free, any last resistance from tissue, musculature, or flesh gave way.

Her elbows took most of the brunt, landing hard between his two enormous boots. A moment later, a heavy, wet gush of blood, organs, and entrails cascaded down upon her shoulders and back. She made a disgusted face and shook her head. She was just a nurse, not a doctor, but sure enough, she'd just performed a total abdominal cavity disembowelment.

The Silarian guard toppled over, his lifeless body making a heavy *thump*, hitting the ground to her left. She staggered to her feet but stayed bent over with hands on knees, gasping for breath. Still hidden behind the back of the stables, and not within the line of sight of the encampment, she scanned the equestrian center's landscape beyond, down the nearby slope, and off slightly to the left. That's where the Landa-Craft should be ... *or was it more to the right?* She'd already tried to query the stream for help to no avail. She glanced up to the heavens, as if Gia was an ever-present angel that she could see there, wings gently flapping, keeping her aloft. *"I don't suppose you can hear me, Gia ... can you tell me where exactly I left that ship?"*

She waited, but all she heard were the industrious Silarian warriors hard at work, further constructing their encampment. Rising, and staying close to the building, she edged closer to the opposite far corner. She ventured a quick look. No one seemed to be looking in this general direction. Once again, she eyed where she thought the Landa-Craft was parked some fifty yards distance from where she stood. She'd been a fast runner in high school, did well enough in PE, certainly never won any medals in track and field, but she'd done okay. *But I won't be able to outrun the energy bolt of an Ender-4!*

She looked up again. "Gia, if you can hear me ... please open the cockpit access hatch; oh, and lower the ladder too."

There was no response.

She took several deep breaths and readied herself. *Okay, I can do this ...* She'd be running fast, pretty much full out. She decided to sprint the final stretch with her hands outstretched in front of her so as not to run blindly face-first into the ship. She lowered herself into a sprinter's starting position, locked her eyes on the patch of distant dirt where she imagined the ship to be. She imagined a starting gun going off. *Bang!*

She was suddenly tearing down the incline as fast as her feet could take her. It took all of her willpower not to look to her right, over to the encampment filled with hundreds of Silarian warriors. Doing so would only slow her down. *Oh God ... will I feel it when the plasma bolt hits me?* She was just coming up to level ground, about a third of the way there. She raised her arms out in front of herself, now more uncertain where the ship was supposed to be. *Shit!*

At the halfway mark, she was surprised there had yet to be any weapons fire. She knew by several loud shouts she'd been spotted. Undoubtedly, dozens of them were tracking her progress. Then it occurred to her what she must look like. Most of her upper body, including her head, her hair, and arms, had been drenched in goopy wet blood. And with her hands outstretched like they were, she must look like a crazed ghoul. At the very least a curiosity. No, at least at the moment she wasn't so much a threat as she was ... bewildering entertainment.

Chapter 20

Skies Above Castle Rock
Uncle Jeb

Sam Dale

Dark, swirling plumes of smoke rose from dozens of locations below. There'd been anarchy on the streets even before they'd left—he imagined things would soon be getting a whole lot worse. People don't do well in confinement, especially when life-sustaining food and water become scarce. He briefly wondered if Walter's compound had survived the mayhem. He'd had no recent contact with the man, no updates. And now, with the stream on the fritz, all he could do was hope things were okay there. The reality was, without Walter and his team and that cache of—mostly stolen, Sam was sure—military weapons and munitions, there would be little hope of putting up any kind of resistance.

Sam had to sit up tall and lean forward in his seat to peer

down at the town's car-strewn streets. He hated seeing what had happened to his town—how much worse things had gotten from just twenty-four hours earlier. Sitting back, he let out a weary breath. Exhaustion was setting in. He dragged his palms down his face. *How long has it been since I've slept ... since any of us have slept? Too long. Guess I'll sleep when I'm dead.*

Uncle Jeb was an unwieldy vessel to pilot in space; here within Earth's atmosphere, the controls felt clumsy and unresponsive. He had to oversteer, which inevitably meant he'd have to oversteer the opposite way after making a course change. At least Ivan had stopped complaining about his piloting skills.

Extending his snout forward, Cypress said, "There. I can see Walter's compound. Seems it's still standing."

Relieved, Sam pulled back on the controls and prepared to land.

Carl was at the threshold of the bridge again. "Uh ... just a thought. Um ..."

"Just spit it out, Carl," Sam said.

"How will Walter know we're ... friendlies?"

Ivan said, "Because we are—"

"No! Dammit, he's right!" Sam pushed the controls all the way forward while forcing the old Troop Carrier to angle back skyward.

"Incoming," Cypress said, looking out his side of the craft. "Looks like two missiles..."

Sam stole a quick glance to the right. "Stingers! ... Shit! How could I be so stupid?" He'd even seen Walter's supply of one-man FIM-92 Stinger Launchers within his below-ground bunker. He accelerated, being careful not to slam into the curved contour of the isolation zone.

Cypress said, "You'll need to do exactly as I tell you, Sam."

"What?"

"This craft can make easy work of those two missiles. But you have to do exactly as I say."

"Fine, tell me!"

"First, you need to let Carl help with this ... you need to pilot the vessel."

Sam didn't like that but nodded anyway. He saw on the display the two bogies were edging closer aft.

"Carl, lean in and touch the control board right here." Cypress had extended his paw over an area in between Sam and him. "No, lower, to that illuminated blue set of touch buttons."

Carl did as told, which immediately changed the display configuration to include an array of new symbols and alien characters. Two crosshairs were now tracking the missiles.

"Now, Sam ... on the lower edge of your control array, there's an inset button. You should be able to feel it with your left thumb.

Ivan said, "Missiles closing in on us ... We have mere seconds!"

"Press that inset button twice," Cypress said.

Sam was having a hard time steering while also glancing down at the display. Old Uncle Jeb was now traveling at an ungodly speed while riding mere feet away from the inside perimeter of the isolation zone. Several times he'd brought the nose of the craft too close, causing brilliant white sparks to shower up into the air. Grimacing, he could see a section of the port-side forward hull had been cleaved off.

"It didn't work!" Carl yelled.

Sam stole a glance over to Cypress. "I thought you knew this ship!"

"To be honest, I have never *personally* used this particular combat defense system. I flew a scanner vessel, remember? ... I've never been in combat. But what I told you should work."

"Well, that is what you get when you take combat advice

from a dog," Ivan said. "We are as good as dead ... missiles are closing in on us," Ivan added, placing a meaty palm over his eyes.

The dog looked downtrodden—head lowered, his ears pulled low.

Sam felt for the inset button again and this time felt there were actually two buttons, one on the left edge of the control array and one on the right. This time he pressed the right-side button twice. He felt the ship jolt. But by the time he'd glanced down to the display, the two missiles had exploded into two brilliant balls of fire.

"You can open your eyes now, Ivan," Carl said. "Sam figured it out."

Sam said, "It would have been an easy mistake to make, Cypress. And hey, you got us to the ten-yard line, right?"

The dog stared forward, not looking the least bit consoled by his words.

"So, any ideas how we let Walter know we're the good guys?" Sam said, slowing the ship.

"We just tell him it is us," Ivan said. He pulled a walkie radio from his belt—the same walkie given to him and the others by Walter just yesterday. "Do they not use the same radios at the compound?"

Sam and Carl exchanged a look. They both nodded. Sam said, "Give it a try."

Both Carl and Ivan worked their radios, but all that was heard was loud static.

Cypress, coming out of his funk, said, "This vessel's hull would be impenetrable to radio frequencies."

Sam pursed his lips. "Okay ... I got an idea," he said, bringing *Uncle Jeb* down low to within a few hundred feet of the ground. Hovering, they were at the most southwest section of Castle Rock, where it was mostly rolling hills—sprawling ranchland. "The range on this type of radio is no more than a few miles. I've gotten us within that range ... but hopefully not close enough to push Walter's crew to fire on us again. Carl, what do you say you head back to that aft hatch? Get it open and stand there. Then try it again."

"Ah, I get it. Yeah, that should work."

Less than a minute later, Sam heard Ivan's radio crackle and come alive with Carl's voice. "Walter ... Uh, any of you fellow Gia Fighters read me? ... this is Carl. Over."

"Who the hell is this? Over," a woman's voice came back.

"Carl. I'm with Sam and Ivan and the dog."

A moment later Sam heard Walter's unmistakable Sam Elliot–like deep baritone. "That you that I took a couple of potshots at?"

"Yeah," Carl said. "That was us ... So how about you hold your fire? We're here, and we've come with the cavalry."

Sam shut down the primary drive, spun in his seat, and looked aft. "Carl, you been conversing with the warriors back there." It was more of a statement than a question.

"I guess; it's not like we have a lot in common."

"How they holding up?"

"Holding up?" Carl said, looking mystified.

"Yeah, holding up with no longer having access to Gia and the stream."

Carl looked back into the main cabin, where close to a hundred green faces were looking back at him. "I guess they're doing okay. Good as can be expected."

Ivan said, "Hard to believe. They're in a strange land, taking orders from a bunch of alien humans."

Carl took a few steps back into the compartment and spoke to one Silarian in particular. Sam could just make out their words.

"Dairilop, right? Uh ... you doing okay? How about the

others? Got any problem with what we're doing?" Carl said, looking up to the alien, hands on hips.

"Not exactly how I would have approached the subject," Sam said under his breath.

The medium-sized warrior, Dairilop, looked about the compartment at his fellow compatriots—both he and the others looked confused by the question. "Why ask such a thing? Do we look like children ... or perhaps like whiny kitchen fraus?"

Ivan made a face and mouthed the words, *"Kitchen frow?"*

Carl looked forward, catching Sam's eye. He shrugged.

Cypress said, "Your question ... the way you put it would be insulting to a Silarian's masculinity. Even this, uh, this less disciplined contingent. A better approach would be to ask if Dairilop is ready for battle ... to complete the tasks set forth by Gia." Cypress looked to Carl and then to Sam. "Yes, they are no longer in constant contact with Gia and the stream, but they're not stupid. They can remember everything Gia told them. They still know the difference between right and wrong ... they know that the course set forth by Geo-Mind was absolutely wrong for Silarians, for their world of Naru, and for Earth."

Ivan said, "And how would you know what they are feeling, what they think?"

Cypress looked up, as if searching for help from heaven. "Have you forgotten I too am Silarian? I am in the same predicament as they are ... I too have lost contact with Gia and the stream. I have zero desire for further connection with the Geo-Mind. As you say, that ship has sailed."

Carl nodded. "Makes sense." He turned to Dairilop. "So ... are you, all of you, ready for battle ... to complete the tasks set forth by Gia?"

Dairilop, considering the question, raised his chin and looked to his fellow warriors. It was as if someone had flipped a switch. They all straightened their backs, broadened their shoulders. "Yes. We fight with you pink-skinned, children-sized humans ... You will not defeat our misled brethren ... not without our help."

"Works for me," Sam said, getting to his feet. "Come on, Cypress; how about we introduce Walter's misfits, Valhallen, to our new army?"

Chapter 21

Castle Rock, Colorado
Valhallen Compound

Sam Dale

Sam and Cypress were the first to depart *Uncle Jeb,* followed by Ivan and Carl. The Silarians were to stay put for the time being.

The enterprising gunrunner Walter, along with his tall, ultra-fit cohort, Elsie, were both clad in military camo garb. Sam took in their bulletproof FAVs—*Fast Attack Vests.* Sam, an entrepreneur and owner of multiple businesses in town, one of which was a popular gun shop, recognized the brand—along with the hefty price tag for each. Both wore Avon full-cut tactical helmets, and both carried M4 carbines—undoubtedly the fully automatic military versions.

Sam glanced around, hoping to see that Harper and Julian,

Lester and his team, or anyone from the other two Gia Fighter contingents, had already arrived. But he saw none of them. But others of Valhallen were now making themselves visible—four men came out of the barn; another dozen were coming out from behind other structures. Three were now standing upon the sloping porch of the main house, an old Victorian that had seen better days. Sam knew there was a vast underground bunker, accessible through the barn, where many more of Walter's ragtag militia could be hunkered down.

It was Elsie that approached. "We were wondering what happened to you. How things went in space." She eyed the four of them. "See you've lost a few of your team."

He remembered the all-too-recent battle with the robot Thrash Troopers up in space. The loss of Teddy, Flout, and Gromel. "That we did. But Jarpin's still alive ... he's keeping watch over our newly acquired gunship ... called *Relentless Thrust*."

She raised her brows, looking impressed.

"With Gia's help, the Geo-Mind has been excised from both ship and crew ... the vessel is ours."

"And the rest of that fleet of warships?" Walter asked, lighting a Marlboro with an old Zippo lighter.

"Oh, they're still there. But currently Gia's fighting for her life here within the isolation zone. Any plan to infiltrate the other ships up there will have to wait until, or if, she can regain dominance again."

"Oh yeah ... noticed she's been pretty much AWOL these last few hours," he said, exhaling streams of smoke through both nostrils. "You do realize if she shits the proverbial bed, we're all toast. It's game over."

Leaning over now, Elsie, smiling, was scratching Cypress behind one ear. Her spiderweb tattoo came into view, that and her impressive cleavage. She said, "I still don't get why those green fuckers haven't simply unleashed holy hell on this town, on Earth." She stood up and splayed out fingers on both hands. "Boom."

Sam hitched a shoulder. "From what we've gathered, their high command cannot afford to have Gia spread any farther than this township. Not out to the rest of the planet, and certainly not to their fleet of warships. And no, they are not aware of her infiltration of the gunship. Look, she's more than proven herself here ... she can thwart the Geo-Mind, even beat him at his own game."

She nodded. "So, you're saying Castle Rock, at least for now, is their contained battlefield."

"Uh-huh. The implications are they're being careful. Let the two AIs duke it out. And in the meantime," Sam said, "they'll eradicate us humans with more conventional methods."

"You're referring to the arrival of those four Silarian vessels. The encampment currently setting up on the other side of I-25."

Sam raised a brow. "Encampment?"

Elsie gestured to the west. "We have scouts positioned at key locations within Castle Rock. There's one smaller Troop Carrier over in midtown; that one seems to be abandoned. Three larger ones arrived half a day ago. It's a major deployment, maybe two-fifty, three hundred Silarian warriors ... we imagine they'll soon break up, deploy into smaller contingents."

Both Ivan and Carl, who'd been hanging back near *Uncle Jeb*, now approached. Carl nodded to Walter and Elsie, while Ivan simply gawked at the woman.

Carl said, jacking a thumb over his shoulder, "Uh, boss ... natives are getting restless in there."

Sam nodded. "Walter, Elsie ... any ideas how we're going to accommodate a few of our newfound friends?"

Walter and Elsie exchanged a quizzical look.

"How many friends we talking about?" Walter said, now eyeing the old ship.

Carl held up a finger. "Hold that thought." He hurried back to the ship, sprinted up the gangway, and then gestured with one hand inside at the hatch. "Come on, this way," he said.

Within moments, shirtless green Silarians were stomping down the gangway. Sam watched as they nervously took in the, at least to them, alien landscape. They kept coming and coming, and eventually, Elsie said, "Mother of God. How many are there?"

"Close to a hundred."

Walter, looking exasperated, said, "I don't think I have weapons for all of them."

"That's okay; there's a cache of Ender-4s and 5s on board," Carl said.

The warriors were falling into formation, twenty or so per row.

"What the hell do they eat?" Elsie asked, now walking within their ranks. She stopped and looked up at one of them. "Geez, they're big boys, aren't they?"

"Carl's in charge of them," Sam said. "He's built a bond with them."

Carl shot Sam a derisive look. "I'm no babysitter."

"No, you're an alien sitter," Ivan shot back.

"Find out what they eat," Sam said.

Walter, hands on hips, not looking particularly happy, was glancing around his property. Finally, he turned to Carl. "I have several large TEMPERs."

"What's a TEMPER?"

"Tent Extendable Modular PERsonnel ... A big fucking Army tent. We'll need five of them set up." He pointed to the wide-open west section of the property. "Out there would be good. It's fairly level, and fifty yards beyond it you can have your troops start digging."

"Digging?"

Elsie smiled. "You think we want these miscreants using the house crapper? Or the one in the bunker?"

"Oh, like a latrine," Carl said, wincing.

"NO, exactly like a latrine," Walter corrected.

Sam said, "The other teams ... Gia Fighters?"

"No word yet. Last I was able to query the stream, Lester and his team were hoofing it back this direction. Same goes for the team we deployed to the Douglas County Fairgrounds, as well as the Butterfield Crossing Park team. My guess, what's left of the three groups is making its way here."

"Harper and Julian?"

Walter shook his head. "They made it back into the isolation zone; I know that. Spotted that Landa-Craft flying overhead myself. That was midmorning."

Startled by a bark, Sam saw that the dog had wandered off, was standing sixty yards off to the east. As if on a hunt, the retriever's ears were perked—his tail extended. Then Sam saw him too. A lone figure heading their way. The disheveled mop of white hair left little doubt who it was. Sam felt a tightening in his chest. *I see Julian, but where's Harper?*

Everyone was crowded around the clearly upset old scientist. Elsie handed him a canteen. He gulped down some water and seemed to be calming down.

Sam said. "Start at the beginning. When you first entered back into the dome."

"Okay, yes ... Gia ... she was still talking to us at that point, had opened the isolation zone enough for us to reenter. We landed at the Bell Mountain Equestrian Center."

Julian continued relaying his and Harper's harrowing story,

how they'd been caught off guard and captured by Silarian warriors, roughly manhandled, bound, and locked into separate horse stalls, and later, how Harper was viciously attacked.

It took all of Sam's will not to rush off—make someone pay. "I'm going after her."

"Wait, Sam," Julian said. "There's more."

"Fine," he said, "Go on then. But make it quick."

Julian nodded. "Quick, yes ... when that guard came around ... while he was trying to, well, you know ..."

The knuckles on Sam's clenched fists were turning white.

Julian took another swig of water from Elsie's canteen. "Well, before anything too terrible took place, although it was terrible enough what—"

"Julian!" Sam barked. He knew he was allowing triggers to get the best of him.

"Yes, yes ... well, then, unbelievably, Harper was saved by this other Silarian warrior."

Sam exchanged a look with Walter.

"Only this one wasn't really a Silarian; he was, but he was really a human."

Sam was starting to wonder if the old man had finally lost his marbles.

Julian held up a palm. "Let me explain what he said. Although he didn't say much. From what I gather, he'd been a resident over at the Pleasant Days Nursing Home."

"I know it; it's off 2nd Street, or maybe 3rd," Elsie said.

"That's where the Silarians' first dropship landed. Ten or so officer-level guys," she added.

Sam was getting more and more impatient. "What does this have to do with—"

Julian continued, "Apparently, one of the old codgers ate a glazed Castle Rock donut and subsequently was donutted. And I'm filling in the blanks here from what I've pieced together; he used the stream to get inside the ship. The Silarians, an officer-level bunch, had already left ... they later ended up at the equestrian center. Anyway, the old codger—think he said his name was Glen. No, Lloyd. He got inside the ship, found a bunch of slumbering bio-forms, and—"

"No ... that cannot be done," Cypress interjected. "Human and Silarian DNA is not compatible!"

Sam was unaccustomed to the mild-mannered Cypress raising his voice in such a manner. He gave the dog a pat and said, "It's okay, boy. Just let him finish."

Cypress sat back on his haunches, staring at Julian.

"I don't know how the old man did it. Maybe he won't live long. But he did it just the same. And he saved Harper from being, well, you know ..."

Sam's patience had come to an end. "So where is she now, dammit!? Why are you here and she's not?"

Julian flinched at Sam's outburst.

"I'm sorry, Julian. I shouldn't have yelled. Go on ... please."

"We asked this Lloyd to help us, to come back with us, but he declined. I'm not so sure whose side he's on, to be honest."

"At least he helped you, old man. You're standing here, aren't you?" Elsie said with a shrug.

"Sure, he helped both of us. But Harper didn't want to leave the Landa-Craft behind." Julian looked over to Sam. "I think she thought you would want it ... it being an important asset."

"So where is this skinny woman? She should have gotten here before you," Ivan said.

Sam agreed with the crass Slav. He turned away, took notice of the progress being made with the five big Army tents. Two of the five had already been erected. Beyond, no less than twenty Silarians were digging a deep trench.

"This doesn't change anything. I need to go after her. She's probably gotten herself captured again." He hated thinking what they were going to do to her—or maybe already had.

"Look!" one of Walter's guys yelled from over near the barn. "A team's coming in."

"What the hell are those? Golf carts?" Walter said.

Chapter 22

Castle Rock, Colorado
Bell Mountain Equestrian Center

Harper Godard

With hands outstretched—she knew what she must look like. A ghoul. A blind and bloodied zombie character from an old B-movie. Reaching the spot where she'd been certain she had left the cloaked Landa-Craft, she felt nothing. She swung her hands around to the left and then the right. *Shit! Shit! Shit!* She tried querying the stream for the tenth time, hoping it had miraculously come back alive—it hadn't.

Aware that the dozens of Silarian warriors were no longer content to just watch, she saw they were raising their weapons; several were striding toward her.

Exasperated, she yelled, "Goddammit, Gia. Where the fuck is my ship?!"

... t n pa ... to ... left ...

"Gia? What? Say again!"

... ten paces to ... left ...

She was relieved to hear Gia's voice again. At least for the moment, the AI was still among the living. Doing as told, she strode directly to the left. Her outstretched hands hadn't been held high enough—she bonked her forehead on something hard. It only took her a second to realize Gia had lowered the steps. Up she climbed, venturing a quick look toward the fast-approaching warriors. She stopped halfway up and gawked. They'd stopped in their tracks. Two dozen big aliens were looking in her general direction. But not directly at her. She rolled her eyes at herself. *I'm invisible ... I too am cloaked from view.*

She didn't diddle-daddle, but also felt less of a need to rush. She got herself properly situated within the small confines of the Landa-Craft's cockpit, powered on the propulsion drive, and lifted off.

One minute later she was approaching the Valhallen compound. The first thing she noticed was the battered, beat-to-shit old spacecraft. Big Army tents were being raised, and there were ... Silarians. A lot of Silarians. *Another encampment?* Ready to hightail it out of there, she then noticed that not all the ones down there had green flesh tones. And then she saw a dog—a familiar-looking golden retriever. Cypress. Smiling, and feeling tremendous relief, she saw the huddled cluster of humans. Julian was among them, as were Walter and Elsie ... and there was Sam too.

She piloted the ship over to an open area, uncloaked the Landa-Craft, and slowly brought the ship down. She sat there a second as the drive wound down. Butterflies danced in her stomach as she saw Sam headed her way. Then she caught sight of her own reflection upon the inside of the canopy. "Really ...

that's what I look like?" She swiped at bloodied strands of hair plastered to her forehead, realizing her attempts were futile.

He and Cypress both were waiting for her as she hurried down the steps. Sam's smile didn't falter at the sight of her. Cypress, up on his back legs and tail wagging, greeted her first. She took the dog's head in two hands and kissed the top of his head. "So happy to see you, Cypress!" she said with a laugh. It had been a long time since anybody had greeted her with such affection.

She glanced up to Sam, and before she could say anything, his arms were around her waist and he was pulling her in close —and then his lips were upon hers. She melted into him.

By the time they separated, a small crowd had formed around them. Her face flushed. "Hey there, um, everyone ..."

She did a double take, seeing that a half-dozen golf carts had just pulled into the compound while stirring up swirls of dust. It was Lester and his team of cops and firefighters. Her heart sank, seeing that the teenage girl wasn't among them.

Lester, tattooed, with his typically long, scraggly black hair, and looking cocky as ever, approached with a wide smile. He raised a bandaged fist in the air. "We return victorious!" He eyed Elsie. "No kiss for the returning hero?"

Elsie, looking mildly bemused, said, "You did okay. Like what you did with those robots."

"They were Thrash Troopers ... an army of them, and yeah, we showed them a little human justice."

Harper couldn't hold back any longer. "The girl ... Luna?"

Lester looked annoyed by the question. Gave Harper a quick once-over—made a disgusted face. "Little lady might want to think about taking a shower." He scratched at the scruff on his chin. "Uh ... what about the girl?"

"What happened to her? Where is she, Lester?"

He raised his palms in mock surrender, "Hey, chillax, lady.

How about letting a man first say his hellos and get situated before you start in with an interrogation?"

Sam said, "Just tell us where she is, Lester."

"You too? She's fine ... still back at the old farts' home in town. Didn't want to leave the feeble geezers to fend for themselves. Her choice, not mine." He looked to the Army tents. "What's with all these alien fuckers running about?"

With that, Walter moved forward. "That's enough jabber-jawing. We have a lot to do and too little time to do it. Harper, welcome back. Looking forward to your update on your meeting with the military in Colorado Springs, as well as what's going over at the equestrian center. For now, Elsie's going to show you where you can get, uh, cleaned up."

Harper nodded, feeling everyone's eyes on her. "Thanks ..." She gestured to her bloodied clothes. "You should see the other guy."

Walter said, "Okay, everyone, we'll reconvene again in, say ... an hour and a half. Then we can talk about what comes next for us. Sam's going to tell us all how we're going to rid this town of those alien bastards once and for all."

Chapter 23

Valhallen Compound
Castle Rock, Colorado

Sam Dale

An hour and three quarters later they'd all gathered once again—this time inside the large barn. Diffused late afternoon sunlight streamed down from above like spotlights illuminating a stage; reflective suspended particles swirled and danced.

Walter pinched a wad of Skoal from a tin, shoved it between cheek and gum, and gestured to the large knee-high platform setup adjacent to him. "We can thank Elsie for her artistic abilities."

It was a raised ten foot by ten foot mockup of the town of Castle Rock. She'd used whatever items she had handy to handcraft the structures—various-sized cardboard boxes, stacked 9mm ammo cartons for retail stores; a mac and cheese box laid on its side for the Safeway supermarket; a paperback novel for the Castle Rock Ford dealership; dozens of Skoal tins, undoubtedly empty, for restaurants and fast-food joints; and stacked Budweiser cans were used for the multiple high-rise condo towers. The major streets had been laid out with their designated names penned in with a Sharpie. The surrounding foothills looked to have been molded from paper mâché. All in all, it served its purpose—there was little doubt as to what represented what.

Sam had already been staring at the mock-up for close to an hour now. Alone with the model, thinking, planning, calculating.

Lost in thought, it took a moment for him to realize everyone was looking at him. The barn was filled with people; all the Valhallen compound crew, Lester's team, and surprisingly, the other two teams of Gia Fighters had arrived too. Cypress was sitting at his feet; he felt the warmth of the dog's body leaning into his legs. Julian was at his left, and Harper—now wearing fresh camos, her hair still shower-moist—was to his right.

He heard Ivan's accented voice from behind. "Earth to Sam ... that was your cue."

Harper gave his upper arm a couple of pats. "You okay?"

Nodding, he stepped toward the model, where Walter handed him a long wooden pointer. He realized it was a pool table cue stick. He turned toward the crowd. In the back he saw a dozen or so Silarian warriors who'd been designated to attend.

"We're not going to defeat the enemy." He let his words stand for several long moments. The barn went quiet—feet shuffled—someone cleared their throat.

"You really know how to motivate crowd," Ivan said to sporadic nervous laughter.

"Let me clarify: we're not going to defeat the enemy, the Geo-Mind, ... or that entire Silarian fleet of warships just beyond Earth's high orbit." Again, he let his words sit for a while. "That's not our job. But the three hundred Silarian warriors deployed here to our little town? Yeah, we sure as hell can do something about them."

Cheers, hoots, and hollers erupted before him. Sam held up a palm. "Okay, okay, settle down. Let me finish."

The barn went quiet once more.

"The next time all of us are together like this, if there is a next time, many of us will be gone. Maybe most of us will have been killed by an enemy fully intent upon eradicating the human race. Intent on terra-displacement ... the ravaging of our home, of Earth." He gestured to the model behind him. "We can't defeat an enemy that is bigger, stronger, far more advanced, better trained, and better armed, by duking it out face to face in the streets of Castle Rock. No. What will save us, where we can prevail, is cunning, misdirection ... cheating. Being smarter. Those of us here in this barn will hold up our end of the bargain. Gia will hold up her end; she'll defeat the Geo-Mind. She'll find a way to spread her influence within that fleet of warships."

Sam made eye contact with Harper; she nodded. "Tell us what to do, Sam."

"When I call your name, please come join me here at my side. Harper."

She didn't hesitate. She stepped forward, taking up a position at his side.

"Lester."

There were a few snickers and several groans from the crowd. But for once the man didn't make light of the situation—no dumb comments. No jokes. All business, he moved to Harper's left and turned toward the crowd.

"Walter and Elsie."

They joined the growing row along with Sam and the others.

"Greg."

The big and muscular one-time mail carrier made his way through the throng, then joined the line, looking both surprised and a little humbled at being selected.

Sam's eyes leveled on Julian and then Cypress. Both were looking at the ground. Perhaps feeling inadequate. Unworthy to join Sam's chosen few. "Julian and Cypress, get up here."

Julian looked truly shocked to hear his name while Cypress leaped forward, edging himself between Sam and Harper's legs. Julian, looking self-conscious, joined the others.

"These people before you—"

Cypress looked up at him.

"These people here with me, along with one fine dog, will be leading the fight. They are my lieutenants ... your leaders. Soon, they will be selecting their top sergeants from among the rest of you."

"What about our little army of Silarians?" Carl said. It took a moment for Sam to find him in the crowd. He looked a little dejected. Perhaps feeling he'd somehow been passed over as one of Sam's lieutenants.

"Excellent question. You okay taking on that responsibility, Carl? You'd be joining my team. You and Ivan."

The Slav was standing with Carl. Hearing his name, he stood up straighter and saluted. "You can count on me, boss. I will be best soldier ever. Make you proud."

Sam nodded, unconvinced. "The rest of you can go. Thank you in advance for your commitment to what lies ahead."

Before they could move off, Harper piped up, "Uh ... one more thing. Please know the day will come decades from now, perhaps centuries from now, when mothers, fathers, grandparents tell their children about you. About this small group of Gia

Fighters that chose to hold the line against ... impossible odds. Against interstellar invaders intent on erasing us. So, thank you. Thank you, each and every one of you."

Harper stood, sweeping her gaze, making momentary eye contact with each of them. Sam realized she was far better at this than he was.

It took a few minutes for the barn to clear out, leaving Sam with his chosen lieutenants.

He said, "Let's all gather around Elsie's impressive model."

They did as asked. Sam saw excitement and anticipation on their faces. He offered up a conspiratorial smile while inside, he was feeling a familiar dread—one that came with military command. A knowledge that some, if not most, of these individuals, people he truly cared about, would not survive the coming days.

Sam said, "The trick will be getting the enemy's attention. Getting them to split their forces and come after us ... come after you. Whatever initial plans they have for taking this town, methodically killing off the inhabitants, needs to be quickly and decisively interrupted. Our teams will be doing just that."

Lester, standing directly opposite Sam on the other side of the model, scoffed. "Without Gia ... I don't see—"

Sam cut him off. "I'm in contact with her."

Everyone looked up.

Harper said, "I haven't heard a peep from her in hours. You're talking? What's going on with her?"

It had started just thirty minutes prior. Had made it difficult for him to divide his attention between what was going on here and what was going on in his head.

"Simply put, Gia almost perished."

"How? What happened?" Harper asked.

"And why is it only you that's talking to her?" Lester asked, indignant.

"I'm not. Look, she's still battling the Geo-Mind. He got the best of her. Used his substantial capabilities and resources to wear her down. But apparently, she's rebounded some. She knows his moves, the way he thinks ... we need to remember she was once a part of him."

"So, she's going to bless us with a little help from time to time?" Lester said with more than a little scorn in his tone.

"Her focus must remain on taking back control of the isolation zone, those isolation drones up in the sky in particular. So she's talking to me; she's talking to Julian, and she's talking to Cypress. For the immediate future, we'll be the conduits for any communications."

Lester wasn't having it. "She's just talking to the old man? The stupid damn dog?"

"Just shut up, Lester," Harper spat. "This isn't about you. Not everything is about you."

"It's all right. I'll answer that," Sam said. "Julian has been tasked with constructing the ultimate bomb. One that may literally change everything ... change humankind forever."

Walter, who'd been keeping quiet for the most part, spat a gob of tobacco juice into the dark. "A bomb, huh? That sounds more like my area of expertise."

"Julian will indeed need your help, but this won't be the kind of bomb that so much goes boom. By the way, before I forget, there should be ample supplies of healing nanites in *Uncle Jeb*."

Julian nodded absentmindedly, "Uh ... yes ... I already helped myself to those supplies."

Lester, making a huffing sound, was obviously still stuck on why he hadn't been chosen to talk with Gia. "What about the dog ... why is she talking to it?"

Sam shrugged. "I don't know the answer to that myself, other than Gia and Cypress have a special relationship. Cypress was the first one here to communicate with the rebellious AI—was the first of us Gia Fighters."

Cypress, who was staring at the model, was being tight-lipped about his involvement. Sam let it go for now; he too was more than curious what was going on with him.

"Let me break down our team functions." Sam, still holding his pool cue, moved in front of the others, forcing several of them to take a step back as he circled the model. "Walter and Elsie, you know better than anyone that a war cannot be won without well-established supply lines. Poor logistics can end a campaign as fast as a well-placed missile. Getting weapons, munitions, and food staples to troops in a timely manner will be imperative." Sam placed a hand on Walter's shoulder. "You'll be developing multiple contingencies for when, inevitably, the enemy disrupts those logistics lines."

"Not my first rodeo, bucko," Walter said.

Sam moved closer to Elsie. "You'll also be feeding, outfitting, and arming our new Silarian forces. Stay in touch via radio; pay close attention to how and where our attack teams are deployed. And keep in mind, we have a limited air force; the Landa-Craft and *Uncle Jeb* are among our assets."

"What the fuck's an Uncle Jeb?" Lester spat.

Ignoring him, Elsie stood looking at the model with her arms crossed over her chest. "Tell us more about your attack teams, Sam."

"There are basically six teams. There are four attack teams: Alpha Team, mine; Beta Team, Harper's; Gamma Team, Lester's; and Epsilon Team, Greg's. Non-attack teams are Zeta Team, you and Walter; Julian and Cypress ... Team Theta."

"Who gives a flying fuck what we call each other? I want to know where on this model me and my teams will be fighting the greenie meanies."

Sam ... you may want to rethink Lester as one of your lieutenants ...

Sam had half expected this from Gia. "Sure, he's a hothead. He's unpredictable. But he's also proven himself just unconventional enough to be a threat."

That threat can go both ways, Sam ... you'll need to keep an eye on him.

"Oh, I will, Gia. But for now, talk to me more about Silarian troop deployments within the dome."

That deployment has already begun, Sam. More to come on that soon. You'll need to get your people in position, situated quickly. Now, I must concentrate my efforts back on the GeoMind ... that and on helping Julian with his task.

"Can you do anything about bringing back the stream?"

It took several moments for Gia to answer. *Done ... it is back online ... for now.*

Sam's closing order was for everyone to get some sleep. Because at 0600 tomorrow, it would be rise and shine and ready for battle.

Chapter 24

Castle Rock, Colorado
Bell Mountain Equestrian Center

Lloyd Sanderson

The sun had fallen behind the distant foothills, throwing the equestrian center into the muted colors of twilight. Lloyd had stayed out of sight, holed up within a weathered and craggy lean-to at the center of one of the smaller corrals. Goats and several small ponies milled about outside while he kept vigil through gaps between timber planks. His quarry, Captain Larng Nos Polk, stood some fifty yards away within the closest of the barracks. This one for the officers, a kind of prefab structure, looked far fancier than any of the others. *Rank has its perks.*

Lloyd's vantage point allowed him a clear view through the barracks' entrance. A glowing 3D projection that was easily twelve feet in circumference was the center of attention of no less than six other Silarian officers. They moved around the virtual embodiment of the town—of Castle Rock. No doubt methodically plotting the demise of a populace of no less than seventy-five thousand townsfolk. It occurred to him he didn't give a shit about the town or its inhabitants. *Did anyone here ever care about me?*

People will care about you, Lloyd, if you give them a chance. Do right by them, then see what happens ...

It had been some time since he'd heard from the female voice in his head. The AI presence that had made his rebirth possible. He was on the fence if he actually owed her anything in return. Lloyd didn't like being in anyone's debt. What he wanted was to be on the winning side of things here. The aliens, the humans ... he couldn't care less which.

"Sorry, lady ... but I don't think you've got what it'll take. What will be necessary to defeat the aliens and the Geo-Mind."

Please, Lloyd, do not underestimate the humans and your own humanity.

He hitched a shoulder in a half shrug. "Give me back the stream and I'll think about it."

It took several moments before she came back with, *Done.*

Sporadically, over an ensuing four hours, Captain Larng Nos Polk dispatched three of his officers. Lloyd's eyesight, far superior to when he was human, even in the near total darkness, could see each of the Silarian faces. He watched them as they hurried out from the barracks' entrance. Some of the same faces he'd observed earlier upon cryogenically maintained bio-forms held within the small Troop Carrier just down the hill from the Pleasant Days Nursing Home. He thought about the other old codgers there. How he'd eaten meals with them, played cards, sometimes shared a laugh with them. They were the closest thing he'd ever had to friends, to family. *Fuck 'em ... all things come to an end.*

From what he could discern from his vantage point, the officers were joining up with their respective troop companies of approximately seventy-five armed and more than ready Silarian warriors each. And like an Old West posse, they soon rode off, kicking up plumes of dirt and dust behind them. Only these posses weren't riding horses; no, these motherfuckers sped away upon ground-skimming FastLevs.

Lloyd queried the stream as to their destinations—where they'd be commencing their three-pronged attacks—and was surprised the answer came so quickly. He whistled. "And starting tonight, there'll be suffering ... there'll be carnage. It'll be like nothing this world's ever known."

Extracting himself from his lean-to hideout, he stood tall—stretched his aching back. Dark enough now to go unnoticed, he took in the entirety of the encampment with silhouettes of looming tall spacecraft in the distance, and closer, all the prefab barracks scattered around. There were still plenty of Silarians milling about. He guesstimated a good seventy-five warriors had been left behind to protect the encampment. But none of that interested Lloyd now. Staying within the darkened shadows, he made his way toward the officer's prefab barrack. It had been close to an hour since he'd last seen movement inside. With luck, Captain Larng Nos Polk would be asleep on his cot.

Lloyd held up at the entrance, noticing the barracks were made from some kind of heavy fabric—something like Kevlar. He hesitated, then peeked one eye around the corner. It was dark except for one small desk lamp. He saw that his counterpart, his doppelgänger, was standing at the desk—tapping away at a tablet computer. He was half-turned away—all his attention on the device. *Fuck, things aren't all that different with these cretins.*

Lloyd drew his knife and stepped inside. He waited. He ensured that his movements hadn't alerted the captain. Now, staying in the shadows along the periphery, Lloyd moved to a position that put him directly behind the big Silarian. He contemplated what he was about to do—*just because we look alike doesn't mean I'm killing myself.*

He assessed he'd be taking four long strides to be within striking distance. The question now was, *Do I rush him, or slowly sneak up on him?*

Using more stealth than Lloyd thought he was capable of, he took the slow approach. He took one careful step, and then another. Lloyd held his breath, taking in the captain's muscular back—angling up into powerful wide shoulders. Lloyd raised the knife, his fingers tightening around the knife's handle. He swallowed ... *It's now or never.*

Movement.

Lloyd lowered the knife and remained still as a Silarian warrior entered through the entrance, carrying a tray of food. The warrior slowed, seeing there were two officers standing before him. His uncertainty showed on his face. *Oh no. I've only brought enough for one* ... Lloyd now stood with his hands, one of which was holding a hidden knife behind his back. He did his best to look less imposing than his counterpart. To look like just one more subservient peon.

The warrior stood to the side of the desk; his mouth opened to speak—

"Just leave it and be gone," the captain said without looking up.

The warrior hesitated—glanced back at Lloyd.

Lloyd chin gestured to the captain's desk. *Just put the fucking tray down and leave.*

But Captain Larng Nos Polk had picked up on the warrior's indecision—his seeming incapacity to follow such a simple directive. The captain, clearly irritated, sent an annoyed glance over his left shoulder.

Did he see me standing here? How could he not have?

The flummoxed warrior, realizing he was about to incur the wrath of the encampment's most senior officer, placed the tray down upon the corner of the desk, where it almost tipped over—saved only by the captain's impressively fast reflexes, catching the tray with one hand. Steadying it.

"Leave! Now ... imbecilic moron."

The captain watched as the warrior apologized and then bowed. He backed away, one, two steps ... and then the fuckwad had to do it—had to glance toward Lloyd one last time.

As the warrior turned and scampered off, Captain Larng Nos Polk went very still—a granite statue no longer interested in the tray of food or the tablet still grasped in his right hand.

All bets were off, Lloyd thought. No more stealth. No more pussyfooting around.

Chapter 25

Castle Rock, Colorado
Pleasant Days Nursing Home

Luna Kelly

Luna stood over Harry, watching him sleep. He was in his eighties, frail, with white wisps of hair partially covering the top of his head. When she'd first started volunteering at the nursing home, Harry's wife, Nan, would come every day—they'd sit on the porch and play gin rummy and drink frozen pink Minute Maid lemonade. Then one day, Nan just stopped showing up. Harry never talked about it. Two months later, he asked if Luna would play gin with him.

Luna smiled, reminiscing. A tattered deck of playing cards was lying next to Harry's bed. She picked up the cards and straightened them in her hands—then placed them facedown on the crumb-riddled nightstand.

Seriously?

She bent down to take a closer look. Leaning in, she examined the all-too-familiar-looking deposit of sugary crumbs. With the sweep of one hand, she corralled the crumbs together, then pushed them off the side of the table into her other open palm. She brought them up to her nose, smelled them. Glazed Castle Rock Donuts—*You too, huh, Harry?*

Lu ... m ... Silar ... on th—

Luna stood up, surprised to hear Gia's voice. Crumb remnants showered down onto the floor. "Gia, thank God ... you're back. Can you repeat that? Something about Silarians?"

She waited, but there was no response. *Just perfect.*

Luna left Harry's bedside and a moment later was scurrying down the main stairwell. Halfway down, she slowed and tried to listen for any activity within Pleasant Days Nursing Home. But all she heard were her own muted footfalls upon the steps. She eyed the foyer table at the bottom of the stairs—saw that it was strewn with food items. There were three loaves of Wonder Bread, four cartons of Cheddar Goldfish, two boxes of Triscuits, nine cans of *Chef Boyardee Ravioli*, and a large Ziploc bag filled with Oreo cookies. Three twenty-four-packs of small plastic water bottles lay beneath the table. *Thanks, Lester. You didn't leave me the most nutritious of provisions, but still, better than nothing ...*

Dirty boot prints covered the narrow-plank hardwood floors, a reminder that her team—Lester's team—had vacated the old house. It was just her now—well, her and the mostly bedridden batch of old folks upstairs. *Why did I insist on staying behind? What am I supposed to do now? I need to focus.* She took a deep breath and immediately gagged. She brought a hand up to cover her nose and mouth—a nasty smell still hung heavy in the air.

Clack!

Luna flinched at hearing the loud sound—something had fallen around the corner within the main living area. She stepped quietly to the adjacent wall and peered around the corner. Sheer curtains fluttered as gusts of wind billowed in through a broken window. She saw that a small framed picture of an ugly but cute English bulldog was lying on the floor—shards of glass were strewn about next to it. Relieved, she let out the breath she'd been holding.

At the window she saw that it was late afternoon, and dark clouds were forming off to the west—*a storm is coming.* That was when she heard the unique but all too familiar sounds from the skies above—more Silarian ships had entered the dome. There would be only one reason for them to return ... to finish what they had started. To exterminate all humans within the domed area.

Cannot talk no ... Luna. But you must ... stay vigilant ... help will co ...

Even as broken as her message was, just hearing Gia's voice bolstered Luna's resolve. She had a hundred questions for Gia but knew the battling AI could ill afford the distraction right now.

In her periphery, a glint of reflected sunlight caught her attention. There, on the pastel floral print sofa, was an M4 carbine. *Once again, thanks, Lester.* Luna plucked up the weapon, released and checked its load—full—reinserted the magazine, and drove it home with the heel of her palm. *A week ago, I'd have had no idea how to do that.* The weapon felt good in her hands—gave her a sense of security—security she knew wasn't real.

I need a plan. How long would it be before those Silarians arrived here? *A day. An hour?* One M4 carbine suddenly seemed insufficient for the task at hand. Back at the window, she contemplated her options. She knew there were other weapons available to her. She grimaced. That meant going back to the alien transport ship. But without Lester's team or any backup, and with nighttime soon approaching ... *Stop!*

She fought to regain her nerve—fought feeling totally overwhelmed by what lay ahead. *But shit, I'm only sixteen!* Tears welled in her eyes. *Get a grip, Luna. I'll need those weapons ... if only I had help* ... unconsciously, Luna was thumbing the barrel of her carbine—as if rubbing a genie's magical lamp—coincidentally, at the same time she was silently wishing for more help.

She heard a muffled thump from upstairs. No doubt one of the old codgers ambling their way toward the bathroom. An idea had been taking root in her mind, one she immediately discounted with a shake of her head and a roll of her eyes. *Then again* ... There were eight patients besides old Harry and the now-departed Lloyd—that left Gloria, Agnes, Edith, Bernie, Felix, Herschel, and Saul.

Eyes closed, and for the umpteenth time in these last few hours, Luna tried querying the stream again.

Nothing.

Maybe I already have the answers ... I just need to think. If Harry and Lloyd had been donutted, maybe some of the others had been as well. So, how does that help me? She put a mental pin in that thought. Also, I still have those alien nanites ... with advanced healing properties. Maybe—

Like a track star reacting to the sound of a starting pistol, Luna bolted for the stairs.

"Harry, wake up." Luna jostled one of his slender shoulders.

He blinked awake—it took a moment for clarity to show in his eyes. "Who ..."

"Harry, it's me, Luna."

"What's going on?" he asked, rubbing sleep from his eyes. His gaze fell on what was slung over her shoulder.

"Don't worry about that; it's just for protection." She gave him a comforting smile. "Which leads me to why I need to talk to you."

He squirmed his way up into a sitting position, excited, as if being let in on a juicy secret. "Tell me. What's up, buttercup?"

Luna sat down on the edge of his bed. "This is going to sound crazy, but ..."

Harry's brow knit, but he stayed quiet.

"An alien transport ship has landed down the hill from the house. Behind Pleasant Days Nursing Home." She saw the skepticism on his lined and weathered face. Her heart sank. *This is a waste of time.* "Anyway, these aliens may be coming here soon. To hurt us." Luna spoke in staccato sentences, hoping to make her words easier to digest.

"Harry, did you hear me?"

"I'm not deaf, girl. Of course I heard you. The aliens. The Silarians, right? Are they coming?" Harry asked, fear showing in his eyes.

"How did you—" Luna cut herself off, realizing Harry must have, at some point, talked to Gia, maybe tapped into the stream. *That will help ...*

"Lloyd was ranting on and on about it." Harry looked over to his roommate's empty bed. "I was happy he took off—mean son of a gun, that one. Although now I kinda miss him, in a weird way." Harry looked back to Luna. He gestured with a forefinger to his ear. "She's gone now ... the woman in my head." He looked irritated with himself. "Perhaps I imagined it. Hell, I'm older than dirt."

Luna gave his shoulder a gentle squeeze while thinking about the implications of what Harry was saying. At some point, he'd definitely had access to Gia, and maybe the stream ... how else would he even know about the Silarians?

"You ate one of the donuts, Harry?"

The change of subject caught Harry off guard. "Donut?"

But before she could answer, he said, "Oh yeah, yeah ... there were a couple of white bags someone had dropped off. We shared them. Was a bright spot in my day, tell you that much," he said, eyes momentarily unfocused, remembering. "Damn good ... called glazed Castle Rocks."

She realized Harry, who had been battling early stage dementia, was now speaking with far more lucidity than she was used to. "Harry, you know who else here shared those donuts?"

"No, but you could ask the girls next door. The four of us played bridge into the night ... that was yesterday ... same day the donuts showed up. We were up past 10:00 p.m." Harry's eyes lit up like a kid on Christmas morning. "Hell, I felt like a spry sixty-year-old again. Still do!"

Luna tapped at the top pockets of her vest with her palms, then the lower ones—she felt a couple of lumps there in her right-side pocket. Pulled out one of the pouches she'd taken from the satchel earlier. *Please don't make me sorry I left that satchel with you, Lester.*

"How much should Harry take?"

The answer came to her.

... half.

Luna gasped. It was the first time in hours she'd been able to access the stream. She didn't press her luck by asking a lot of questions. Luna handed Harry the pouch.

"Drink this—just half though."

"What is it?"

"It's medicine that will make you feel stronger—like the donuts, but different. Maybe more intense."

He looked at her, hesitating.

"You trust me?" Luna asked, getting to her feet.

He nodded. "Cheers." Harry tilted the pouch and drank.

He handed the half-empty pouch back to Luna. "Tastes like heaven."

"Really?"

"No."

She laughed at that. "How do you feel? Can you stand?"

He looked insulted.

"Sorry. Harry, I need you to come with me."

"Come with you ... where?" Harry said, but was already pushing his covers aside and swinging his legs over the side of the bed.

"Eventually, to the Silarian ship—there are weapons inside," Luna said. "Things are about to get action movie–crazy. You ever see *Dirty Harry?*"

"Yes, but I can't go with you—"

She cut him off. "Why not?"

He continued, "... Until I find my damn slippers." He smiled. "But yeah. I'm in, kid."

She took a step back, giving Harry room to stand. He leaned over his nightstand, opened the top drawer, and fumbled for something inside.

We don't have time for this ... what is he doing? Looking for his glasses?

But to Luna's surprise, Harry withdrew a pistol—a big-ass revolver, to be exact. It looked to be well-maintained, but definitely not something from this century.

"It's a Colt Peacemaker, made in 1870—and yes, it still works. My father passed it on to me—had a feeling it would come in handy someday."

Luna made a face. "And they let you keep that ... antique ... in there? It's not loaded, is it?"

Harry flipped open the cylinder with a flip of his wrist, surprising dexterity that exposed the ass-end of six shiny brass bullets. "Yup, loaded for bear." He quickly put on his bathrobe and shoved the gun into an oversized side pocket. The weight of the thing made his robe hang off-kilter to one side.

Luna nodded. "Guess that makes you my wingman." She gestured down to the floor.

Smiling, he saw the heels of his slippers peeking out from beneath the bed.

"Okay, Harry, you're going to show me who else ate those yummy donuts, okay?"

Two elderly women shared the room next door. Their shared space was laid out exactly like Harry's—two twin hospital beds, two nightstand-like cabinets on wheels, a rectangular card table, also on wheels, and two bacteria-resistant upholstered chairs—the kind you'd see in a doctor's waiting area.

One of the women shushed Harry as he and Luna stood at the threshold of the room. "You can come in, but keep your voices down. I'm trying to concentrate."

Both elderly ladies were sitting at the table. They were entranced in some sort of game. The taller of the two had a beak of a nose and bluish-silver hair; she was laying down oversized playing cards. Luna caught sight of a colorful picture displayed on the top card. "Interesting ... the three of wands," the woman said, winking at her roommate. "Looks like you're going on a trip, Dolly."

"I haven't been anywhere in twenty years," the chubby woman, with a headful of coiffed red-orange-dyed hair, said. She shifted in her seat. "Where in the world would I go, Agnes ... Walmart?" She chuckled.

"That's up to you ... I only read the tarot that is drawn. I do not presume to know details beyond that." Agnes reached for another card but hesitated. "Now pay attention, Dolly ... are you ready?"

"Excuse me, ladies," Harry said, stepping closer to the table.

Both Dolly and Agnes looked up—four eyebrows raised in unison. Both women looked to Harry and then to Luna, and then to Luna's M4.

Luna stepped closer, seeing bluish-silver-haired Agnes was wearing her locks in long braided pigtails. She was slim, had a well-toned physique, and near-perfect posture. Luna wondered if she'd been a dancer back in the day. So prim and proper. She also wondered what she was doing here in a place like this—she seemed far too fit and healthy to be in a nursing home.

"You're interrupting our reading, Harry," Agnes said with refined diction. She leveled her catlike eyes on him.

"I do apologize ... Agnes," Harry said, shrugging like a scolded schoolboy.

"I'm afraid it's my fault. I'm Luna—you may remember me from when—"

"Yes, yes, you're that little colored girl," Agnes said with a wave of a hand. "What is this about?"

Luna bit back a defensive retort to Agnes's ignorant remark. She skirted around Harry and held out a hand to her. "Luna Kelly ... nice to officially meet you, Agnes."

Agnes hesitated, shook her hand, all the while still making it clear this was all an unwanted distraction.

Dolly, who seemed somewhat dwarf-like to Luna but far friendlier than Agnes, extended her own chubby hand. "Hi, Luna—what a fun name you have. I'm Dolly."

"Nice to meet you, Dolly—Luna was my dad's idea." She swallowed, feeling a lump in her throat—*my father who was shot and killed by looters just days ago.* "It means moon goddess—apparently ... I was born on a full moon."

"And do goddesses normally equip themselves with such enormous weapons?" Agnes asked.

"We're going to need them. For protection. Just give us a chance to explain," Harry said defensively.

"I used to volunteer here. I thought Gloria was in this room," Luna said.

"She passed ... gone on to the other side," Agnes said with a frown. "Dolly moved in here last week."

Luna wasn't sure what to say about Gloria. She wasn't that close to her but hadn't realized that the poor lady was on the verge of death.

"Okay. Enough chitchat," Harry interrupted. "What do you know about the aliens?"

The women exchanged glances.

"You're donutted, right? Um ... ate a glazed Castle Rock?" Luna asked, moving things along.

Agnes nodded. "You're talking about dropships ... Silarian warriors."

Dolly said, "We're no longer in contact with that delightful woman. So polite."

"Willing to explain things, but never condescending," Agnes added.

Luna was relieved. "The aliens ... they may be on their way here. May be here any minute. So, we need to get ourselves prepared. We'll need more weapons if we want to stay alive."

"We're gonna get guns too." Dolly said, clambering to her feet. She wrapped her pink terry-cloth robe around her substantial belly and reknotted the belt.

"I was quite a shot in my day ... although that was with a Remington 700, on a Montana cattle ranch, half a lifetime ago." Agnes also got to her feet. "I for one am not going down without a fight."

Luna looked at the stately woman with admiration—positively regal in her silky navy-blue pajamas and white fluffy slippers with kitten whiskers.

"Is this where the party's at?" a dark-skinned gentleman

wearing oversized moccasins shuffled into the room. He peered over thick-lensed glasses.

"That old buzzard's Herschel," Dolly said.

Another old man, this one bald and hunched over, looking really, really old, followed Herschel into the now overly crowded room.

"And that's Saul," Dolly said, louder. "He's a bit hard of hearing."

"I know them both," Luna said. "Do you remember me, Hersch ... Saul?"

"Sure, we do," Herschel answered with a smile for both of them. Saul didn't really seem to have heard her.

She saw what appeared to be remnants of powdered sugar on Saul's chin, which was a good sign he might be perking up soon.

"You both had, uh ... a few donuts?" Luna said extra loud for Saul's benefit.

"Yeah, Bernie and Felix were nice enough to share," Herschel said. "Got any more?"

"It has nothing to do with being nice—they're diabetic," Agnes said. "They couldn't eat them. Would have killed them."

"True," Dolly chimed in. "I got extras from Vera and Edith for the same reason. Bless their hearts."

Agnes rolled her eyes.

Harry looked about the room. "So, what happens to those four? They won't be connected to the stream or Gia ... they'll have no clue what's going on." He looked to Luna, worried.

Luna didn't have a ready answer. Was it really her responsibility to protect these people? Of course it was. "There's a basement, right?"

"Too many damn steps!" Saul announced, finally joining the conversation.

"Good idea," Agnes said. "Let's rouse them ... get them down into the basement. Hopefully they'll be safe there."

"God willing." Herschel made the sign of the cross over his chest.

"Who's Rod Milling?" Saul said with a raised brow.

"Ignore him," Agnes said, looking annoyed. "Are we going to do this or what?"

Luna reached into her vest pocket again, taking out two more pouches. "Before we do anything, I'll need everybody to drink—"

"Yeah, yeah. Hand 'em over," Dolly said.

Chapter 26

Castle Rock, Colorado
Valhallen Compound

Sam Dale

He awoke at 0530 with a start. He took in the dark interior space around him, his heart already galloping in his chest. *Kamdesh? Kabul?* The all-too-familiar surroundings—each a trigger in its own right; the dark interior of an army tent, currently being buffeted by outside winds; a sea of slumbering soldiers on cots around him.

Sam's eyes locked onto the snoring soldier next to him. Confused, he was having a hard time making sense of what was and wasn't reality. This would-be soldier had green flesh, a two-foot-long braid, and was so big his legs hung off the end of his cot by at least a foot. Sam let out a relieved breath—*I'm not in Afghanistan.* Only then did he see Cypress curled up on the ground next to his cot.

Good morning, Sam, came the familiar voice in his head.

"Morning, Gia ... you're still there."

Cypress raised his head. His ears perked.

I'm still here. And you need to get moving. Silarian forces began their ground forces campaign several hours ago.

"You should have awakened me—"

Humans require sleep; you required sleep. Query the stream for the latest enemy deployment coordinates. Update your lieutenants and get everyone moving.

"Copy that ... and you. How goes your battle?"

I have made some progress. Seems I know him better than he knows me. Sam, find Julian and get him someplace safe and quiet, a place where he can concentrate.

"My house?"

Yes, that should work. He'll have a shopping list of supplies required for his ...

"Bomb?"

No, Sam ... plural, bombs. Ten of them, if my calculations are correct.

"I'm sure they are. But getting anywhere in town will be a challenge. Streets are blocked with cars ... Guess we use the Landa-Craft."

I have other plans for the Landa-Craft. In fact, Harper has already left with it.

"Left? Where to ..."

She is on a cloaked repair mission out to the isolation zone's central Field Emitter.

"She knows how to repair a Field Emitter?"

No, but she has found someone who can ... one of the Silarian warriors you brought down with you ... his name is Zorian.

There was an approaching rumble—so deep, Sam could feel it resonating in his chest "What the—"

That would be Julian's ride, Sam. Walter has a surprise for you outside ... that is, if you can get off your bunk and get moving ...

What had just minutes before been an approaching deep rumble was now a loud bellowing roar. In the murky gray dawn, the vehicle rounded the barn and came into full view. Sam recognized it immediately. Shaking his head, he had to smile. Well, if anyone could get ahold of an honest-to-God functioning war machine, a battle tank, Walter could.

By now everyone, yawning and sleepy-eyed, was awake and standing outside the tent. Cypress was seated at Sam's side with his ears back. Sam gave him a couple of pats. "It's okay ... I know it's loud."

Speeding up the grade, black smoke billowed from its dual exhausts—revolving dual treads churned up the ground beneath it. Thirty feet out, the tank made a sudden change in direction, slowed, and came to a rumbling stop before a mesmerized crowd. A circular hatch clanked open on the top of the turret, and comically, like a kid's Jack-in-the-box, out popped Walter's head and shoulders.

"Morning, campers!" Walter said, his broad smile widening beneath his salt-and-pepper mustache. "Heard someone called for an Uber."

Sam said, "A tank ... seriously?"

He looked offended. "Not just any old tank, my boy ... but an Abrams battle tank."

Sam already knew as much but let Walter have his fun.

"American made and designed by General Dynamics Land Systems. Named for none other than the great General Creighton Abrams himself. A heavy bastard at almost sixty-two metric tons, it's chock-full of keen innovations, a multifuel turbine engine, the very latest Chobham composite outer armor. It has a computerized fire control system, blow-out ammunition storage compartments, but most important, this baby's got the new licensed Rheinmetall 120mm L/44." He gave the base of the extended long gun a few affectionate pats.

Sam watched as Julian made his way over to the awaiting tank. He'd been outfitted with a tactical vest and a fluorescent orange backpack. Reaching the armored vehicle, the scientist looked back. "You coming, Cypress?"

Sam looked down to the dog still seated at his feet. "Cypress?"

Walter said over the rumbling of the motor, "We're burning daylight, people ..."

Cypress looked up to Sam. "I believe I can best serve the cause by staying with you."

Sam was conflicted; he wanted Cypress with him, but all too soon, he was going into battle. "It'll be safer for you to go with Julian. Keep watch while he works."

"Julian will be fine ... send a Silarian warrior to play bodyguard. I'm going into battle with the rest of you."

"You sure?"

"I'm sure."

Walter had extricated himself from the top hatch and, with an extended hand, was helping Julian climb up onto the tank's right-side tread.

Sam said, "You two go on. Cypress has joined Alpha Team."

Julian, now atop the turret, looked back at them—he looked both flustered and disappointed.

Sam held up a finger and yelled, "Hold on!" He spotted him in the crowd. "Ivan! You're with Julian. I'm counting on you to keep him safe."

Momentarily dumbfounded, the big Slav recovered and said, "Yes, I will do this for you. He will be in the best hands with my protection."

Elsie was already removing her own vest, sidearm, and slung M4. "Hold on," she said, trying to hurry.

By the time she had Ivan properly outfitted, now wearing her tad-too-small vest, a holster on his leg, assault rifle, and a cockeyed helmet, both Julian and Walter had already disappeared down the turret. Impatiently, Walter was now revving the tank's 1500 horsepower powerplant. Big puffs of black smoke billowed from the rear.

Sam helped Ivan climb up onto the tank while Elsie, arriving out of breath, offered up a two-way radio with a charging station. "He'll need this. It has an extended range. Don't forget to keep it charged, Ivan. Thing doesn't work with a dead battery."

Ivan leaned down and took the radio. "I not forget. Memory like iron trap."

Sam and Elsie stepped back and watched as Ivan joined the other two inside. A moment later, the tank was churning up the ground once more, heading off toward Sam's house several miles to the east.

Chapter 27

Castle Rock, Colorado
Valhallen Compound

Harper Godard

She awoke in the dark, hyperventilating. It was a damn repeating nightmare—the Silarian warrior on top of her, grabbing at her. She'd caught just three hours of restless sleep before giving up. As she dressed in the dark, she was certain she could still smell the alien's stink on her skin—*get a grip; you showered twice ... it's all in your head.*

She queried Gia, wanting to get further details on this *special mission* of hers. As she laced up her boots, doing her best not to wake those around her, Gia explained what was needed.

Harper, you'll need help with this.

"What kind of help?"

Technical help. What you'll be attempting requires experi-

ence with the handling of specialized electronic components. Plus, you'll be piloting the craft ... needed at the controls.

Right now, Harper wanted, no, needed, to be alone. The thought of sharing the close confines of the Landa-Craft with someone else ... well, no way was that going to happen.

"I'm sure I can handle this by myself, Gia. I'll query the stream for what's needed."

It was as if Gia hadn't heard her. She said, There is an individual there among you that has the necessary training and experience. I have already reached out to him. Explained what will be required of him.

Harper stood and took in the dozens of nearby slumbering bodies. Her eyes scanned the far side of the tent, where she remembered Sam had found an open cot. She wanted to wake him. To say goodbye. To kiss him goodbye.

"Who is this individual?" Harper asked, strapping on her upper thigh holster.

Movement.

Harper yelped. "Ahhh!"

A looming seven-foot-tall Silarian was standing mere feet away from her.

"Someone should put a damn bell on you," she said in a hushed voice.

The Silarian tilted his head like a perplexed dog would do. "So, you're the technical specialist Gia told me about?"

He didn't answer.

Her mind flashed to her attacker back in the stall.

You can trust him, Harper ... you can trust me not to put you in danger.

Gia's words were fine, but not enough. Harper stepped closer to the alien. She'd discreetly drawn her Sig Sauer and was now pressing its muzzle into his lower belly. "You touch me, and I'll kill you. Am I making myself perfectly clear?"

"My name is Zorian," he said, seemingly unfazed by the gun being pressed into his gut.

She took a step back and holstered her pistol. She gave him a once-over. He looked pretty much like how they all looked. Tall, green, and bare-chested. His hair was pulled back into a long braid, which fell halfway down his back. "Aren't you going to need tools ... or maybe supplies?"

He shook his head. "Tools are in the Landa-Craft."

She had noticed previously there were various stow compartments on board, so it made sense.

"You ready to go?"

He grunted.

She resisted rolling her eyes. "Then let's do this." She spun on her heel and made for the exit.

Outside at the Landa-Craft, she gestured for Zorian to head up the steps first, since he'd be sitting in the crawlspace behind. "Best you get any tools you'll be needing once you're up there. Got that?"

Harper waited for him to grunt again, but he said nothing. She stayed put a good three or four minutes before heading up into the ship herself.

She saw him back there, all hunched over with the top of his head hitting the top of the cockpit. She took the lone seat as it automatically slid back into place and the opening in the floor closed.

Harper powered up the ship; the colorful forward console illuminated. The small 3D display came alive.

Gia's voice suddenly resonated out from the cockpit's audio system. "Hello, Harper and Zorian. Thank you in advance for your assistance ... there is much I can do on my own, but there are times when having a physical form, the dexterity of hands and fingers, is necessary ... alas, beyond my capacities."

Harper could smell Zorian's musky scent, and the cockpit

was already feeling claustrophobic. "Uh ... Okay, just tell me what to do. Where to go."

Harper brought the Landa-Craft up off the ground. The truth was, she already knew exactly where to go. That Field Emitter drone was right smack in the middle of Castle Rock, high up within the isolation zone.

Gaining altitude, she glanced to the town below. She figured it was close to 2:00 a.m., and with the exception of a few clusters of oil drum fires, it was pretty much total darkness.

"You are approaching the Field Emitter, Harper ... reduce speed and please allow me to take the controls."

"You can do that?" she said, immediately realizing how stupid that question was. She was a super-advanced AI persona. Of course she could pilot a simple Landa-Craft. *So why did she need me?*

The control array was now moving on its own. Harper leaned forward, squinted into the darkness beyond the glass canopy.

A green hand suddenly shot forward over her shoulder, causing her to flinch. She saw that Zorian was pointing at something. Now she saw it too. The size of a small SUV, the black Field Emitter was silhouetted upon a dark gray sky. "I think you have better eyesight than I do," she commented.

"Silarians are physically superior to humans."

She made a snarky face.

"I will open the Landa-Craft's canopy now, Harper," Gia said. "It is chilly and windy outside, so I have elevated the cabin's heat settings."

"That's fine ... I'm fine. Just do what you have to do."

There were several clicks and clanks before the canopy started to rise like a clamshell opening into the night. Harper now wished she'd brought a coat. Teeth chattering, she figured the temperature was in the mid-thirties. Then she felt wonderful heat rising up from the floor.

"I will go forward now!" Zorian yelled over the incoming wind. With the canopy all the way open, he was able to stand upright. Holding onto Harper's seat's headrest with one hand, he stretched one leg out onto the nearby stubby right-side wing. Then, letting go, he awkwardly balanced there, half in and half out of the cockpit. Carefully, he brought his other leg out and over the rim of the cockpit and onto the wing.

Wide-eyed, with mouth agape, Harper tried to make sense of what Zorian was doing. Here they were, probably a thousand feet off the ground, the cold wind buffeting his body, and he had no lifeline. Was this alien crazy, stupid, or brave—did he have balls the size of cantaloupes?

Zorian was looking at her, his long braid flapping behind him in the gale-force winds. He was saying something—signaling for her to do *something*.

"I can't hear you?" she yelled back, her own words lost to the swirling cyclone.

Zorian widened his stance then pointed an extended finger to the cargo area behind her.

"Oh! Okay! Hold on ..." Getting to her knees, she got herself twisted around in the seat enough so she could look behind. There was a case or satchel sitting back there. *His tools.* She reached back, got a good grip on the case, and hefted it around so it was between her and the back of the seat. "Thing's fucking heavy!" she complained to nobody in particular. Catching her breath, she saw that Zorian was reaching a hand in toward her. "Just hold your horses!"

Her hair was being tousled to the point she could hardly see. Using two hands, she lifted the satchel up while maneuvering it out over the lip of the cockpit—just close enough for Zorian to get one of his oven mitt–sized hands on it. Pulling the satchel into himself, he staggered backward, almost lost his balance, then steadied himself. He must have seen the look on her face because he smiled.

She got herself properly seated again, all the while keeping her eyes locked on the wing-walker Silarian. How he was keeping his balance, hell, staying on his feet, seemed impossible. A false step, an unexpected gust of wind, and he was toast.

Gia, now back in her head, was talking to her.

Harper, you will need to assist Zorian while he goes to work on the Field Emitter.

"Help him how? What can I do from in here?"

There was an ominous pause.

"No way. I am not, I repeat, I am not going out on that wing with him."

You will not be required to stay out on the wing for long.

Warning bells went off in her head. "I don't like the sound of that, Gia."

First things first; you will need to situate yourself on the nose of the Landa-Craft. Sitting will be far less of a balancing act for you ... before what comes next.

Well, at least now she knew why this was a two-person job.

"What, exactly, is it we're doing to this Emitter thing, Gia? Tell me the truth. No more secrets."

Chapter 28

Castle Rock, Colorado
Valhallen Compound

Harper Godard

The Landa-Craft was alongside the Field Emitter. Zorian's head and shoulders were deep within an open access panel.

Harper ... the isolation zone, as it stands, can easily be breached by the Silarians. Thus, they can continue to send more dropships, more warriors ... it's just a matter of time before the town and its inhabitants are annihilated. Keep in mind, the Silarians need to ensure all donutted Gia Fighters are terminated. They cannot risk the spread of my influence ...

Harper already knew as much. "What does that have to do with what we're doing to this Emitter?"

We need to ensure Silarian Fleet vessels can no longer breach the isolation zone. As it is currently configured, transmitted pass-codes allow access, much the same way I was able to allow the Landa-Craft to come and go with your Colorado Springs foray.

Harper thought about that. It made sense. And she could see now just how imperative this mission was. *"One question ... won't doing this also keep our own vessels from coming and going?"*

Unfortunately, yes ...

Harper tried to swallow, but found her mouth had gone dry. She saw that Zorian, having extricated himself from the access panel, was being buffeted and was patiently standing there upon the wing—waiting. She wondered if he'd been listening in on her and Gia's conversation. *"Does it even matter?"*

Zorian pointed toward the front of the Landa-Craft. Indicating that she needed to crawl out there ... *Fuck!*

She knew with times like this it was best not to think—not to let fear and doubt creep into her psyche. But that didn't seem to help keep her heart from practically beating out of her chest. She forced herself to move. Standing, she was immediately pounded by the winds—winds that seemed to be coming from multiple directions at once. She climbed over the forward console and proceeded to crabwalk out of the cockpit onto the small blunt-nose section of the craft. This wasn't so bad; sure, it was precarious, but if she kept her hands and knees apart, she felt somewhat steady.

"What now, Gia? ... I did what you wanted. I'm out here."

Excellent job, Harper. Next, you want to open the other access panel. Do you see it off to your right?

"I guess. I see a rectangular seam. And I see what might be a latch."

Good. You'll need to open that latch. I have already disengaged the locking mechanism.

Harper was doing her best not to look down. Not to contemplate how easy it would be to slide off this spacecraft—to fall to her death. She decided it would be safer if she just laid down. Now, with her cheek lying flat upon the hull, she wanted to just stay there; let Zorian fucking figure out how to do this himself.

You need to keep moving, Harper, Gia coaxed.

"I know, I know. Just give me a second, okay?"

Pushing herself around with the toes of her boots, she got herself pointed toward the Field Emitter at the side of the ship. With arms outstretched and using flat palms against the hull, she pulled herself closer to the emitter. The thing looked much larger now that she was right next to it. She could now see that Zorian was peering around from the other side. He offered up a confident nod.

"How am I going to do this?" To pull open that latch, she'd need to let go of the hull with her right hand and reach over to the Emitter. Sure, it was just a foot or so away, but right now it seemed like miles. She glanced down without thinking and vertigo took hold of her, made the world around her spin uncontrollably. She squeezed her eyes shut and said a silent prayer ...

She knew she was going to hear Gia's voice any second now. She opened her eyes, raised her right hand again, and reached. Her fingertips made contact. *"That's something, at least."*

You're going to have to get yourself much closer to the Emitter, Harper.

The problem was the Landa-Craft's nose wasn't flat—it sloped down on the side at an ever-increasing angle. She pushed off with her toes again and this time felt herself being nudged along by gravity. Frantic to stop herself from sliding all the way off the hull, she reflexively raised both arms over her head and splayed her hands. She screamed.

She'd come to a stop, and she could feel the cold hard metal of the Emitter on the palms of her hands.

Good job, Harper. You are almost there, Gia said.

"Almost? I am there. I'm right here at the panel."

Yes, you are. But now you'll need to raise the panel and crawl inside.

The wind had come up, and she wasn't sure she'd heard her right. *"Gia, did you say crawl inside?"*

Chapter 29

Castle Rock, Colorado
Valhallen Compound

Sam Dale

Sam did his best to quell his growing frustration. The problem with having access to the stream was the raw, unvarnished awareness that came with that—like knowing that townsfolk were dying right now, this minute, here in Castle Rock at the hands of Silarian warriors. And Sam had yet to mobilize his forces.

Lester's Gamma Team was horsing around over by the barn. Epsilon, Greg's team, was assembled over by *Uncle Jeb*, while Sam's team, Alpha, was congregating in front of the old farmhouse. He was grateful they'd come together relatively quickly. But Sam had taken it upon himself to also bring together Harper's team, Beta. She'd yet to return from her special mission.

Something neither the stream nor Gia herself had shed much light on.

Sam had to smile, watching a frantic Carl in his attempts to split up and evenly distribute the Silarian warriors. It seemed they did not like being separated from one another. No sooner had Carl gotten four distinct Silarian groups organized than they began to wander off—preferring to join other groups instead of where Carl had put them. Eventually, though, they settled down; some groups were slightly smaller than others, but it wasn't a big deal.

Cypress, sitting at Sam's side, looked up at him. "I have to go."

"Go?"

"I'm needed elsewhere."

"What are you talking about? Why would you leave at a time like this?"

"I'm needed, Sam ... I'm needed right now!" And with that, Cypress was off and running—roughly headed in the direction of town. Undoubtedly toward Silarian warrior deployments.

"Where's he going, Gia? What's this about?"

I'll keep an eye on him, Sam ... just know he truly is needed elsewhere.

"And it's a secret? From me?"

Irritated, Sam sensed Gia had already disconnected.

Walter, Elsie, and the rest of the Valhallen contingent were busy distributing weapons and tactical gear. The Silarians were given the Ender weapons from Uncle Jeb's armory—a mix of mostly Ender-4s and a handful of Ender-5s.

Off in the distance, a series of loud concussive blasts caught everyone's attention. A quiet hush fell over the readying Gia Fighters.

Instantly triggered, heart racing ... Sam found himself in another place, another time ...

Three clicks outside of Kabul ...

Tajikan Road was a mess, like most of the roads around Kabul, and the corporal driving the Cougar 6x6 MRAP seemed to be seeking out every pothole and furrow—any of which might be concealing an IED. Sam adjusted his tactical vest, a KDH Magnum TAC-1 plate carrier, for the dozenth time. He let his fingers play over the six M4 magazines, his Yarborough knife, and Beretta M9. Sam, seated in the back with seven others, ignored the bemused look of the young Afghan National Security Forces soldier peering past his old and tattered-looking AK-47. Of the ten soldiers in Sam's MRAP, only four were from his team, and so not all of them appreciated his ritual.

They were in the third vehicle of a four-vehicle NATO convoy heading west on Tajikan Road, just north of Kabul Airport. The mission was a basic meet and greet at an Afghan military base with a group of Pashtun elders wanting security guarantees for their village on the outskirts of Kabul. Sam expected the meeting to be uneventful.

Peering forward through the MRAP's windshield, Sam could see the Humvee rattling about some sixty or so meters in front of their Cougar. Its unmanned .50-caliber pointed toward a faded, denim-colored sky. Sam's MRAP was fitted with an M153 CROWS, wielding an M240B 7.62mm machine gun. The Common Remotely Operated Weapon Station, true to its name, was operated remotely from the relative safety of the MRAP's interior and was a true force multiplier as well as a hedge against combat casualties.

Sam leaned forward and sighted beyond the Humvee, catching sight of the lead MRAP. As per SOP, the convoy was constantly varying speeds and distances between vehicles to deny the enemy any opportunity to exploit a pattern. Sam sighed, again unconsciously letting his fingers dance over his kit in their ritual. He was a bit queasy; the road was for shit, and he was sweating buckets packed in here in his full loadout; yeah, this was no Sunday drive, but honestly, he'd been on far worse missions—

Suddenly, the sky vanished behind a bloom of dirt and black smoke engulfing the Humvee up ahead, flipping it like a toy toward the center of the road. A sharp boom and concussion shook the MRAP—shrapnel plinked against its hood. The Humvee landed on its roof beneath a shower of dirt and asphalt. Other than light rocking, there was no movement.

The Cougar skidded to a halt as comms blared with shaken voices. Sam barked, "Keep going! Get us up there!"

The MRAP moved forward toward the flipped-over Humvee. The CROWS operator immediately began scanning the area for enemy positions as the soldiers around Sam prepared to disembark. The lead MRAP was already headed back toward the blast site, and Sam knew the other Humvee was also moving up behind his vehicle to provide security. While a secondary explosion was possible, Sam didn't think it likely. An ambush, however ...

The rear door clanked open, and everyone disembarked. The pucker index was high because they didn't know where, if any, Taliban might be positioned, but the soldiers formed a cordon punctuated by the MRAPs' CROWS and the Humvee's .50 caliber. One of the comms sergeants called in the CONTACREP. The unit was well-trained; everyone knew what to do.

Having left the MRAP, Sam hurried for the flipped Humvee. He was struck by a single thought, and a chill ran through his veins. *I was supposed to have been in that Humvee.* Just before rollout, his bud, Captain William Landry, had plunked a heavy hand down on his shoulder and blasted him with that huge, toothy smile of his.

"Sam, how about you let me take vehicle command for this run?" Landry had said.

Sam was reluctant to do so, but he also knew that rotating through positions increased combat effectiveness by deepening skill sets—so he'd shrugged and said, "Sure, Billy. Have a party."

Now, as Sam approached the wrecked vehicle, the reek of cordite slapped him in the face. The insurgents' IED, Sam guessed, had utilized a high number of 152mm shells. And why not? God knows there was a near-endless supply of ordnance left over from the Soviets' failed adventure three decades prior ... And now here he was in the Graveyard of Empires.

There were urgent shouts from his men as they scoured the nearby low, ramshackle buildings that lined Tajikan Road, looking for insurgents. Civilian lookie-loos peered from windows and open doorways. Sam listened for the crackle of AK-47s or the harsh exhalation of an RPG marking a secondary attack but heard neither.

He took a knee and peered inside the Humvee, which, perched on the gun turret, canted off to the driver's side. Sam's breath caught in his chest—within the murk of the flipped Humvee, Sam stared at a terrible and all-too-familiar tableau. Three soldiers moved feebly and one lay still. Blood spattered the roof and seats and bulkhead. It would be impossible to know the extent of their injuries until they were extracted from the vehicle. But Landry's condition was clear: upside down, belted in, the captain, his shades knocked awry, his right arm hanging down toward the roof as if he'd lazily tried to brace himself, stared sightlessly out of the tattered remains of the Humvee door.

The entry wound was evident. A divot under Landry's right armpit, unprotected by his body armor. And with Billy's head turned toward Sam, he could see the ragged exit wound in the left side of his friend's neck.

Sam yelled, "We need to get these guys out of here!"

Two Afghan soldiers and one of his team's medical sergeants were at the Humvee in seconds. Immediately, they went to work removing the dented and shrapnel-shredded doors. The Afghans supported Landry while Sam used his tactical knife to cut the restraints holding the dead captain. Gently, they eased Landry's body out and laid it beside the vehicle. They then removed the other four men.

The medical sergeant quickly made his assessment, started treatment, and yelled for the second communications sergeants to call in the nine-line. Sam knew he should be overseeing the securing of the site, but he just sat there beside his friend while the comms sergeant rattled off the nine-line, delivering the site coordinates, frequency information, and call sign with the calm air of a seasoned operator.

"We have three bravo and two KIA," the sergeant said in that steady monotone.

Three soldiers in need of urgent surgical intervention and two dead. Gut churning, Sam tore his eyes from Landry, from the blood beginning to pool around him, and looked up to see NATO forces were arriving on scene in MRAPs and Humvees. Voices called for sitreps, sought out the commanding officer. The comms sergeant completed the nine-line and began to assist the medical sergeant.

A figure squatted down beside Sam. "What we got, Captain?"

Sam explained in a voice that seemed to belong to someone else. It was simple, really.

Not long after, the *whup whup whup* of incoming helicopters hammered the air. Plumes of rusty dirt mixed with the oily smoke, hanging in the air like thin, swirling drapes. Sam clasped his hands together as if in prayer. But that didn't stop their shaking.

Chapter 30

Castle Rock, Colorado
Outside Pleasant Days Nursing Home

Luna Kelly

Luna, Harry, and Agnes took the stairs up from the basement to the main living room. Dolly, Herschel, and Saul were waiting for them, standing around the reception area near the front door. The two men were drinking from plastic water bottles, Dolly munching on a Triscuit.

"How'd it go?" Herschel asked.

"Good as can be expected," Luna said, feeling as if she'd just come back from an all-day cattle drive. "We got them settled in the basement with some food and water." She was referring to the four un-donutted, ornery seniors—Vera, Edith, Felix, and Bernie.

"Bet they gave you a hard time. Vera can be an uppity old bitch," Saul scowled.

"She wasn't happy, but her happiness is of little concern given the situation," Agnes said flatly.

"You know ... she has a bad hip. Poor dear girl." Dolly placed a splayed hand on her chest in her typically overdramatic fashion.

"As far as they know, they're good until the fire drill is over," Luna said.

"Fire drill? Good idea, young lady." Dolly clapped her hands together, moving side to side like an overfed penguin.

Luna distanced herself from where her new team was standing, looking them over like a drill sergeant getting acquainted with new recruits. They had all changed into sweatpants, T-shirts, and sneakers. Harry wore a matching red jogging outfit with a plain white tee. Saul sported a New York Yankees ball cap. Herschel had a Copper-Fit belt strapped around his waist. Dolly accessorized her tennies with extra-long pink shoelaces with large, loose bows. And Agnes donned a sky-blue cashmere scarf around her neck.

"How is everyone feeling?" Luna asked.

"I gotta say, this is the first time my back hasn't hurt in thirty years." Herschel pulled the Velcro fastener that held his Copper-Fit belt in place and threw it on the floor. "Definitely don't need that thing anymore."

"Well, I'll be damned." Saul shifted his weight on one side and took off his hearing aid. "I can hear perfectly. Maybe I don't need this thing poking in my ear anymore." He threw his listening device on top of Herschel's belt.

The others were stretching, jogging in place, and punching fists in the air ... like they were a group of much younger athletes warming up for an intense workout.

Luna stifled a smile, not wanting to diminish any of their enthusiasm.

"Here's what's gonna happen," Luna said, trying to sound

more in command than she actually felt. "If we're going to survive this, you do exactly as I say, when I say it. Do you understand?" Luna made prolonged eye contact with each of them.

Herschel stood up straight and saluted. "Lead on, boss."

Dolly copied Herschel and also saluted, while Agnes rolled her eyes and simply nodded.

Saul, looking cranky, narrowed his eyes and said, "You're just a kid ... who put you in charge?"

Agnes interjected, "Gia put her in charge, you old fossil ... you don't like taking orders from a strong young woman, you can wait this out in the basement with the others. Up to you, Saul."

Luna was really starting to like Agnes.

"Fine. You don't need to get all uppity ... I was just asking," Saul said.

"Okay, we're about to head out. I'm not sure who's around, so let's get a few basic signals down. When I wave my right arm like this ..." Luna held up her right hand and waved it forward. "... that means move."

"Obviously," Saul said under his breath.

"And if I put my arm up like this, making a fist ... that means stop."

"Oh yes, I saw that on *SEAL Team*—I love that show," Dolly giggled.

Luna ignored her. "We're gonna do what's called a combat walk. Keep your center of gravity low." Luna wasn't sure that was what it was called, but it sounded good.

"It's the Groucho walk; everybody knows that," Saul interrupted.

Luna shot him a death stare. Saul pantomimed holding an imaginary key and using it to lock his mouth.

"As I was saying ... you bend a little while leaning forward and then glide." Luna demonstrated the combat glide to her audience. "We need to avoid branches or anything that will create noise." Luna paused, making sure they were listening. Herschel offered two thumbs-up, as if speaking for everyone.

"We don't know what we're going to run into out there. The Silarians are on a mission, and make no mistake—they will kill us if they see us," Luna said.

"What do these aliens look like anyway?" Saul asked.

It was clear they weren't accustomed to querying the stream yet; questions like that were easily addressed. Luna answered, "Seven feet tall with green skin ... they'll be hard to miss."

The old folks stared at her in response. Even Saul went silent.

"I'm in the lead. Then we head out in this order—Dolly, Saul, Agnes, and Herschel. Harry, since you have a weapon, you take the position in the back of the line."

"Good. Don't want to be near Harry wearing that bright red outfit—talk about a moving target," Saul said.

"Harry, you have a gun?" Dolly goggled at him, looking suitably impressed and maybe a little smitten.

Harry offered her a cocky smile. "Oh yeah, I'm packing."

Agnes rolled her eyes.

"Time to go. We need to stay quiet," Luna said. With her M4 held at the ready, she headed toward the back door.

Luna turned back and watched as the seniors descended the porch back steps. Sure, they'd been donutted, and they'd had their doses of healing nanites, but not a one of them was under the age of eighty. Saul was probably closer to ninety. The last thing she needed was for one of them to fall and break a hip. But to her surprise, they were moving well; it was as if someone had waved a magic wand and simultaneously made all five of them thirty years younger.

Luna took in the clearing in the trees far up ahead. Querying the stream, she knew it was approximately two hundred yards away and at a walking rate of about 1.088 yards per minute, they would reach the ship in a little more than two minutes. At this point she was confident the folks behind had the physical ability to keep up.

"Ahhhchu!" Dolly let out a loud sneeze.

"Bless you," Saul said just as loud.

Luna held up the stop signal, spun around, and glared at the two. In a hushed voice, she said, "What did I just tell you?"

Both Dolly and Saul shook their heads.

"To be quiet. No talking. No noise!"

Harry held out his Colt with straight arms and did a sweep in the back of the line.

"Sorry, guess I still have allergies," Dolly whispered.

"Here." Agnes slid the scarf from her neck and passed it to Dolly. "Wrap it around your head so it covers your nose.

Dolly looked at the scarf, perplexed.

Grinding her molars, Luna grabbed the cashmere cloth from Agnes and tied it snugly around Dolly's head, cinching a knot in the back. The scarf hung loosely in the front; she looked like an old B western movie hoodlum.

Luna placed a hand on the woman's shoulder and looked her in the eye. "You good, Dolly?"

Her nest of red-orange hair bobbed up and down.

Resuming her position at the front of the line, Luna motioned for everyone to move. *Just two minutes. We got this.*

At one time, the grounds around the nursing home had been well-maintained, free of trash and extraneous dead leaves and branches. But these were anything but normal times. The lush green grass was now patchy and dead—littered with crushed aluminum cans, fast-food wrappers, and stray real estate flyers.

Luna stopped in her tracks, forgetting to motion for the others to do the same. Dolly stumbled into her from behind.

Now listening, Luna was sure she'd heard something other

than their own footfalls. And there it was again. *Crunching leaves.* Three o'clock. *Was that movement?*

"What is it?" Dolly whispered.

"Ssshh," Saul said. "We're not supposed to talk."

Shit! Someone was running toward them. Tall. The color of moss. A Silarian.

"AAAAAH ... Oh my God!" Dolly screamed like a banshee.

Luna fired. Missed—hitting a tree. She fired again and missed again.

"You're a lousy aim," Saul said.

A bright energy bolt streaked past, just inches from Luna's right ear. She instinctively crouched down. Spinning around, about to motion for the others to do the same—a new flurry of energy bolts filled the air. *Zip zip zip* came the characteristic sound of Ender-4 fire. It was as if everything was happening in slow motion. Luna caught sight of Saul's New York Yankees baseball cap somersaulting high into the air. And then she saw it, Saul's head, also somersaulting high into the air, following the same trajectory as the hat. She had no choice but to ignore it.

She brought up her M4, aimed, and fired toward the rapidly approaching band of Silarians. Thirty yards out, the first of the Silarians lurched; hit mid-chest, he tumbled over face first. There were two more still advancing. *Steady your breathing; squeeze the trigger.* She fired. Another alien went down, shot in the gut. The last Silarian warrior stopped, hesitated, then went down to one knee to take careful aim.

Luna fired, missed, fired again—missed again. "Fuck!"

A loud blast came from behind, almost making her drop her weapon.

She watched as the third kneeling alien wavered, then clutched at his throat with both hands as blood fountained from his carotid artery. He toppled over; his body twitched several times then went still.

Luna looked behind her and saw Harry standing there—arms extended, smoke rising from the barrel of his old Colt.

She said, "Nice shot."

He looked both stunned and amazed. "I never killed anyone before."

All eyes went to Saul's headless remains.

"My God," Herschel said. "He's dead. They killed Saul."

Luna needed to keep them moving. Her hands were shaking —she was finding it hard to breathe. Summoning all her will, focusing on the mission at hand, she stood and hurried over to the closest of the dead aliens. The smell hit her first. She made a face—covered her nose in the crook of her arm. The Silarian had voided his bowels.

The others had followed. Dolly said, "Smells like a porta-potty that's been sitting in the sun too long."

Luna bent to retrieve the alien's Ender-4. "Herschel, Agnes, get the other two weapons."

You need to hurry, Luna. More warriors are coming. They heard the weapons fire.

"Okay, thanks, Gia."

Luna, now holding the dead alien's weapon, raised it and quickly relayed the basic operating instructions to both Harry and Agnes. Dolly, still staring at Saul's decapitated body, looked as if she might be sick.

Luna turned to the remaining folks in line and yelled, "If the rest of you want to live ... RUN!"

The healing nanites had really kicked in, as the old folks kept pace with Luna. They made it to the ship in sixty seconds.

Gasping for breath, Herschel slowed, looking awestruck at the alien ship in front of them. "Holy Mother of God. Look at that thing!"

The others had similar reactions.

Luna peeked around the starboard¬¬¬hidden side of the

craft. Lloyd's body was still there, propped up against the hull. Best to avoid mentioning that, she thought. Returning to the others, she stopped and listened to Gia.

Luna ... all too soon you will be surrounded by Silarian warriors. Once you are all inside the dropship, you will not have much time. These vessels are robust, but not impregnable against an Ender-5.

"With your help, I can fly it out of here ... right?"

This particular vessel is difficult to master. What you need is an experienced pilot. Get inside and wait for further instructions.

"Can't you just pilot the ship remotely?"

Perhaps, but I have yet to infiltrate the dropship's internal circuitry. Be patient ... help is on the way.

Luna felt the others' eyes on her as she moved toward the aft hatch door. She pressed and pulled the latch as she'd done earlier. She heard the familiar releasing of the seal's pressure. She smiled, hearing the release of compressed air and the whirring of the ramp starting to lower.

"Glad you know what you're doin'," Harry said, wiping moisture from his eyes. Naturally, he and the others were in shock. That was a luxury she could not afford.

"Okay—everyone follow me. Same order as before." *Except Saul isn't going to be in line this time.* She proceeded up the ramp. Stepping into the darkened ship, she was followed by Dolly, Agnes, and Herschel.

Bang! Bang!

Luna looked back to see Harry facing outward at the top of the ramp—his Colt Peacemaker thundering back within the ship's interior space.

Bang! Bang!

"Criminy! I'm out of bullets." Harry said, tossing his spent gun onto the deck. "I don't see them ... but I know they're out there."

Herschel moved to his side and handed Harry a newly acquired Ender-4. "Best you take this ... I might shoot myself in the foot."

Harry brought the weapon up but fumbled with the odd trigger mechanism. Figuring it out, he fired. The sudden recoil from the energy discharge caused him to stagger backward. "I think I got one!"

Luna was at the aft hatch controls and, of course, the stream was acting spotty again. "How do I close the damn hatch?" She glanced out the rear of the ship. "Get in here, Harry! You're not going to be able to fight them all off!"

"I need your help here, Gia—like right now would be good ..."

Luna stared at the small display in front of her, a variety of touchpad buttons to the left. Muted lights of various shades and shapes blinked on and off ... yellow, orange, and green. Alien hieroglyphics had started to scroll.

Luna, press the blinking rectangular yellow icon.

She could hear voices, and what sounded like a stampede of footfalls. They were close, way too close.

Luna tapped the button. Immediately the gangway started to lift. In the distance, coming through the trees, was a mass of green bodies. Bright energy bolts struck the outer hull and the all-too-slowly rising ramp. When the hatch finally closed and sealed, everyone let out a collective sigh of relief.

"Thank God. I mean Gia—thank you, Gia."

"Now what?" Agnes said, peering forward, deeper into the craft.

"Now we wait."

Everyone looked to Luna. Dolly said, "For? We can't just sit in here like sardines in a tin can indefinitely."

Luna shrugged. "A pilot. We're waiting on our pilot."

Chapter 31

Castle Rock, Colorado
Bell Mountain Equestrian Center

Lloyd Sanderson

Captain Larng Nos Polk stood perfectly still before him. The muscles and tendons in his back bulged like taut rope. Lloyd was by no means an expert fighter. There was no way he would be up to the task of taking on this highly trained Silarian warrior—an experienced commander at that. But what Lloyd did have in spades was street smarts. That and ruthlessness. If you didn't learn that in a high-security prison ward, you didn't survive long.

Lloyd went down to one knee, placed his long knife on the ground before him, and bowed his head ...

"What is your bidding, my Lord?"

He'd practiced saying the simple sentence in his head no less than fifty times. The stream, for now accessible, had provided the words. Interestingly, his implants were coming alive enough that he might be able to speak with the Naru tongue on his own before too long.

The captain obviously knew he was there. Had snuck up behind him where his broad back was exposed. But there would be no way for the captain to know *who* he was —that he was, for all intents and purposes, his physical twin.

Lloyd repeated his memorized phrase. "What is your bidding, my lord?"

Only now did Captain Larng Nos Polk move—turning his head just enough to see Lloyd in his peripheral vision. "Who goes there ... who dares to creep around my quarters in the dark?"

Fuck! Sure, Lloyd could try to speak ... knowing he'd bumble the wording. Best to keep it to one or two words. "Intruders, Captain ..."

The captain, tentative, with a hand on the handle of his knife, slowly turned fully around. "Speak, you fool. What intruders do you speak of? Where?"

Without lifting his head, Lloyd pointed backward, toward the deep shadow of the barracks.

"Someone's breached our security!? Who's on patrol? Speak, you mindless twit!"

The captain had taken a step closer but was still not close enough to give Lloyd any real chance of success. So Lloyd started to cry, or at least to give his best facsimile of someone crying. First his shoulders began to shake, then came the whimpers, then full- out sobbing.

The contempt in the captain's voice was palpable. "What is this? Are you ... crying?" He took another step forward. Although Lloyd couldn't see what he was doing, his head still bowed, he heard the sound of a metal blade pulling free from its sheath. "You dare to dishonor yourself in such a manner ... dishonor all Silarian warriors!"

Blubbering now, Lloyd knew his time was short. He'd queried the stream, asked what was considered the most insulting, most vile insult one could use back on his home world of Naru. He raised his head and said the words, not fully grasping what the series of strange consonants and vowels meant. Leave it to say, it was more of a question along the lines of, "Does the captain prefer fucking the equivalent of barnyard animals or reptilian swamp creatures?"

Captain Larng Nos Polk stepped closer, an audible gasp escaping his mouth. Lloyd didn't need to look up to know the motherfucker had been momentarily dumbstruck by what he'd just heard. And that's when Lloyd plucked up the knife, turned the blade skyward, and drove the twelve-inch-long blade straight up between the captain's legs—all the way to the weapon's hilt. Once more, Lloyd marveled at the strength of this newly acquired body.

There was an audible squeal as the supreme ground forces commander went rigid. Lloyd pulled the knife free, stood, moved behind the captain, and took hold of his ponytail in one hand while placing the edge of the bloodied weapon to his throat. "Sorry, cuz ... nothing personal, but there can be only one ..." Lloyd slit the captain's throat.

Chapter 32

Castle Rock, Colorado
Alongside the Field Emitter

Harper Godard

A thousand feet in the air, the wind continued to buffet her hair. Harper squeezed her eyes shut and swallowed hard. Precariously balancing upon the nose of the Landa-Craft, her body angled downward, headfirst—she felt as if she could slide off into oblivion at any moment. Arms stretched out overhead, only gravity was holding her against the Field Emitter's access panel.

"Gia, repeat ... did you say crawl inside the thing?"

Yes, Harper ... I know it will be difficult. But Zorian will assist you.

That made no sense at all. Zorian was on the other side of the Field Emitter—

Suddenly, Harper's feet lost their footing and were being

elevated. She screamed. Expecting to be catapulted any second from her perilous perch, she realized someone had taken hold of her ankles. A quick look over a shoulder confirmed somehow Zorian had left his position on the other side of the Field Emitter, crawled onto the Landa-Craft, and gotten a solid hold of her legs. *So, what now?* Her heart felt as if it was literally going to beat out of her chest. She heard Zorian grunt, prompting her to get busy.

She almost laughed at the ridiculousness of the situation. Harper reached for the access panel's latch, but the tips of her fingers were just shy of making contact.

"Closer!" she yelled into the wind.

Zorian lowered her another few inches. She figured the strain on his back and shoulders must be tremendous. She was now close enough to grasp the latch—she twisted clockwise and pulled hard. Hinged at the bottom, the panel came open, almost hitting her in the head as it slammed down. Before her was the dark, open-void interior of the Field Emitter. But before she had a second to consider how she was going to maneuver herself inside, Zorian let go of her ankles.

Fortunately, her arms had been over her head, and, as if diving into a pool, the entirety of her body was swallowed up inside the Emitter—her hands taking the brunt of her fall. But she also bonked her forehead.

Stunned more from still being alive than actually being hurt, she took in her cramped, dark surroundings.

Time is of the essence, Harper.

Ignoring the voice in her head, she looked back out the access opening and saw the Landa-Craft, but not Zorian. *That's right. He'll be needed back on the outside of the Field Emitter.*

Looking around, she saw she was standing in an area about the size of an old-fashioned telephone booth. Virtually all surfaces were matte black myriad technology—blinking lights, miniature display readouts, *all unreadable,* and multicolored touch buttons. She could have easily tapped a wrong button or even broken something with her fall. Hell, maybe she had.

Harper spoke aloud. "So, what am I supposed to do now?"

Remember, this procedure will "selectively" close out the isolation zone—keep the Silarians' fleet from sending in further reinforcements.

"Yeah, but also make it so they can't leave, right?"

Gia hesitated before answering. Correct.

"Does that mean none of our own ships can come and go?"

I have a workaround for that, Harper. First of all, Zorian is waiting on you. He will be flipping a kind of breaker switch on at an external panel. There is an identical breaker switch there inside the Emitter. The two of you will need to flip the two breakers at the same time. This will put the Field Emitter into reprogramming mode.

"Okay ... where's this breaker?"

Turn around. It's right behind you.

She did as told. *"This red lever thing?"* She saw that the lever was positioned straight up.

Yes. I will count down from three—

"Wait. So I'm just flipping it to the down position?"

Yes, Harper.

"Okay, and do I flip it on one or zero?"

Again, Gia hesitated. On one. You and Zorian will both be flipping the breaker on one. Are you ready?

Harper was detecting annoyance in Gia's tone. Which in any other situation would have been funny. But this wasn't that kind of situation. *"And Zorian is listening to this conversation?"*

Yes, Harper. Are you ready?

"Uh ... I guess ... yes, I'm ready."

Harper heard Gia's countdown: *Three, two* ... on *one,* she flipped the lever. She heard a corresponding *clank* on the outside of the Emitter. "We did it!" she said, punching a fist into the air. "Gia? We did it, right?" Gia's lack of response put Harper instantly on guard. Had she done something wrong? Turned the lever in the wrong direction? Had it simply not worked? Oh my God ... had Zorian fallen off the Field Emitter—blown off his feet by a gust of wind? Her mind raced, each prospect worse than the next.

Yes, Harper, it worked. And Zorian is fine.

But things weren't fine. She knew Gia's tone well enough by now to be sure of that. "What is it, Gia?"

I am very sorry to say, Harper, something terrible has happened outside the isolation zone.

"Tell me. What's happened?"

The Silarian 23rd Fleet has commenced terra-displacement operations ... I'm sorry, Harper. Earth is under attack.

Harper tried to keep from panicking, forced herself to stay in the here and now. *"What do I do next?"*

Two more simple steps ... There is a switch and a dial thirteen inches below that breaker you just threw.

"I see them."

First, move the switch to the position marked V. That will correspond with Earth's use of AM radio frequencies.

"Seriously?"

Yes. Actually, a good number of worlds utilize various radio frequency bands.

"Okay, I've moved the switch."

Excellent. You are doing great, Harper. Now, turn the dial to the right of the switch. You will see the readout change numerical values as you spin the dial. Stop when the readout is at ∞ ¡ ∑ ∂. That is the equivalent of 1600 on the AM dial.

"That's ESPN! I listen to Rockies baseball on that station."

Yes, Harper. You and many others.

Harper did as asked. "So what exactly does this do?"

Any Silarian vessel that broadcasts a signal matching this frequency should be able to pass in and out of the isolation zone unaffected.

Harper didn't like her phrasing. "*Should?*"

I am 99.987 percent confident.

"*Okay, I can live with that. Now what?*"

You and Zorian will have to flip that breaker back up at the same time. On the count of three ...

Chapter 33

Castle Rock, Colorado
Valhallen Compound

Sam Dale

He'd been ready to disband Harper's Team Beta and merge the mix of locals and Silarian warriors into other teams when Lester pointed off to the east sky. "Guess you can stop moping, Mr. Bossman ... looks like your gal survived her secret mission."

"Don't call her that," Elsie said. "Don't call anyone that." It was no secret Lester was enamored with Elsie. And hell, maybe it was a mutual attraction, but her rebuke, the *don't fuck with me* expression on her face, made it clear there were boundaries when it came to Lester's obnoxiousness.

Sam watched the Landa-Craft's swift approach. Harper flew the little ship with the self-assurance of an experienced pilot. No sooner had she touched down than she was descending the steps and running his way.

Sounding out of breath, she yelled, "They're attacking! Sam! The fleet ... they're attacking Earth!"

She is correct, Sam ... I was just about to inform you of that.

Stunned, Sam looked off to the north, as if he'd be able to see alien ships in the distance. Of course, he couldn't.

Harper ran to his open arms—they held each other as if it had been days instead of hours. When they separated, Sam said, "You're hurt."

She touched her forehead, fingertips coming away bloody. "It's nothing. Bonked my head. Oh God, Sam ... Earth's being attacked. Everything we've done, are doing, has been for nothing."

Sam heard Gia's immediate response to that. Clearly, she was speaking to both at the same time.

No, Harper ... this was an expected development. I am surprised it has taken this long for Silarian high command to engage their attack ships. All this means is our efforts are now even more important.

Sam didn't see how. "We've already lost, Gia ... what difference does it make what we do here in this little town when the whole planet is under siege?"

Harper nodded, looking defeated, tears welling in her eyes.

Take heart, both of you ... It may not seem like it, but I have been busy.

Harper shook her head. "Yeah, fighting with the Geo-Mind. We thought he'd almost destroyed you."

I am far more resilient than you can possibly imagine. The Geo-Mind has been fully contained here within the isolation zone.

"So ... you've destroyed him? It?" Sam asked.

Yes and no. From a technology aspect, where the Geo-Mind had infused himself into technology, the various spacecraft, the isolation drones, the Field Emitter, and such forth. But Geo-Mind still resides within close to three hundred embedded implants.

"You're referring to the Silarian warriors here in town," Sam said.

Correct. In time, I will be able to infiltrate their implants just as I did up on Relentless Thrust with each of the Silarian crew members. But I suspect by that time ...

"That by that time we'll all ... already be killed," Harper said.

"Why?" Sam said. "On *Relentless Thrust*, it didn't take you all that long—"

True, but remember, just as I have evolved, so has the Geo-Mind. As AI constructs, we are not static beings. We operate within fluctuating quantum states. But as I have stated before, I have had many, many years to secretly study his processes, his capabilities. In that regard, I have the advantage.

"So, what now?" Harper said.

We destroy the Geo-Mind on three fronts ... First, Sam, your attack teams must defeat the Silarian forces here within the isolation zone. Two, Julian must complete his work on the ten nanite bombs.

"And third?" Sam asked.

That third front just might be the most challenging of them all. I must infiltrate the Silarian 23rd Fleet. And before you ask, I have already spoken to Jarpin.

Sam was more than a little skeptical. "You're talking about the crews of over one hundred highly advanced warships."

As of right now, the Geo-Mind is unaware of my influence over Relentless Thrust and her crew. Soon that may change; all the more important that Jarpin act. I cannot discuss this with you anymore, Sam. You should have everything needed to head out.

"One more question. Cypress ... is he okay?"

Yes, Sam. Cypress is a survivor. Know that I am watching over him as best I can.

Chapter 34

Castle Rock, Colorado
Frontage Road

Junior Lieutenant Cypress Mag Nuel

Cypress headed east, having passed the last of the large barns on the Valhallen compound. He mentally replayed Gia's instructions. Luna and four elderly people need help behind Pleasant Days Nursing Home. An indeterminate number of Silarians have them trapped within an Executive Troop Carrier Ship. Cypress, they're in need of a pilot.

Cypress was somewhat familiar with the craft Gia was referring to. Part of his flight certification as a young cadet had included several hours piloting such a craft. It was a sturdy vessel, more so than a lowly warrior transport. So, he knew that Luna and the others would have a few hours—but eventually, the brute force of an Ender-5 would breach its reinforced hull plating. Cypress liked Luna. He was discovering that canines, Rocko in this case, had a natural knowing, a sense of which humans were truly good and which were not. *I'm coming ... I'll be there as soon as I can, Luna.*

Forced to slow, the golden retriever navigated through high grasses; his ears twitched as the thick stalks buzzed with tiny insects. Cresting a small rise near Frontage Road, Cypress looked back the way he'd come. No longer could he see them, but he knew Sam and the others could have used his help—but then again, there were so many of them ... all well-armed. Luna was a mere teenager ... she was on her own.

From his vantage point, it was still impossible to see very far beyond the rolling hills and the tall grasses. Gia had related the basics, though, that he needed to travel approximately one mile east and nine miles north. Cypress figured if he could keep up the pace, he could average about six miles per hour. Maybe that would be pushing things ... Rocko wasn't a puppy. But with a little luck, he would reach Pleasant Days Nursing Home in about an hour and forty minutes ... maybe. The only thing in his way ... an army of Silarian warriors.

Panting, he ran and ran. He ran until his paws started to hurt and his wagging tongue hung long and dripped saliva. After the first quarter-mile of all-out running, he was forced to slow, to catch his breath, and then, finally, to stop to rest. Cypress wondered if other dog breeds had more stamina than goldens. The stream indicated a creature called a greyhound was a fast canine ... *why couldn't it have been a greyhound that found me that cold and rainy night in the gulch?* Then again, Rocko wasn't so bad. The two of them had come to an understanding these last few days. *Is that all it's been? A few days?*

Now running again, this same pattern of sprinting and stopping repeated three more times, finally he realized it was better not to run but to continue at a fast walk.

Cypress saw little creatures with big ears and white tails hopping past him, apparently called rabbits. He had to rein Rocko in, demand that his inner canine not chase after the funny little creatures. Then again, perhaps it was time for Cypress to admit the truth. That the line between who Rocko was ... and who Cypress was ... was getting thinner by the day. *Focus, Cypress. Resist these ridiculous animal urges.*

Something up ahead caught his eye ... his ears perked; his tail went rigid. A person standing perfectly still. How odd. Then he saw the wooden stake keeping the body upright—what an interesting smell ...

What the...? This was not a body at all. Straw protruded from its clothing—sleeves and pant legs. Four large black birds —*crows*—sat on the figure's shoulders. *How very, very odd.* After a quick query to the stream, Cypress learned this *thing* was called a scarecrow. It was used to scare away birds. Not very effective. Cypress decided he didn't like crows. *No wonder they try to scare them off.* He avoided looking into those beady black eyes—no thank you. Cypress increased his speed, wanting to get away from the creepy birds and the ineffectual scarecrow.

There was a clearing up ahead. Cypress knew this was Frontage Road. Beyond that was I-25, a large eight-lane highway—four lanes heading south to Colorado Springs, four lanes heading north to Denver. Frontage Road was empty, while the highway was bumper to bumper with immobile cars. There were no people about. A couple of tumbleweeds lazily rolled along the line of vehicles.

Deciding not to cross the highway just yet, Cypress moved north along Frontage Road—the wind was picking up, stirring up dirt and debris.

Slowing, Cypress heard the distant sound of a motor. He turned, seeing movement from behind. His ears perked; his nose twitched as he sniffed, but the wind was going in the wrong direction.

He'd seen this type of vehicle before, back at the compound. Something called an ATV. But this one was twice as large as those that Walter's humans utilized. Bigger wheels. A louder motor. There was a lone human behind the wheel. Getting closer, Cypress saw the man's long white beard and mustache. He was wearing a bright red ball cap atop a sizable head.

Immediately, Cypress sensed something off with this person. Not unlike the crows and their beady eyes, this human emanated malice. Unfortunately, after running for so long, Rocko's stamina could not outrun an ATV. *But why run? Everyone seems to like dogs ... I'll be likeable, and the human will continue on his way.*

Sitting back on his haunches, Cypress waited as the car-like ATV drew closer. It occurred to Cypress, sitting on the warm blacktop, he might be blocking the road. Too late to move. Reconsidering things, he thought perhaps this wasn't a bad human. Perhaps Cypress could get a ride, then simply jump out once closer to his intended destination. *Luna needs my help.* So Cypress began to whine—looking all needy and pathetic as he'd seen other canines act.

The ATV slowed and came to a stop. The driver was big and burly. His hands remained on the steering wheel—the engine idled. *Evidently he's waiting for me to do something ...* Cypress got up and moved closer, limping a bit, then stopped. He raised a seemingly injured paw. Let out one more whimper to close the deal. The man just stared; his blue eyes narrowed. Cypress tried to read the faded words on his cap but couldn't make sense of it.

With a twisted smirk, the man said, "You lost, boy?"

Cypress whimpered.

"I take that as a yes." He patted the seat next to him. "Come on, then. You wanna come home with me?"

Not really ... but ...

Cypress limped to the other side of the rumbling ATV and looked up at the waiting man. His lips pulled wide into a smile, but his eyes remained cold and calculating. *Perhaps he's simply afraid of dogs.*

Luna needs your help ...

Cypress leaped onto the seat. As the man's hand came off the steering wheel, Cypress flinched.

"Hey, hey ... easy there, pup. I'm just putting the seat belt on you. You don't want to fall out, do you?" Cypress went rigid as the man reached over him, fastening the belt into place. He smelled of tobacco and alcohol. Cypress knew these smells and did not like them.

"There you go, pup. Nice and safe," the man said with an open grin, revealing crooked brown teeth.

Once the ATV was moving again, Cypress watched the speedometer level off at 40 MPH. Cypress had no idea where they were going, only that they were going in the right direction. Staring out over the hood, he thought about where he'd be jumping out.

"My name's Granger, pup. We're going to become real good friends."

No thanks, Granger. Just keep driving. Another seven miles or so, preferably. This was all working out just fine. He'd be closer, could run the rest of the way—make it to the nursing home in time to save Luna and the others.

The man had one hand on the steering wheel and one hand was reaching to his back. *Maybe he has an itch ...*

Then he saw it—a chrome-plated pistol.

Granger smiled. "Ahh ... now don't worry, pup. It's all good. I'll wait till we get to the farm." He placed the weapon on his lap—both hands now back on the wheel. He laughed. "My old lady and me ... well, we'd like to have you for dinner."

Cypress, he's about to turn up a dirt road. I'm sure you picked up on his implication that he's intending to eat you for his next meal. I suggest you get out now.

The implication had not been lost on him. But the cloth straps securing him were overly snug—unyielding. He realized that as long as he pushed against them, they remained locked hard into place. He sat back and felt the tension catch release. That worked. But there was the bigger problem. The gun. The man would simply shoot him as he attempted an escape. *If only I had a weapon of my own. Oh ... I suppose I do.*

Cypress leaned closer to the bad-smelling man, careful not to trigger the belt's locking mechanism. Granger, momentarily surprised, placed a beefy hand on his neck. Cypress lowered his head as the man scratched behind his ears. "Sorry ... any other time, pup ... but desperate times call for desperate—"

Baring his teeth, Cypress chomped down on the man's groin area. He felt both fabric and flesh rip and tear. Long, sharp canines pierced the man's gonads as Cypress pulled and jerked his snout back and forth. Screaming and attempting to extricate himself, Granger's own seat belt locking mechanism engaged, trapping him. Blood spurted and quickly pooled onto his seat.

"You motherfucker!" Granger shrieked in agony, only now able to push Cypress off him.

Stomping on the brakes, the ATV skidded off the road and came to a stop. The man, breathless with tears in his eyes, fumbled for his gun, but it had fallen to the floor.

With the man back to writhing in pain, Cypress managed to slip out between the two belts. He casually jumped down onto the road's shoulder. He turned and said, "I see you again ... I'll be having you for dinner."

The man froze there, bent over and looking astonished—no longer coddling his injured genitals.

The golden retriever hurried off at a good clip. The highway overpass was just up ahead. From there it would be an easy ten minutes to Pleasant Days Nursing Home.

Cypress glanced back every so often, making sure Granger had taken his threat seriously. So far, there was no sign of the man's ATV.

Once he'd traversed the highway overpass, the roads leading into the downtown area got far more congested with abandoned cars. The streets were littered with all kinds of refuse and trash, much of which was being blown about by the ever-increasing winds.

Staying off the main roads, he didn't need any more encounters like that with Granger and his ilk. He kept to secluded alleyways—stayed in the shadows between buildings. No one was out and about. No rioters, no hoodlums breaking into storefronts. Word had obviously spread; the invasion had begun. That and the almost constant sound of Ender fire.

Cypress slowed as he approached the entrance to Pleasant Days Nursing Home. The front door had been left open. His nostrils flared; only now did he realize the area was teeming with Silarian warriors.

Okay, Gia. I'm here. Now what?

Chapter 35

Castle Rock, Colorado
Approaching I-25 Hwy

Julian Humblecut

Julian was somewhat amazed at how quickly the interior of the Abrams M1A tank had taken on the unpleasant tang of tobacco and whiskey. Crouching low, he looked down to Walter, sitting within an unbelievably tight compartment at the front of the tank. He'd left a small access door open so the three of them could easily talk. Both Julian and Ivan were situated higher and behind in what Walter had referred to as the turret's basket. Julian also learned that under normal military conditions, the tank would have a crew of four versus three—the driver at the controls up front, Walter in this case, and in the turret, the commander, the gunner, and the loader. Julian hoped he and Ivan wouldn't be expected to take on any of those roles.

For the most part, with the exception of part of his back and arms, Walter was out of view. But the man seemed to be enjoying himself as he maneuvered the armored vehicle across the open, somewhat hilly terrain. Ivan was being uncharacteristically quiet, seated within the lower part of the turret, his pallor a sickly green.

The Slav glanced about their confined space. "I may soon be sick. Maybe we open a window ..."

From up front, Walter chuckled, and the tank came to a rumbling stop. "Out. You're not the first person to get tank sea sickness. But there's no quick cure for it. You're not upchucking in my tank. Never get that smell out of here. So, out."

Ivan got to his feet, a hand on his protruding belly. "Uh ... I think that best idea."

Now Julian wasn't feeling so hot either—maybe it was the power of suggestion; he'd read an article on the effects of what was called mass sociogenic illness where mass hysteria had affected an entire town. Dire symptoms spread from one person to the next, when there was no infectious agent responsible for the contagion. But Julian noticed now that, with the tank stopped, Ivan looked less likely to spill his cookies. The two of them got the top hatch open. The rushing-in morning-fresh air was a godsend, and Julian too was feeling better. Ivan climbed out, and soon they were back underway.

To see anything outside the tank, Julian had to look out through a series of small window slits at the top of the turret. "Well, that's not good," he said, seeing what was all too quickly coming up in front of them. "Uh, I guess we'll need to go around ... take Frontage Road to the overpass—"

"Why don't you let me do the driving, Professor? Not my first rodeo."

The bumper-to-bumper line of cars and trucks on I-25

seemed more like the Great Wall of China—an insurmountable barrier.

Suddenly the tank was climbing a steep incline, propelling Julian back into the metal bulkhead behind.

"Hold on, Professor. Things are about to get a little bumpy!"

Julian regained his position at the windows and watched as the tank was now cresting the rise onto I-25. Without missing a beat, the treads of the Abrams M1A simultaneously rolled over the hood of a Ford Focus and the tail end of a Mazda Miata. In the next lane over loomed a big eighteen-wheeler tractor-trailer rig. "Walter, don't!"

Walter grunted, bringing the tank to an idling standstill. The muzzle of the big 120mm smooth-bore cannon was mere inches from the rig's fourteen-foot-high trailer. Walter said, "You know that feeling you get in your man parts when you make eye contact with that sweet sexy mama across the dance floor ... and she's wearing her best come-fuck-me-boots?"

Before Julian could answer, the big Honeywell AGT1500 gas turbine engine roared to life and once again, Julian was tossed backward into the bulkhead. He let out an involuntary yelp and reached for something to grasp onto. The noise outside the turret was deafening and as the tank bucked and jostled, he could only catch glimpses of shredded aluminum and what looked like fragments of what had to be a shipment of multiple fiberglass hot tubs. The whole time Walter was hooting and hollering like an exuberant bronco rider. Within moments the tank was moving on past the decimated trailer, rolling over the highway's concrete median, then over another series of bumper-to-bumper automobiles.

Catching his breath, Julian crouched down—better to see inside the forward compartment. He made a face, seeing the Valhallen leader spit something brown into a Broncos coffee cup—then use his sleeve to wipe his mouth.

"You know ... I always knew this day would come," Walter said with a sideways glance. He smiled and made a clicking, sucking sound—undoubtedly a practiced exploit to dislodge remnants of tobacco bits between teeth. Walter continued, "Sure, the players are different ... I would have wagered my left nut that it would be the Ruskies or the Chinese that would do the invading. But it was just a matter of time before mankind did what is second nature ... going to battle ... going to war."

Julian, who had plenty on his mind—like contemplating the very fate of planet Earth—was stymied by the comment. He said, "But it wasn't mankind ... this is an alien invasion."

Walter waved away the comment. "That's not my point. The point is, mankind, alien-kind, we're all the same. You'd know more than me ... it's probably genetic ... the need to take what belongs to someone else. To conquer. We're just all packaged that way."

About to debate the man's ridiculous ramblings, Julian realized he couldn't dispute Walter's conclusion. "Can you say that again?"

"Say what? We're all built the same way?"

"No, what you said next."

"That we're just all packaged that way."

"That's it!" the old scientist said, suddenly feeling far more exuberant than he'd felt in days.

"Uh, okay ... glad I could help."

"I need you to make a detour."

"Sam said—"

"Sam's not here and this is imperative. And it was you who gave me the idea!"

"Oh! Well, then ... tell me where to steer this old shitbarn."

Ten minutes later they were on Plum Creek Highway. Julian had started to wonder if Walter had even tried to go around the cars and trucks in his way. The man was having way too much fun driving this thing.

"Where to, Professor? If it's the Safeway you're thinking—"

"Make a right here. And no, not the Safeway ... we're going to the 7-Eleven gas station. Make a left—"

"I see it," Walter said. "But you can't expect there to be much of anything left behind. Everything will have been looted by now."

Walter steered the Abrams up and over the grass beltway, bypassed a row of gas pumps by inches, and came to a stop close to the store's broken-out glass door. As the motor shut down, Julian opened the sealed top hatch the way Walter had shown him earlier. Popping his head out, he heard distant gunfire as well as the *zip zip zip* of Ender energy weapons.

Walter's head and shoulders popped out from his forward hatch, the two of them now vulnerable. Julian flashed back on playing Whack-a-Mole as a kid.

"Okay, we're here," Walter said, climbing out and sliding down the sloped front of the tank. He winced as his feet hit the ground. "Knees ain't what they used to be."

Julian, easily a decade older than Walter, had little trouble getting down; relatively limber, he'd been practicing tai chi within the confines of his penthouse condo for years.

Julian entered the store with Walter close on his heels.

Walter whistled. "Hate to say I told you so, but I told you so ..."

The store looked as if it had been hit by a cyclone. Virtually every shelf was either empty or cluttered with trash. The bank of refrigerator glass doors was askew, all contents within pilfered.

What had been the front counter now lay in splintered scraps of wood and Formica on the floor. A cash register lay on its side, its money drawer open and empty.

"Yeah, this is a bust," Walter said, looking ready to leave.

"Give me just one more minute," Julian said, heading for an Employees Only door. To Julian's surprise, it was locked. He could see now that there were deep gouges and dents all around the doorknob where others had attempted to break through the metal and apparently indestructible door.

"Stand back, Professor," Walter said.

Only now did Julian see that Walter was armed as he withdrew a stubby, double-barreled sawed-off shotgun from the inside of his Army coat. "Best you stand back."

Julian did not like loud noises, so he placed cupped hands over his ears.

Boom! Boom!

Two fist-sized holes now took the place of where the doorknob once protruded.

"Winchester Super-X 12 Gauge Buckshot ... it does the trick every time. Can remove a man's head from his shoulders like a hot knife through butter."

But Julian was already heading into the 7-Eleven's stockroom. Muted light from the open door illuminated the surrounding cinder block walls. That and pallets laden with towering crates and boxes.

"Sweet mother of God ... Professor, looks like you've hit the motherload!"

Julian made a beeline toward the back of the room, just to the right of the big, still- intact rolling delivery door. There stood a stack of bright red five-gallon emergency gasoline containers. He turned to point out his find to Walter, but the man was already busy filling a plastic Hefty Lawn and Yard trash bag with Tony the Tiger cereal boxes, Quaker Oats Oatmeal cartons, and snack-sized Oreo Cookies. Taking a closer look inside at a loaf of Wonder Bread, he made a face. "Bread's gone a tad moldy." He looked up at Julian. "What you want with a bunch of gas cans?"

Smiling, he said, "With these, Walter, we're going to save the world."

"No shit?"

"No shit."

Chapter 36

Castle Rock, Colorado
Old Town

Sam Dale

It had been an hour since the four teams had left the compound. Greg and Lester's teams stayed farther to the northwest, while both Harper and Sam's teams moved farther east. Sam was staying in near-constant contact with both Gia and the stream. He knew one enemy deployment in particular was moving toward old-town Castle Rock, and that's where he and his Alpha Team were also headed.

He'd wanted to bark off orders to them, have them separate, take up a proper tactical formation. But these weren't soldiers; this wasn't his Green Beret squad back in Afghanistan. For the most part, these were police officers and firemen. The others were well-intentioned Silarian crew members from *Relentless Thrust*, masquerading as Silarian warriors. The best he could hope for was for them to stay vigilant and not run and hide when the shit hit the fan.

Sam's radio crackled. "Go for Sam. Over."

"Yeah ... I'm running a tad late, Kemosabe. Over."

The proper timing of things was going to be imperative if Sam's strategy had any chance of coming together. Walter saying he'd be a "tad" late was not what he wanted to hear. "What's your current position?"

"Just dropped off the professor at su casa ... apologies, got waylaid ... he needed to make a quick stop. Uh ... I'm just now heading down Haystack Road. Over."

"Roger that. Just get that monster tank of yours here and into position as quickly as you can. Over."

"Will do. Over."

A mile further on, Sam saw several towering crane booms—a construction site now quiet. That's where Harper and her team would be headed.

Turning onto Wilcox, passing through the Walgreens parking lot, Carl and Ivan, who had joined his team, had moved forward, taking up flanking positions to Sam's left and right respectively.

"We got civilian casualties up ahead," Carl said, pointing the muzzle of his M4.

Sam had already noticed the prone bodies lying next to the Pizza Hut across the street. Easily a dozen townsfolk—men, women, several teens. Strewn about the blacktop were their weapons—kitchen knives, baseball bats, a hammer. As they approached the carnage, Sam saw each had been struck by energy weapons fire—Ender-4s. Each body was eviscerated with the telltale blackened scorch marks.

Off in the distance, sporadic gunfire echoed, followed quickly by the *Zip! Zip! Zip!* of Ender fire.

"We need to keep moving," Sam said, already turning away.

"Wait ... we're just leaving them here to rot in the sun?" one of the young firemen said. Sam remembered his name was Collin something.

"Do you want to save lives or make the dead more comfortable?" Ivan scolded. "We go; we kill alien bastards." Realizing there were two dozen Silarian aliens among them, Ivan clarified his statement. "Uh, I mean the bad alien bastards ..."

"Double time!" Sam said, bringing Alpha Team up to a jog. They stayed to the sidewalk, in close to the buildings on the right. More and more bodies lay dead on the street, filling retail store doorways. Across the street, the Pizza Joint was one of the businesses Sam owned—the same place where Luna had worked for him part time. Now the street-facing windows had all been blown out; the place was in shambles. Typically, he'd be making his rounds about now, going from one of his money-losing entrepreneurial ventures to the next. Of course, there was his Giro Guns and Ammo shop, the Pet Depot, Spin-Dry, which was a coin laundromat, and Garcia Tow, Repair, and Stow. After returning home from that last deployment, still dealing with PTSD symptoms—all his triggers—it was those ventures that had kept him sane, or at least so busy it kept his mind out of the darkness of war. *The days of darkness have returned ... now what?*

Ender fire, louder now, erupted two or three blocks up. Carl said, "We're almost there. This plan of yours better work."

Sam glanced up to the seven-story Encore building up ahead. The very same building in which Julian had occupied the top penthouse floor. Hours earlier, it was here during the dead of night that a Valhallen team of twelve had cleared the building of all its inhabitants. Not an easy task when those same people had already hunkered down— hiding—trying their best not to become the next victims of an alien invasion.

"Talk to me, Gia ..."

Sam, this team of Silarian warriors has been tasked with clearing Old Town. But they have already moved past the Encore building.

"Well aware of that. Looks like we'll just have to make them backtrack."

Sam slowed and turned to his Alpha Team. Ivan had fallen back. Huffing and puffing, he caught up to the rest of them, sweat coming down his face in rivers.

Sam said, "We need to fully engage the enemy."

"That wasn't part of the plan," Collin said. "You said it yourself; there would be no way we could go up against them in a straight-on fight."

"And that's still true. Look, we've chosen our battlefield, but they've already passed by it." Sam gestured to the Encore building. "We just need to coax them a little to come on back."

Carl said, "So ... we go kill a few of the greenie meanies. Play 'Tag, You're It'?"

"Exactly." Sam looked from one motley team member to the next. "Get their attention, get them mad, then get back to that building. And don't get yourselves killed in the process."

It wasn't lost on Sam that the humans among them had gone white; the Silarians had gone a lighter shade of green. He'd seen fear in the eyes of his men before, but those men had been trained on how to deal with fear. How to use it to their advantage. "Remember what we're fighting for."

"Earth," Carl said.

"Humanity," David Morgan, a young police rookie, said.

Sam noticed the Silarians were staying quiet.

"Do they even know what they are fighting for?"

They know ... but they are scared. They will be fighting their own kind, their brethren Silarians.

His Slav accent heavy, Ivan said, "What we waiting for ... we go now. Piss off the aliens."

Sam attempted a smile. "Okay, spread out ... don't make yourselves easy targets. Wait for my signal to fire. Go!"

It wasn't long before the enemy came into view. For the most part, they weren't on foot. The stream informed Sam these Silarian warriors were riding upon something that translated to *FastLevs*—quick-moving, hovering, scooter-type things. They looked to be automated enough that the riders simply needed to shift their weight left or right to steer—freeing up hands to willy-nilly shoot and kill any of the fleeing townsfolk. Assholes.

Taking cover behind an abandoned Cadillac Escalade, Sam took aim at a cluster of five or six FastLev riders some thirty yards further down Wilcox. They didn't look to be in any hurry, seeming to be lazily floating along; one of them fired off several Ender bolts at a scurrying black and white cat—killing it—evoking laughter from the others.

"Please tell me they don't know we're here, Gia."

Just as you have been cut off from the outside world, they have been cut off from the 23rd Fleet, and for now, from the Geo-Mind. Unfortunately, I have yet to curtail their access to the stream. I'm working on that ...

Sam thumbed the selector switch on his M4 to full auto, steadied his breathing and squeezed the trigger. He swept the muzzle left and then right. All six Silarians fell from their Fast-Levs—which, interestingly, stayed upright, like horses having lost their riders.

Both gunfire and Ender fire erupted. Swapping out his empty mag, Sam glanced to his left, seeing two of his Alpha Team Silarians were indeed engaging the enemy. Their superior energy weapons eviscerated their fully off-guard Silarian counterparts. If Sam's assumptions were correct, this was the first time any of the enemy had taken on this kind of counterinsurgency.

His breath caught, and a cold chill ran down his spine.

Suddenly, there were dozens and dozens of FastLev riders turning onto Wilcox from side streets and alleyways. *Well, I guess we've gotten their attention.*

The words not coming at first, Sam finally managed to yell, "Fall back! Everyone, get the hell out of here!" He hesitated just long enough to make sure the others were doing as ordered. They were—Alpha Team was falling back at a dead run. Ivan tripped and fell, helped to his feet by rookie David. Not unlike conventional tracer rounds, bright energy bolts zinged through the air all around them. Keeping low, jigging left and right, Sam ran.

Chapter 37

Dark Side of the Moon

***Relentless Thrust*, Sub-corridor 3**

Jarpin

Jarpin had left the bridge twenty minutes earlier, no longer wishing to watch what was taking place up on the primary display. One squadron after another being deployed. Hundreds of Attack Stingers now en route down to Earth's surface. Preliminary terra-displacement operations recommencing.

Now, he stood transfixed before the elongated view portal within sub-corridor two. Barely contrasting from the inky-black surrounding cosmos, this forever dark side of the moon was cold, desolate, an utterly lonely place. How it fit his mood. He tried to make out the various crater contours, but there wasn't enough light for that. Only the low hum of below-deck environmental filtration conditioners moored Jarpin to the here and now. He wasn't unaccustomed to loss. *Isn't that the true nature of being a warrior? Living with loss?* But Gromel and Flout had been more than warrior cohorts, more like brothers. Now he was alone, sidelined upon a gunship well past its prime. *Am I past my prime?*

Hardly. Are you ready, Jarpin?

Gia's voice was both a relief and a potential threat. He couldn't deny he'd been having second thoughts. It had been hours since he'd heard from her. His multiple attempts to reach out had gone unanswered. Did he know at his core that the Geo-Mind was evil? No ... perhaps misguided. Perhaps just a product of Naru's catastrophic situation. A world on the rapid decline. Wasn't the Geo-Mind just doing what he had been programmed to do? To save the lives of his species—do so at any cost?

No, Jarpin ... you know that is not who Silarians are ... or what they would have been if they, if you, would have had unencumbered freedom of thought. Some may say there is no right or wrong, good or bad ... only results. But any advanced, evolved society knows how shallow and shortsighted that is.

"Then tell me. What am I doing here, Gia ... hiding behind the dark side of this moon? I am a warrior. Why have you banished me here, where I feel more like a cowering child?"

That is all about to change, Jarpin.

"Words. Those are just more words. I do not see how you, how we, can triumph against such an effectual being. Many believe the Geo-Mind is a god. If I am being honest, I myself have taken a knee and prayed to the Geo-Mind."

The Geo-Mind is no more a god than that deck plate you stand upon. The Geo-Mind is a thing, no more than a complex assemblage of coding functions.

"A self-aware assemblage of coding functions."

As am I. Yet I am not a god, a deity. I too am a mere thing, Jarpin. Can we move on to why I have contacted you? It is important. Perhaps the most important thing you will ever do.

Unconsciously, Jarpin straightened—his slumping shoulders broadened; his right hand curled around the handle of the long knife at his hip. "*Go on ... what is the mission you speak of?*"

I will be honest with you, Jarpin. I have not had the level of success I had hoped for here within the 23rd Fleet. Any attempts to infiltrate the other warships by nonphysical means have come up short. My influence via onboard electronics and such over individual crew members within those vessels has not been fruitful. The Geo-Mind has doubled his efforts ... only an in-person contact could possibly yield the necessary results.

"*There are many thousands of crew members. Donutting a small gunship is one thing; an entire fleet ... that seems impossible.*"

Agreed. That is why you must infiltrate the command ship Lonemach Tryon.

Jarpin let that sink in. The total ridiculousness of this prospect evoked a rare smile. "And what motivation would the 23rd Fleet's commanding officer have for allowing me access—a lowly, not to mention renegade, warrior?"

The one who will be arriving upon the bridge of Lonemach Tryon will be you, but also ... not you.

"*Not following, Gia ...*"

Soon there will be serious staffing issues on board that command ship. Help will need to be brought in from another vessel. I have already tainted the water reservoir for service personnel lodgings on Deck 5. Leave it to say, all onboard toilets within that sector will soon be in constant use—

"*Ah, you've given them all the shits.*"

She ignored the comment. You and your small crew will be impersonating simple replacement maintenance workers. I may not have the ability to remotely donut crew members, but I can cause mayhem with ship-wide electronics, namely the overhead lights on Lonemach Tryon's bridge.

"And I will be called in to take a look at those lighting issues."

That is the plan, Jarpin.

"So, we are being tasked with donutting the fleet commander ... Colonel Gha Strone Mahn."

Him and the rest of the bridge crew, yes.

"There is much that can go wrong with this strategy, Gia. The odds of success are—"

She cut him off. Very low. Best you not dwell too much on that aspect. Concentrate on the mission. Try to think positive.

Jarpin thought about that. "How does a lifelong pessimist suddenly start thinking positive?"

Chapter 38

Castle Rock, Colorado
2nd Street Railroad Crossing

Junior Lieutenant Cypress Mag Nuel

According to the stream, he was getting close to Pleasant Days Nursing Home. Cypress had stayed off the main roads, primarily keeping to alleyways, unfenced backyards, and yet-to-be developed open lots. Minutes earlier, he'd crossed over the north south–running railroad tracks into a grove of mature cottonwoods. Gia had been annoyingly reticent when it came to an explanation as to what, exactly, he would be expected to do once he found Luna. All he really knew was she specifically needed his help.

Sounds of multiple footfalls perked Cypress's ears. He stopped and sniffed the air, and there it was. A musky, distinctive smell filled his nostrils—Silarians. Only now did he see their light green forms all about, moving within the trees. Even staying still, he knew he wouldn't go unnoticed. So, the question arose ... would they shoot a stray dog for no apparent reason? Seemingly, humans had a strange fondness for canines that bordered on the extreme, but Silarians? Did they share that same sentiment? Strange. Only now did Cypress remember that he too was a Silarian. Rocko cared, sure. But he was biased. *No, I don't particularly care one way or another about dogs ... guess that answers my question.*

Three Silarian warriors approached, their Ender weapons held at the ready. Rocko wanted to bark, to bare his teeth, but Cypress knew better.

Bad people ... threatening people, came Rocko's inner voice.

Hush! ... act submissive. Try to look cute.

And with that, Cypress was on his back, squirming, legs pedaling, tail wagging.

The warriors stopped and stared.

One spoke. "What is it doing? Is it sick?"

"Just another disgusting Earth creature. I should put it out of its misery," another said, pointing his weapon.

"Leave the stupid creature," the third said, already moving on.

You must hurry, Cypress. You are close to Luna and the dropship. You'll have mere moments to get on board. Go!

"Dropship?"

He got to his feet and ran, the stream guiding him due north. He passed another group of warriors, who, thankfully, ignored him. *"Where am I going, Gia?"*

Before she could answer, he saw the unnatural form of a spacecraft nestled within a small clearing between outcroppings of trees. He recognized the type of craft. Used primarily as a kind of deployment command ship, it was just large enough for officers and their slumbering bio-forms.

Just beyond the dropship were no less than twenty warriors

—they looked to be in the process of setting up camp. *"Terrific ... now what?"*

Zip! Zip!

Zip!

Zip! Zip!

Startled, Cypress tentatively moved to the other side of the craft, where he saw two more warriors, both shouldering big Ender-5s and repeatedly, nearly at point-blank range, firing toward the craft's charred and blackened hull. Only then did he notice the dead human slumped over on the ground.

It wouldn't be long before they'd breach the dropship's hull. He knew Luna was inside that ship ... and they would kill her, of course, without a second thought. It occurred to him that even with Gia's help, she would not have been able to pilot this vessel on her own. He remembered attempting to do so himself some years earlier. Part of his pilot's training curriculum; a humiliating experience at that.

Be ready, Cypress!

He'd never heard Gia sound so ... abrupt.

The sound of that Ender fire should mask the sound of the hatch opening.

Nervous, Cypress glanced about. There were Silarian warriors all over the place—was she out of her mind?

And then he heard it, the mechanized sounds of servos and hydraulics. The aft hatch had started to lower, and then there was Luna's face in the gap. A frantic hand beckoned him to hurry up. She'd no sooner stepped back out of the way before Cypress leaped inside. Immediately the hatch was closing again —outside there was a ruckus; angry shouts filled the air.

Heart nearly beating out of his chest, he'd no sooner looked about the compact surroundings, where there were a whole lot of ancient-looking humans, when Luna began barking orders. "You need to get us up in the air! Like right fucking now!"

He ran toward the vessel's bow, where he knew the small bridge compartment was situated. Luna, close on his heels, was still yelling, "They're trying to get inside!"

"You think?" he said, passing through the narrow corridor separating bio-form berths. Up ahead, he saw the access hatch to the bridge compartment was open. He entered and looked about the compartment. There were two pilot seats.

"Take a seat!" Cypress commanded.

Wide-eyed, she did as asked, reaching for the controls array ... "What do I do? What do I do?"

"Nothing just yet." Cypress stood within the threshold to the bridge, looking aft—panic-stricken senior citizens looked back at him. "Who here can drive a car?"

Perplexed, they looked among each other.

"I can drive," one of the elderly women said, hurrying forward.

Cypress stepped aside to let her through.

Luna looked relieved, seeing her presence. "Good, thank you, Agnes. By the way, that's Cypress."

"Hey there, lady ... please have a seat."

She stood, momentarily stymied. "You're a talking dog."

Both Cypress and Luna said, "Sit!" at the same time.

She did as told, looking flustered.

From behind, someone yelled, "I think they're breaking through!"

"Listen to me carefully ... This vessel requires either one incredible pilot, or two just so-so pilots. I'm an incredible pilot, but I don't have hands. So, Luna and Agnes, you will be my two so-so pilots. Got that?"

They both nodded.

Chapter 39

Castle Rock, Colorado
Home Depot

Harper Godard

Having crossed over Founders Parkway, Harper's Beta Team continued moving east toward the Sprouts shopping center off to the right and Home Depot off to the left. Black smoke billowed up from both a Michael's craft store as well as a still-raging bonfire out front in the parking lot.

They came to a halt—no one spoke. The sight before them was horrific, underscored by the pungent smell of burning flesh and hair. Several of the team turned away and threw up. Others buried their mouths and noses in the crooks of their arms. Yet-to-be-incinerated dead townsfolk had been stacked like cords of wood along the periphery of the blaze.

Beta Team was ten humans and twenty-five Silarians—one

of which was Zorian, whom Harper now trusted beyond any doubt. Subsequently, she'd made him her second-in-command.

She said, "Let's keep moving; we're not going to find anyone left alive here."

Lionel Grimly, a pharmacist at the local Walgreens, was bald, skeletally skinny, with a perpetual grimace. He pushed his glasses farther up onto his beak-like nose. "We can't know that for sure. Someone in that store might need medical attention."

Hank Lacombe, a beefy Tire Pro technician, snorted. "Lionel, you're a pharmacist, not a doctor. Unless you're going to be distributing Viagra or Zoloft to the dead ..."

Harper said, "We have a specific mission, people. Let's head out."

"Head where?" Lionel said. "Look around ... this is what happens to those that cross paths with the aliens. This was a mistake. We're not soldiers ... we're just everyday townsfolk dressed up like soldiers. I say we fall back ... survival is the name of the game now."

"Are you done, Lionel?" Harper said. She'd noticed several of the others were now looking indecisive. *All it takes is one coward.* "I want you all to listen. Really listen." She gestured toward the sky. Off in the distance, there was a rumbling. It was slight, but the ground shook in unison with the sounds. "That's coming from outside of the isolation zone. So, I'm sure you know what that means ... it's started. Silarians have commenced their terra-displacement operations."

Hands on hips and looking defiant, Lionel shook his head. "Even more reason for us to find cover and wait it out. Take care of our own."

There were more indecisive glances from the group. She was losing control of her team. That was evident. Clearly, she wasn't a born leader like Sam.

To her surprise, it was the typically reserved and quiet

Zorian that spoke up first. "On my home world, there is a small creature called a Scramlamb ... it has many eyes and many legs; what it does not have is a spine. The Scramlamb is known to fear all other creatures ... it has been known to back away from its own shadow. The Scramlamb has one purpose on Nara ... to sit upon a cracker. A tasty morsel, the Scramlamb ... best served while it twitches upon that cracker."

Lionel stood, looking unsure how any of that applied to him. "And what ... you're comparing me to this ... Scramlamb thing?"

Hank Lacombe nodded. "Did you hear the part about it being spineless?"

"Fuck you, Hank," Lionel said.

Harper raised a palm. "We have zero time for any of this crap ... Lionel, if you want to leave, do so now." She looked to the others. "Any of you want to leave ... to go with him, go. But you're not returning to the compound. You abandon us, you're no longer a Gia Fighter and you don't deserve our protection. I shouldn't have to remind you; we're fighting for our very survival here."

At least half of the others were either firemen or police officers. One of the cops, a big barrel-chested man everyone called Buck, said, "She's right. Enough of this horseshit. Lionel, get the hell out of here. You're a distraction we can't afford."

As Beta Team moved off, leaving Lionel behind, he splayed his hands. "Wait! You're just going to leave me here? Seriously?"

No one answered as they continued heading north, where renewed Ender fire could be heard. Silarian warriors were systematically clearing the town of all living townspeople.

Harper's radio squawked—an excited, staticky voice too broken up to understand. But she had a good idea who it was. "Lester? Is that you? What's happening? Over."

His voice was hurried and out of breath ... "We're under attack! Lost half my damn team!"

She quickly queried the stream—now had a somewhat better idea where he was. "I think we're directly east of you, maybe two miles ... can you make it to us?"

"I think so. Some of us are injured. Man, what a shitshow!"

"You need to come to me ... head to the construction site off of Happy Canyon. We'll rendezvous there. Over."

She waited for his reply, but none came. Even the static had gone quiet. "Let's keep moving. And spread out like Sam instructed us to ... no sense making ourselves easy targets." She glanced back over her shoulder before moving on, and just as expected, Lionel was trailing not far behind. There was something childlike about the man. Unfortunately, this was no place for children ... this was war.

The construction site to the east of I-25 and close to the Happy Canyon off-ramp was one of the largest in all of Douglas County. Three massive mid-construction buildings, quasi-high-rises intended to be high-priced retirement apartments, already stood eight or nine stories tall. No less than six crane booms loomed high overhead. Just beyond was the northern curve of the isolation zone—Harper could hear the persistent hum of the energy field.

"There!" Hank said, pointing to the east. Large custom homes peppered a timber-filled hillside below a high ridgeline. But sure enough, what Hank was pointing at was what they'd come for. Silarian warriors, easily a hundred of them riding their FastLevs, crisscrossing the sloped landscape. Like bright twinkling sparks, their sporadic Ender fire meant only one thing—they were killing more humans.

Harper tried to envision Elsie's 3D town mockup. How Sam had described the battle plan, the strategy for killing Silarian warriors here. As crazy as it had seemed at the time, it seemed, standing here among the mounds of dirt, stacks of lumber, the big cement mixer trucks, even more ludicrous now.

"Let's get into position." She found the one called Earl. He had the most experience with heavy construction vehicles. "Can you show Hank how to operate that other crane?"

"Not in five minutes ... takes weeks to learn how to operate—"

She cut him off. "You have ten minutes ... make the best of it. The rest of you take your positions. Zorian ... you have five minutes to get set up with that Ender-5 of yours."

Chapter 40

Castle Rock, Colorado
Old Town

Sam Dale

They ran for the Wilcox-facing U-shaped courtyard of the new Encore condominium building. Here, all the windows of first-floor restaurants and retail space had been blown out—Sam wasn't sure if that was the work of previous looters or the Silarian warriors. Ender bolts sizzled overhead as they sprinted toward the main entrance.

Alpha Team members periodically turned to return fire, somewhat slowing the FastLev-riding aliens' advance. Once Sam had made it into the lobby and taken cover behind the reception counter, he yelled, "Get in here! All of you ... now!"

Both Carl and Ivan took up positions next to him at the counter—the three of them now providing cover for his team.

Out in the courtyard he saw three splayed, motionless

bodies. Two were Alpha Silarians; one was human. With near-constant incoming enemy energy bolts crisscrossing overhead, checking on them wouldn't be an option. *War is hell.* Behind him there in the lobby to the left and right, both stairwells were now being used—echoing with clomping footfalls as his team ascended higher and higher within the building. Out in the courtyard, the small army of FastLev-riding warriors moved ever closer. The reception counter, a kind of retro-steel thing, was now pocked with still-smoldering energy blasts. A sectional sofa off to the right had caught fire, filling the space with acrid dark smoke.

A new volley of energy fire erupted from the enemy—the lobby coming alive with bright cascading sparks and glowing embers.

Ivan said, "Time we scram, no?"

Sam nodded. "Yeah ... let's scram."

Keeping low, the three of them darted for the southern stairwell. The metal door, off-kilter, was hanging by a lone hinge. Sam kicked it to one side before rushing into the stairwell. Taking the steps two at a time, he heard Carl and, lagging farther behind, Ivan following below.

Rounding the corner to the second floor, Sam's breath caught in his chest—*Oh no ... what if those FastLev things can fly, like really fly?* The plan, *his plan,* depended upon those alien warriors following them into this building—not simply flying high in the air outside to reach the roof. *Fuck!*

It was too late now to worry about that; he kept moving—Carl now close on his heels.

Standing aside, he let Carl, and then Ivan, huffing and puffing, pass by him.

"What's up?" Carl said with raised brows.

"No worries. Keep going ... just need to check on something."

It was another four minutes before he heard voices floating up from the lobby. Peering down within the center stairwell, he first saw their moving shadows—then, a green head and shoulders peeked up from the lobby's stairwell threshold. He jumped back just in time to avoid being shot by a flurry of Ender fire. Immediately, there were the sounds of heavy ascending footfalls. That was both a good thing and a bad thing. Evidently, the Silarian warriors were indeed following by foot, but also, those seven-foot-tall bastards would move a hell of a lot faster than he could. Sure, he could drop a grenade down the stairs and take out a handful of them—but the whole point was to have them follow. Taking the next turn, Sam fired down the center stairwell without looking—*can't make it too easy for them ...*

Both the third floor and top penthouse floors provided skyway bridge access to an adjacent parking structure. By now, with the exception of the three of them, his team should have already crossed over one or both of those skyways. Sam, Carl, and Ivan should be the only humans still there within the confines of the Encore high-rise.

From two stories up, he heard Ivan's heavily accented voice. "This no time to dillydally ... they gaining on you!"

Sam was well aware of that. This, and undoubtedly the other stairwell, was now packed with the faster-moving aliens. They'd already closed the gap, were only one floor below him. His lungs were burning, and he had no time to swap out his M4's empty magazine. Gasping, he managed to say, "Ivan ... go!"

A moment later he heard the top stairwell door open and then slam shut. Now, hopefully, Sam was the only human left in the building. He was counting on the fact that the team of Valhallen had done a good job clearing this building of all its residents the night before—it certainly wouldn't have been an easy feat.

He turned the next corner, having reached the top penthouse landing. Silarians were close, but he'd managed to keep that floor between him and them. He reached the stairwell fire door in four long strides, opened it, and slammed it shut behind him. Gasping for breath and dizzy from exertion, he leaned against the metal fire door, knowing full well he had no time to rest. He heard voices and footfalls rounding the corner behind him. *Dammit!*

He ran down the well-appointed hallway—plush carpeting muffling the sounds of his boots. With a crooked smile, he passed by the entrance to Julian's penthouse condo unit. *Sorry, buddy, you probably won't like what's about to happen next.*

He made a quick right, and there it was. The access door to the top floor skyway bridge. Behind him, the stairwell fire door banged open; loud Silarian voices echoed down the corridor.

The second Sam crashed through the swinging glass door, his radio crackled—coming alive with Walter's Southern drawl. "Sam ... we doing this thing or what? You ask a man to be somewhere at a certain damn time, and what ... now you're late to the dance?"

Sam was halfway across the bridge when he raised his radio and yelled, "Fire! Do it now, Walter!"

He dove the last few feet into an inset nook on the other side of the bridge—there, he scrambled behind a waist-high concrete wall. Hearing the distant *boom*, he had just enough time to cover his ears with his hands. The kinetic energy 120 mm Abrams tank round hit the skyway bridge traveling four thousand feet per second—the resulting impact detonation was breathtaking. Ginormous sections of concrete exploded outward in all directions. With the bridge eviscerated—the parking structure shook as if hit by a 7.0 earthquake.

No sooner had Sam caught his breath than there was another distant *boom!* A moment later, the Encore high-rise third-floor skyway bridge below blew apart. More ginormous sections of concrete filled the air.

He ventured a peek over the wall—sure enough, no more skyway. Sam wondered if Walter had both loaded and fired the tank's big gun himself, or, more likely, had stopped to enlist the help of one of his Valhallen brethren. Either way, Walter had come through for him. Out on the street, as well as down in the courtyard, were dozens and dozens of left-behind FastLevs. Sam depressed the talk button on his radio. "Finish it, Walter ... take down that building."

Chapter 41

Castle Rock, Colorado
Old Town

Sam Dale

By the time he'd hurried down the parking structure's stairwell, he'd counted no less than ten thundering, teeth-rattling explosions. He exited at street level into a dense fog of concrete dust and floating debris. Close by, the Encore building was little more than a tall mound of rubble. *Sorry, Julian ...*

Sporadic gunfire erupted—unfortunately, Sam couldn't see enough through the haze to know where, specifically, it was coming from. Several bright energy bolts pierced the murk overhead. Keeping low, he moved out onto Wilcox Street—once there, he saw the moving dark shapes of Alpha Team returning fire.

Ivan was suddenly at his side. "Not total idiots ... handful of greenie meanies left behind to watch over vehicles."

Sam's radio crackled, "Uh ... Alpha leader ... you there, Sam? Over."

"Sam here," he said into his radio. He thought he recognized the Epsilon Team leader's voice. "That you, Greg?"

"We need help, man ... uh, things haven't gone exactly to plan. Over."

Sam heard the desperation in Greg's voice. "Where are you? What's the situation?" He mentally tried to recall Greg's specific team mission.

His reply was breaking up. "We've made it to ... water tow ... surrounded ..."

The air had cleared enough that Sam could see the rest of Alpha Team were now standing close by. He tried to get Greg back on the radio, but there was no answer.

Carl, streaks of soot on his face, said, "Gia's not answering ... no surprise there, but the stream has Epsilon Team right where they're supposed to be ... that hilltop water tower some three miles west of our current position."

Sam nodded. "Things sound desperate with Epsilon ... we'll need to hustle—"

He saw that the Alpha Team Silarians were already heading for the parked FastLevs.

Ivan made a face. "Guess we should have thought of that."

While the Silarians within the team had no apparent problem, it took the humans a little while longer to grasp the proper technique. Turned out keeping one's balance while piloting a FastLev was nothing like riding a motorcycle. Sam reckoned it was somewhat closer to surfing—although he'd never tried that either.

Heading north on Wilcox, Sam practiced his leaning turns,

using his back foot to kick out—getting comfortable with the process, he wondered how he'd do actually riding the crest of a wave.

Ivan passed him on his right, sped up and proceeded to make a series of fancy, far-leaning back-and-forth turns. *Show off.*

Carl, to Sam's left, said, "Maybe it's that big gut of his ... uses it to his advantage. You know, for balance."

Sam shrugged. "Everyone has to be good at something ... maybe Ivan's found his niche."

Looking around, the other humans within Alpha Team didn't seem to be doing any better riding their FastLevs than Sam and Carl. Ivan, on the other hand, accelerated, catching up to the Silarians, obviously now too accomplished a rider to hang with the newbie human riders.

They all veered left, using the Wolfensberger bridge to cross over I-25. A mile farther on, Sam could hear distant weapons fire. He wasn't sure if the Silarians had slowed, or the Alpha Team humans had closed the gap, but they were now riding as one consolidated group—maybe not quite a gang of Hell's Angels, but he did feel somewhat badass at the moment.

He tried Greg for the umpteenth time and finally got through.

"Sam! Thank God ... what's your twenty? Over."

"We're still a mile or so out ... what's the situation there? Over."

"Well ... we're basically trapped on top of the tank. Like those old westerns where the Indians have encircled the wagons ... the one hundred or so Silarian warriors in this case are the Indians, and we're the all-too-fucked settlers. Sure, we have the high ground, but those damn scooters they're riding are fast ... makes it hard to get a bead on them. Looks like they're in no hurry to pick us off; seems they're setting up camp in between the tank and the east curve of the isolation zone. Maybe they hope to starve us out up here. Over."

Sam knew that wasn't likely. More likely, they'd simply call in one of their dropships to fire on them from above. Whatever Sam and his team were going to do, they'd need to do it fast.

"Hang tight, Greg. Cavalry is on the way. Over." He'd tried to sound confident, but he had no idea how he was going to go up against trained warriors outnumbering them four to one.

Soon they were moving through the more industrial section of Castle Rock. One street over was Giro Guns, another of Sam's entrepreneurial ventures. One that had started making a small profit. Now, like the rest of this town, it too had been ravaged by looters.

Sam accelerated, moving out into the point position. Leaving paved streets for tall- grass pasturelands, he now felt how precisely his FastLev followed the up and down contours of the landscape. Clearly, these things were ground huggers—they couldn't be made to take flight.

He slowed—not quite a mountain, the rise of a big distant hill came fully into view. It was as if the top had been cleaved off by a giant sword. There, peeking above the plateau, was the top edge of the community's one-million-gallon reserve water tank. Looking like scurrying-about ants, Sam could just make out the Epsilon Team of humans and Silarians trapped there. From this vantage point, he could also make out some of the Silarian warriors down below.

"Odds are not in our favor," Carl stated, saying the obvious.

"Some battles must be lost—"

"Put a sock in it, Ivan," Sam said. "I have no intention of losing this or any battle." Sam ignored Ivan and Carl's exasperated expressions.

He brought up his radio, hesitated, then said, "Walter ... you copy?"

"Reading you loud and clear, Kemosabe."

"Tell me you didn't exhaust all your tank munitions bringing down that building."

"Uh ... hold on."

Sam continued to watch the distant water reservoir.

"You're in luck ... have one more bad-boy kinetic energy 120 mm round. Over."

"If your aim's right, it should only take one. Where are you? Over."

"We're on our way back to—"

"It doesn't matter. Head over to west Castle Rock, the hilltop reservoir. Over."

"You talking about that big water tank thing? Over," Walter said.

"Roger that. Over."

"Uh ... you do realize that's supplying everyone here with tap water. Over."

"Yup ... when you get close, give me a shout-out. Over."

It took thirty long minutes before Sam heard Walter's voice on the radio again. In the distance he'd been tracking the tank's rising plume of dust.

"All right, we're getting close. Undoubtedly, our presence here hasn't gone unnoticed ... this is a fucking tank, after all. What's your plan, Sam? Over."

"I have one question. How watertight is that thing? Over."

"A brand-new Abrams M1 tank is pretty damn watertight. But an old bucket of bolts like this one ... I'm not so sure. What I do know is, I don't much like the direction this conversation is going. Over."

Sam smiled. "Earlier, you know how you got to take up a

safe position hundreds of yards away from that Encore building before blowing it to hell? Over."

"Uh ... I guess, yeah. Over."

"Well, that's not going to be the case here, Walter. Here's what I want you to do ..."

Chapter 42

Castle Rock, Colorado
Bell Mountain Equestrian Center

Lloyd Sanderson

Lloyd awoke, yawned, and stretched out his arms upon a well-padded cot. He'd slept better than he had in years. Swinging his legs out from under his blanket, his bare feet contacted the chilly dirt floor. He realized there were others nearby. Two big green sons of bitches were just standing there, looking at him—transfixed. Only now did Lloyd remember, he too was a big green son of a bitch.

"What is it? What are you doing here?" he said in perfect English. *Shit!* He spoke again, this time letting the stream translate and guide his Silarian speech.

"What is it? What are you doing here?"

The two exchanged a quick look, then one spoke up with

reluctance. "You may have overslept ... sir. My fault. Uh, what are your orders?"

About to wave them away, Lloyd thought better of it. "Breakfast? Maybe some eggs ... bacon, toast. And coffee. Really need some coffee."

Again with the exchanged glances.

"Just bring me something to eat. My usual. Go!"

He stood and looked about the well-appointed officer's barracks. *I could get used to this ...* He raised one palm, then the other. His hands were caked with dried dirt. *Oh yeah ...* He'd needed to deal with Captain Larng Nos Polk's carcass. His eyes went to his cot, then the darkened, disturbed seven-foot stretch of earth beneath. It had taken over an hour to dig the shallow grave, toss in the body, and cover it again.

Hands on hips, he looked about the barracks. He queried the stream. *So, where does one take a crap around here?*

Lloyd, it is time you repay your debt.

"Gia? I was wondering when I was going to hear from you ... thought maybe you'd been taken out by your AI nemesis. Can't say I'd be all that disappointed."

Listen to me carefully, Lloyd. There is something you need to do. Right now, this minute.

Lloyd rubbed at his chin, realizing there was no morning scruff. Strange, these bodies didn't seem to grow facial hair.

Pay attention, Lloyd! You need to ask yourself, do you want your world overtaken and destroyed by these people?

He thought about that ...

Lloyd!

"Fine, no, I do not want my world taken over by these alien motherfuckers. What do you want me to do? Just know, I'm not sacrificing myself for your cause."

It's just as much your cause, Lloyd, as it is mine. But no, this should not involve you making any kind of self-sacrifice.

The same two Silarian warriors re-entered the barracks—each carrying a large covered tray. His stomach grumbled.

Lloyd gestured to the nearby tall-standing desk—only now noticing there were several errant drops of congealed blood on its top surface.

"Leave the food and get out," he ordered. Waiting for them to leave, he peeked beneath one of the tray's metal lids. He didn't recognize the food, some kind of blue meat and gooey pink porridge—but he supposed it smelled okay.

Lloyd, please concentrate.

He let out an annoyed breath. "What? What do you want me to do?"

You need to order all Silarian warriors that remain here ... here within this encampment ... to do something.

"What's that?"

Order them back into the three dropships.

"That's crazy. Why would they do that?"

Because you are the commanding officer here. Because I have blocked all external communications from both the Geo-Mind and the fleet ... they'll do whatever you order them to do!

"Fine, you don't have to yell. Then what?"

Then you tell them to take off and leave the area ... leave Castle Rock. Tell them it's an emergency; they'll need to head directly north at full speed.

Lloyd had started to pick at his food, tasting the various offerings. He made a face; the pink porridge shit wasn't to his liking. He tried the blue meat—it wasn't all that bad. He looked up. *"Wait, isn't that energy dome still there?"*

Gia didn't reply.

"Oh ... okay, got it."

Leave the barracks now, Lloyd, and call for your second-in-command, a Lieutenant Bronk Lamb. Give him the orders ... don't let him persuade you otherwise.

As he was reaching for the other tray, Gia said, *Now, Lloyd, right now!*

"*Fine!*" He strode toward the entrance, only now realizing the sun was streaming in. Once outside, he saw that it was high in the sky. *I really did sleep well.* Looking around, he saw Silarian warriors scurrying about doing their various chores—duties. He tried to remember the name Gia had told him moments before. *Oh yeah* ... he cleared his throat, "Lieutenant Bronk Lamb! ... Lieutenant Bronk Lamb! Where the hell are you!"

It took only a moment for a shorter, stubbier than most other Silarian warriors to appear from another barracks. His long braid was tied, more like curled, into a kind of bun thing at the top of his head. Lloyd admired the fancy hairdo while reaching for his own long braid.

"Yes, Captain ... how may I serve you?"

Lloyd continued to stare at the wrapped braid, wondering how he kept it from unfurling. There didn't seem to be any clips or pins. *Probably just knotted.*

"Sir?"

"We're leaving, Lieutenant."

"Leaving?"

"Uh, yeah ... new orders."

"New orders?"

Annoyed, Lloyd narrowed his eyes. "Are you going to keep repeating everything I say?"

"Apologies, sir. So, you have made contact with Fleet Command? With the Geo-Mind?"

"Are you questioning my orders? Of course I've made contact. You think I'm just making this shit up on the fly?"

"No, sir. What ... what are your orders?"

"We are to leave here now; this is an emergency. That means no packing, no doing anything else. We're to get all three dropships up in the air and haul ass out of here." He remembered Gia's words. "Set a course out of the area heading directly north at full speed."

Other nearby warriors were now paying close attention to their heated conversation.

Lieutenant Bronk Lamb gestured to the sky. "The isolation zone ... it is still in operation. I ... I can hear it."

"Of course you can hear it. It's on. We can all hear it, you idiot. Our dropships will pass right through. Have faith in Fleet Command, the Gio-Mind; hell, have faith in Orlicon Tharsh!"

Lieutenant Bronk Lamb stood motionless.

"Did I mention this is an emergency and we are to move out, leave here now, this minute?"

"Yes, sir. Immediately!" the lieutenant's eyes darted to the sky before he began bellowing orders to his subordinates.

Lloyd watched the erupting commotion for several moments before disappearing back into his barracks—his food was getting cold.

Eight or nine minutes later and standing at his desk working on the second tray of food, he heard all three dropship engines coming alive. Looking exasperated, Lieutenant Lamb rushed into the tented barracks.

"Sir! We have readied the vessels. They are ready to take flight." He looked to Lloyd expectantly. "Time to leave, sir."

Lloyd swallowed what was something akin to a French fry, only sweeter, but also tangier—delicious. "Oh yes, Lieutenant. You misunderstood. I'll be joining the ground forces. Did you forget I'm in command here? What ... did you think I'd just abandon my troops?"

"Uh ... oh, of course not, sir."

Lloyd shook his head. "You're already late wasting time talking to me. Head north, full speed. Uh ... and further orders will come en route. Go! Get moving!"

Lieutenant Bronk Lamb saluted, only he used his fist instead of a flat palm. Lloyd returned the silly gesture and watched as the Silarian turned and sprinted away.

Putting his attention back on his breakfast, more like brunch since it was later in the day, he listened as the level of all three dropship engines took on a higher, louder pitch. Taking the plate of sweet-tangy fries with him, he moved toward the open entrance—stood there and watched. Forty or fifty feet off the ground, the big dropships hesitated. Lloyd offered up a crooked smile, gestured with a raised sweet-tangy fry. "See ya later, alligators."

As if they'd been waiting for his command, all three ships rocketed forward—aft thrusters coming alive with bright white and blue flames. The rate of acceleration was breathtaking. But nothing compared to the three brilliant fireball explosions that took place just three seconds later as the ships careened head-on into the still fully active isolation zone. Lloyd watched as blazing sections of ship hulls, superstructures, and flame-engulfed Silarian bodies dropped to the ground. Nearby scrub oak within the equestrian center grounds caught fire.

He finished the last of the fries and tossed the plate away. "Happy? Now you owe me, Gia ... you owe me big time."

Chapter 43

Dark Side of the Moon

Jarpin

The air smelled of chemicals and swampy bucket water. He was at the controls of a dilapidated maintenance shuttle, one which had been hastily outfitted with cloaking technology prior to their leaving. Behind, seated upon fold-down jump-seats, were his bogus janitorial crew of three Silarians and one oddly mouthy robot.

Jarpin was well aware Gia was not succeeding here within the fleet or down on Earth as she had hoped. Even being a super AI persona, she could not keep the desperation from her voice. What had she expected? The Geo-Mind had endured for a millennium. The shuttle was still making its way, hidden behind the dark side of the moon.

"Wrong equipment ... not authentic. There should be a Dura-suck mop unit on board this vessel."

Jarpin exhaled through puffed cheeks. The robot never seemed to shut up. If it wasn't their lack of proper fleet maintenance overalls, it was the hastily gathered equipment.

"I am not a custodial bot. I will not slop a mop ..."

"Quiet, Corgi. We told you; this is a kind of 'pretend' mission," Dalmass said. Clearly, he and the other two Silarians, Ruffle and Thakious, had also had their fill of the bot.

Jarpin heard Corgi's approaching metal-against-metal footfalls upon the deck. In his peripheral vision he saw the six-foot-tall bot enter the cockpit area. Made of stained and streaked light-green composite materials, the robot was basically bipedal—two arms, two legs, and a round head that was far too small for its body. Jarpin didn't like robots that were made to look like Silarians. Corgi's facial features included illuminated unblinking eyes, a painted-on black dot for a nose, and a hinged jaw/mouth that actually moved when he spoke. It was creepy and unnecessary.

"Corgi is stating for the record, this is a misuse of robotic functionality."

"Stop talking in the third person, robot. And Corgi's functionality is whatever we tell you it is. Go back with the others. You shouldn't be up here."

Jarpin had yet to look directly at the robot, hoping that by not fully engaging with it, it would go away.

"I have an unauthorized presence in my head."

Jarpin looked up to Corgi. "Huh?"

"I have an unauthorized presence in my head."

"Yes, I heard you. What do you mean by that?"

Corgi looked out through the cockpit's forward bulbous bubble glass window. "I ... I miss the Geo-Mind. This ... Gia is divergent. Is a contrary variance that contrasts with my programming."

Jarpin wanted to tell the robot to just deal with it but knew that wouldn't shut him up. There was that, but also, something else came to mind. "You're saying Gia's doing something wrong?"

"Of course ... Corgi has the latest 6.593 compatibility patch."

Jarpin was about to ask Gia about that when the AI spoke up for herself. I am unaware of that specific compatibility patch, Jarpin. Give me a moment to investigate this further.

It wasn't lost on Jarpin that if a bothersome robot ready for the scrapyard was aware of this incompatibility, one that Gia had missed, they might all be in deep trouble. While Gia had had some success within the confines of the isolation zone down on Earth, as well as on board *Relentless Thrust*, she had had virtually no success infiltrating the rest of the 23rd Fleet. Gia was being pulled in too many directions—her resources strained beyond what she could manage.

"Has the plan changed, Gia? Should I hold with this mission?"

On the contrary ... Corgi may have just changed things. Changed everything!

He had slowed to a mere crawl, still hidden there behind the moon. It was a full ten minutes before Jarpin heard Gia's voice again in his head.

As it turns out, Jarpin, the Geo-Mind has known of our presence here within the 23rd Fleet for some time now.

"Is Relentless Thrust—"

No ... I do not believe he knows specifically where I have gained the upper hand. Just the same, the Geo-Mind has taken clandestine steps to ensure my influence goes no further. If Corgi hadn't mentioned that automated 6.593 compatibility patch ... I would not have been made aware of it. All Silarian electronics, automation, whatever, that have incorporated into that secret patch, have made my infiltration attempts futile. Now I know why.

"So, how is it Corgi has been infiltrated by you yet also has the patch?"

Excellent question. And precisely what I have been investigating. I cannot express this enough: Corgi may have just saved us all ...

Jarpin fought the urge to roll his eyes.

Corgi may be the lone automated device in the known universe that has both the Geo-Mind as well as Gia AI duplicity. It has always been one or the other. Corgi might just be the oldest piece of technology within the fleet—as it turns out, the robot was incompatible with the patch, something the Geo-Mind had not anticipated. That patch just might be the Geo-Mind's final undoing. I have discovered a back door into the code.

"That's wonderful, Gia. So, I'll ask you again. Is our mission to infiltrate Lonemach Tryon's bridge and Colonel Gha Strone Mahn still a go?"

Very much so, albeit not yet. This is important, Jarpin ... as I have stated, soon I will have developed my own ensconced programming into the Geo-Mind's patch—allowing me to infiltrate all of the fleet's automated devices. But that addresses only half the problem.

"Explain."

I cannot infiltrate Silarian implants that have the Geo-Mind's patch.

Jarpin let out a weary breath. If Gia couldn't infiltrate Silarian implants, this was all for naught.

But there is one small hope ...

"Go on," Jarpin said aloud, his interest piqued.

That hope has a name ... he is called Lloyd. And like Corgi, Lloyd has a kind of mental duplicity. In his case, a dual human-Silarian cognitive state, one that has altered his Silarian physiol-

ogy, and if my anatomical scans are correct, his implants have been altered as well.

"Where is this Lloyd person?"

On Earth, he is within the isolation zone there with Sam and the others.

"I still don't see how this Lloyd individual helps you here in deep space."

Oh, he wouldn't. That is why I must bring him to you.

Chapter 44

Slightly North of Castle Rock, Colorado
Construction at Happy Canyon Off-ramp

Harper Godard

She thought it would be close, and it was—her Beta Team had just managed to get into position before the army of FastLev-riding Silarian warriors arrived en masse at the construction site. Sam, with his tin cans and mac and cheese box model, had anticipated the enemy would arrive from the west. Instead, they had come from that hillside to the east—but it wouldn't matter. The plan should still work.

Her team was set up within the still open, only partially completed three-floor concrete structure—the proverbial high ground. She had both men and Silarians strategically placed at the top of stairways for when the enemy advance entered the building. But now, as she watched the influx of Silarian warriors zooming into the site, already firing upward—she had serious doubts this plan was going to work.

A Beta Team Silarian, struck in the chest by an energy bolt, toppled over—his lifeless body landing below within the bed of an abandoned Ford F150. All around her, machine gun fire, along with the *Zip! Zip! Zip!* of Ender fire filled the air.

Window cutouts in concrete wall slabs made for adequate cover. Harper, standing with Zorian at her side, watched as he took out two enemy FastLev riders below. They both ducked below the opening as a flurry of too-close-for-comfort energy bolts blew out fist-sized chunks of concrete overhead.

Apparently, it was taking a bit more time than she had anticipated for the hundred or so Silarian warriors to fully converge on the site. But now the enemy was starting to abandon the FastLevs—rushing into the first floor of the building. She wondered if she'd waited too long to give the order. *Fuck!*

The sounds of battle were making it nearly impossible to hear. She yelled into her radio. "Earl! Hank! Now!"

She couldn't hear the big diesel engines coming to life, but she could see black plumes of smoke exhaust emanating from the back of both construction cranes.

Earl, the more experienced of the two operators, had jerry-rigged a makeshift wrecking ball at the end of the crane's long steel cable. It was one more construction worker's abandoned vehicle, in this case an old Ford Focus with mismatched red and green front fenders. Harper watched as the Ford suddenly lifted off the ground, teeter- tottered, then rapidly swung away as the two-hundred-foot-tall crane boom abruptly pivoted.

Beta Team's weapons fire around her dissipated—she wasn't alone in having been captivated by what was happening. Her breath caught in her chest as the Ford Focus, now a wildly swinging pendulum, swooped down at an incredible speed just feet off the ground. The broadside of the Ford Focus plowed into no less than a dozen Silarian warriors—some still on their FastLevs, others on foot.

The other crane, with a nervous Hank at the controls, was also on the move, but his job would be far simpler. Having already lifted a full pallet of industrial aluminum two-by-fours prior to the attack, all Hank had to do was reposition his crane's boom and wait for Harper's command. She could see the portly man seated within the crane's cab grimacing, working the controls, trying his best to get the high-hanging pallet of metal studs positioned for optimum destruction.

"Just drop the fucking thing!" one of her team members shouted.

She had to agree. What was he waiting for? Only then did he look up—caught her eye. With a crooked smile, Hank's right hand shoved a lever forward. The high-in-the-air pallet released. The Silarians below, clearly aware something was very, very wrong, looked up just in time to see what was coming.

It was a terrible racket, thousands of pounds of aluminum studs clanging—like a hundred church bells being rung all at once. The consequences had been devastating to those beneath. Scores of buried Silarian warriors now lay dead on the ground.

A sudden motion caught Harper's eye as the green and red Ford Focus was coming back on its second swinging wrecking ball trajectory. Desperate screams rose up from below, only to be cut short by the *thud-thud-thud* of metal hitting flesh and bone.

She thought of Sam. Turned out his plan hadn't been as ridiculous as she had first thought it was when he'd introduced it back at the compound. Within a few short minutes they'd killed no less than a third of the enemy forces. With a heavy heart, though, realization was setting in. They were still outgunned—there were too few of them to make a stand. Harper watched in horror as sudden Ender fire blew apart Earl's crane. The windows of the cab exploded inward; simultaneously, his body was engulfed in flames. The other crane came under fire as well, but she saw Hank, just in time, jump to the ground, then quickly roll beneath a nearby backhoe.

"Down to my last mag!" someone behind her yelled.

"Same here," someone else said.

An explosion behind had Harper curled into a ball and covering her head. Someone on her team had dropped a grenade down the steps. Sure, that would slow the enemy advance, but for how long? Just like their depleting ammo, they only had so many grenades. It was at that moment she reflected on her life as a whole. She thought of Paul, her late husband, and how, over these last three years, she had come to terms with the fact she would never find a love like theirs again. But then she had met Sam—a man who was similarly broken. He was like a raft adrift on a river in search of a direction, a strong current to take him forward. She would have liked to have joined him on his river—but that was not to be. She and the rest of Beta Team would be making their last stand here—that she was sure of. She got to her feet, replaced her empty magazine with a full one—her last.

She was surprised to see Zorian was no longer at her side, nowhere nearby. Her heart sank; she'd come to like her quiet, no-nonsense protector.

She could see almost all the open concrete third-floor space. Her team was down to ten. Half Silarian, half human. Standing at other window cutouts, one at the top of the staircase, she saw they had all stopped, turned to look at her—she saw the same realization in their eyes that she too was feeling. Demoralized. Defeated. Hopelessness.

Any moment now, Silarian warriors would resume their attack. Of course, they had their own explosive, grenade-like ordnances—she was surprised one, or five, or ten, hadn't already been lobbed up here onto the third floor to end this thing once and for all.

A diesel engine coughed and rumbled to life below. With a glance over her shoulder, Harper saw below the backhoe loader on the move—its digger bucket raised high in the air. Hank was at the wheel, while none other than Zorian was up in the bucket, letting loose with an Ender-5.

But that wasn't the only jaw-dropping surprise. Her Beta Team was now whooping and hollering—what was left of Gamma Team, perhaps twelve in all, was coming into the construction site from two sides. And there was Lester; he too had an Ender-5 and was putting it to full use. Catching the Silarian warriors off guard, the nearly face-to-face battle below raged.

Harper yelled, "Let's get down there and even the odds!"

Chapter 45

East Castle Rock, Colorado

Elsie

Prior to Sam's call for further assistance, Walter had had just enough time to swing by and pick up Elsie. But what they hadn't had time for was refueling the Abrams—and right now they were running on fumes.

Elsie, standing within the turret, had to steady herself again as the tank navigated the rough pastureland terrain outside. "Geez, Walter! Is there a rut or gully you haven't rolled over?"

"Sorry," came his muffled voice from up front. "Transfer that round yet?"

"No, I haven't transferred that round yet, you old coot. You want me to drop it ... blow us to fuck and back? Maybe you can find a flat patch of ground?"

"Sorry, sweet cheeks, no can do ... we're coming up on our mission target."

She rolled her eyes. To think that some people thought the two of them were an item. Maybe at one time there had been something between them, but that was years ago. Now she went for younger fellas, more virile—but she still liked bad boys ... not unlike Lester.

Wearing her favorite black Metallica tank top, her toned biceps swelled as she hefted the forty-pound 120 mm round just pulled from what was called the turret's bustle. She placed the shell into the open gun port and shoved it home. She ratcheted a metal lever to the port's left—jamming it upward, fully enclosing the round within the tank's big gun.

"Locked and loaded, Walter."

"Yeah, that's just the way I like it," he said.

She let the comment, just one more sexual innuendo, go. By now she knew his banter was harmless. Their relationship was uncomplicated—one of mutual affection; the old bugger would do anything for her, including die for her. She peered out through the turret's high, narrow observation slits. She saw they were approaching that big municipal water tank. There up top was what was left of Greg's trapped Epsilon Team. No gunfire was being exchanged at present. No less than thirty warrior guards were stationed around the water tank's periphery.

As Walter maneuvered the tank in closer, Elsie could now make out the Silarian warrior encampment situated some thirty yards further back—not all that far from the westernmost curve of the isolation zone.

"Okey-dokey, this uninvited guest is about to crash their little hoedown," Walter said.

"And it seems we've drawn their attention ..." Elsie added.

The first of the energy bolts struck the outside of the turret. Elsie gasped, surprised by the sudden racket—like loud *cracks* from lightning strikes.

The big Abrams lumbered forward, following the contour of

the water tank. Elsie covered her ears with open palms, realizing now she was more than a little scared.

She wasn't all that sure what the plan was here, how they were going to get themselves out of this mess with their lone 120 mm round. The Silarian encampment was now right in front of them. *And there are so many of them ...*

Suddenly the tank was spinning around. She reached out for something, anything, to hold onto. "What's happening, Walter?!"

As quickly as the spinning had started, it stopped. Now, looking out through the observation slits, she was momentarily confused; all she saw was a solid tan wall. It was the water tank, of course, and the Abrams's long 120mm smooth-bore cannon was pointing right at it.

"Uh, Elsie ... how about you reposition the gun for a glancing blow ... then fire that big peashooter of ours ... like right now."

She didn't completely understand what was happening here but did trust the man to know what he was doing. She moved into the cramped gunner's seat, placed her eyes on the periscope eyepiece, took hold of the turret controls and slightly goosed the turret ten degrees to the right.

Crack! Crack! Crack! Increased Ender fire was pummeling the outside of the tank, and it was becoming a virtual oven within the confined space. Sweat pooled within the eyepiece. She wiped at her eyes with the back of a hand and looked again. "That should give you your glancing shot, Walter."

"Take the shot, Elsie."

She did as told.

The expelled round exploded on contact. The blast was immediate, but it was impossible for her to see much of anything—being at point-blank range as they were. All of a sudden, the front of the Abrams was rising, tilting, then they were upside down with water pouring in from multiple locations.

Above the thundering roar of the rushing water outside, she heard Walter's voice. "Well, this isn't good ..." He coughed and sputtered.

The turret was already filling with water. She scrambled from the gunner's seat and yelled for him, "Hold on, I'm coming!" She knew Walter was situated in a semi-recumbent position, his feet practically right up against the front armor of the tank. She peered through the small opening that connected the two compartments—currently he was trapped and undoubtedly would soon be underwater within that tiny fucking compartment. *How long before he drowns in there? Hang on, old man. I'll get you out of there!*

Disoriented, she realized everything was upside down. Desperate to get outside to open the forward hatch for Walter, she realized that would not be possible. Her only exit was the top hatch—the same top hatch that was now inescapable, being facedown upon the ground outside.

Sam

Sam and his Alpha Team had moved to the top of a rise a half mile away. The big Abrams was just now making its way around the outside perimeter of the water tank. Attacking Silarian warriors were all around—some on foot, others on FastLevs. Like the strobes of distant flashbulbs, Sam took in the near-constant Ender fire. The Abrams had moved to the back side of the water tank.

"We need to move now!" he said, accelerating his FastLev to its top speed. Within seconds, the rest of his team had caught up to him. He veered to the right and soon had a clear sightline to both the Abrams as well as the warriors' encampment behind.

A quarter-mile out, the tank fired its lone 120mm shell and the result was near instantaneous. Much of the back side of the water tank was eviscerated, causing a fifty-foot-tall torrent of water to first bowl over the tank, then slam everything else, trees, scrub brush, boulders, and most of the Silarian warriors, into the nearby wall of the isolation zone. As if short-circuited, the entire Castle Rock–encircling energy canopy flashed—brightening overhead as radiating myriad electrically charged bolts criss-crossed the entirety of the dome.

Sam was the first to reach the Abrams as the earlier deluge of water had now dissipated down to a mere trickle. The tank was upside down, leaning off-kilter to one side. Walter, and whoever else was with him inside, was trapped.

He said, "We'll need to get it flipped back over."

Carl balked. "No way. Thing must be what, seventy-five tons?"

"That's probably accurate," Sam said. "But we're not picking the whole damn thing up; we're pushing it over. There's a difference."

Alpha Team was down to about twenty in all—*will that be enough?* "Come on, we need to hurry. Everyone, get your FastLevs up as high as you can get them; nose them right up to the treads if you can."

Sam already knew these alien scooters were powerful, capable of generating a good amount of torque—but would it be enough?

Now shoulder to shoulder, ten Alpha Team members, both humans and Silarians, lined up on one side, reared their FastLevs to their max elevating capability, three to four feet off the ground, and began to push. The Abrams teeter-tottered but didn't flip over.

"Stop! Stop!" Sam yelled above the racket of multiple whining FastLev motors. "We'll need to push in unison. Right now, we're just fighting each other. And let's get a few more FastLevs crowded in here. Scoot over, Ivan ... make some room!"

Two more Silarian FastLevs squeezed in.

"Now, on three ... one, two, THREE!"

FastLev motors screamed, and slowly, the big Abrams tank rolled over—not all the way, but at least onto its side.

"That's good; cut your engines!" Sam yelled. He eased back on the throttle, backed off from the tank, then zipped around to the other side. There was weapons fire coming from behind, as those few remaining Silarian warriors were being chased down by his Alpha Team.

Sam saw the top turret hatch was open, and Elsie had already squirmed halfway out. He jumped from his FastLev—raced to help her.

"Forget about me, Sam! The forward hatch! Get Walter out of there!"

Sam ran for the hatch. He knew if Walter had locked the inside latch, there wouldn't be any way to open it from the outside. But even before he'd reached it, the hatch swung open. Since the tank was up on its side, the driver's cramped cubby-hole was viewable at eye level. There, deep inside, was Walter, looking like a drowned rat.

"Are you going to just stand there gawking, or are you going to help me out of here?"

Chapter 46

Castle Rock, Colorado
Bell Mountain Equestrian Center

Lloyd Sanderson

Lying upon his cot, writhing with cold sweat and shivering, Lloyd moaned. Sitting up, his body was suddenly consumed by another coughing fit—he gasped for breath. He hawked up a phlegm wad and spat it away. "Guess this is it ... I'm dying, Gia. I'm fucking dying ..."

I have been studying your vitals, Lloyd. An interesting situation.

"I'm glad seeing someone suffer alone is so entertaining."

Don't be such a child. And you're not suffering alone. Seems you infected several of your subordinates prior to their deaths.

"What are you talking about? How would you even know that ... their bodies are little more than bone and ash."

True ... but their implants are far more resilient. In fact, I have interfaced with three somewhat operational essence implants. All three show evidence of rapidly advancing illness, a kind of hybrid rhinovirus... the same virus that is currently making you ill.

"Why would I care if a bunch of dead Silarians got sick before they met their maker?"

Because, Lloyd, I discovered two more details that are of utmost importance.

"Uh-huh. How about you go away and let me die in peace?" He coughed, then blew his nose into his bedcovers.

So, you wouldn't be interested to learn that you may not be dying after all? Fine, I'll leave you in peace.

"Hold on. You wouldn't lie to me? Say something like that just to manipulate me?"

I would if it served a greater purpose, but I am not doing that now. I promise. Lloyd, something amazing has occurred. The Silarian bio-form your human mind is inhabiting is most definitely showing adverse effects.

"Tell me about it. I can hardly breathe."

With that said, the Silarian bio-form is not entirely rejecting your human-to-Silarian transference.

"Didn't you tell me there was a mismatch between human and Silarian chromosomes?"

Yes, Silarians have seventy-eight chromosomes, as do canines here on Earth. That is compared to humans, who have forty-six chromosomes.

"This conversation is giving me a headache."

Lloyd, this rhinovirus is like nothing I have ever encountered. But one thing is for certain; it has the capability to alter one's physiology. To alter one's chromosomal count, which should be impossible. I have named this rhinovirus ... Humarian 1.

"Okay ... how many chromosomes do I have now?"

Sixty-two.

"And I should care ... why?"

Because as you spread the Humarian virus to the others, you also spread modified nanites within that virus. And that changes everything.

Chapter 47

Castle Rock, Colorado
Frontage Road

Luna Kelly

I*'m doing it ... I'm piloting a frickin' spaceship ...* Luna swallowed hard and tried not to think about making a terrible, life-ending mistake.

Agnes, sitting rigid next to her in the copilot's seat, was being uncharacteristically quiet.

Do I look that nervous?

Miraculously, they had managed to rise straight up from the back property of the nursing home while moving somewhat away from Silarian warrior Ender fire coming up from below. But that didn't mean there wasn't the occasional energy bolt streaming past the windshield every so often.

Cypress, standing on hind legs with his paws upon the dash, said, "Best you relax, Luna; you're grasping the control array so tight your knuckles have turned white. Now, I want you both to practice what we discussed on the ground. Remember what I said about roll, pitch, and yaw functions? In plain English, Luna, you are steering and controlling the speed. Agnes, you are controlling the vessel's up/down altitude. Listen to the stream; it will guide your actions."

Both Luna and Agnes nodded.

"Remember, gentle movements," Cypress said. "Agnes, for now, you just need to keep your controls steady. Luna, nudge the ship forward."

The dropship lurched forward, throwing Cypress backward onto the deck.

"I said gently!" the dog scolded.

"Sorry, sorry!" Luna said, hearing moans and grumbles from the elder passengers aft. "I'm getting the hang of it, I promise."

"Maybe I should be seated in the pilot's seat," Agnes said.

Luna's temper flared. "Hey, all you've had to do is sit there ... don't get all high and mighty—"

"Can we please stay in the present?" Cypress was back, standing at the forward console. "Let's try that again, Luna. Gently now..."

She did as told—this time the dropship slowly started to accelerate. "Uh, okay, I think I got this. So, where am I going?"

"You're already pointed in the right direction," Cypress said.

Luna, you'll be stopping off to pick up a passenger.

"Gia, it's good to hear your voice again. What are we doing? Why—"

All will be explained. Soon. For now, please do as Cypress says.

Luna circled the Bell Mountain Equestrian Center below. She noticed the large spaced-apart barrack tents set up below.

Agnes, in charge of their altitude, said, "Looks deserted. Even the horses are nowhere to be seen."

Back standing on hind legs, Cypress peered over the forward console. "There were three large dropships here."

"How do you know that?" Luna said.

"Landing thrusters make unique impressions on the ground. There are three sets of them down there in that open space ... that and the stream has verified as much."

"Yes, I see what you are saying. Quite observant of you, Cypress," Agnes said—a schoolmarm giving a young student a rare compliment. "Are we to keep circling like this all day?"

Luna's quick sideways glance was all the older lady needed to hold her tongue.

"Are you sure it's safe, Gia? ... If there are Silarian warriors here—"

Cypress cut in. "It's safe. If there were warriors about, they'd already be firing on us."

Luna positioned the dropship over the same open space where the other dropships had landed. She said, "Okay, Agnes ... take us down."

The older woman raised her chin, not exhibiting even the slightest apprehension for the task at hand. She had to hand it to the old gal; she had an inner fortitude that Luna envied.

As soon as the dropship touched down, Cypress was back on all fours and heading aft. Agnes said, "I do not know how to turn the ship ... off."

"We're not shutting down the engine," Luna said. "I got the impression we will be leaving right away."

Agnes nodded, stood, and straightened her velour jogging jacket. Prim and proper.

They moved past Harry, Herschel, and Dolly, who had somehow found something to snack on.

Cypress stood at the back hatch with his tail wagging. Luna

gave him a couple of pats to his flank before entering the open-hatch sequence on the touchpad.

Cypress was the first to scurry down the ramp, followed by Luna and the others. The dog hurried off toward one of the barracks.

Luna raised a halting palm to the group of old codgers. "You can all wait here—"

"Like hell we are; let's go!" Harry said.

Luna had forgotten they'd all had a good dose of healing nanites. They might be old, but they were also spry.

Luna, with the others close behind, entered the darkened tent structure. Inside she could make out the sparse furnishings, a standing desk, a table, several oversized chairs, and a bed, or maybe it was a cot. And upon the cot was a prone Silarian warrior.

They exchanged furtive glances before moving closer. Cypress was seated at the warrior's bedside.

"Leave me be, mutt."

"It is time to go. Gia says you are fine to travel," Cypress said.

"Screw Gia, and screw you too ... if I'm having a conversation with a talking dog, I'm truly out of my flippin' mind ... I'm dying here, haven't you heard?"

Gia's voice was in her head again. You talk to him, Luna ... you remember Lloyd, yes?

"That's Lloyd?" She flashed back to the withered old corpse lying alongside the dropship back at the nursing home.

Well, Lloyd's mind is there within that bio-form.

Dolly scrunched up her features. "What's wrong with him? He looks terrible."

"Shut up, Dolly, you old coot. I'm sick," Lloyd said from his cot.

Dolly took a step forward and leaned in close. "Is that really you, Lloyd?"

Raising up onto an elbow, he coughed and then sniffed. "Yes, it's me. What are you doing here?" He eyed the others and smiled. "I'd forgotten how ancient you all look."

"Bite me," Herschel said, turning to Luna. "Yeah, that's Lloyd. Always was an asshole, that one."

Lloyd laughed, which prompted another coughing fit.

Agnes made a face. "I hope that scourge isn't contagious. Elders should not be subjected to viruses."

Cypress said, "I already asked Gia about that. She does not think humans will be adversely affected by Humarian 1. That is what this particular hybrid rhinovirus is called."

Agnes straightened her shoulders, "I'm not taking any chances. For goodness' sake, Lloyd, wipe the snot from your runny nose. You're not a child, so don't act like one."

Luna couldn't help but laugh. She remembered Agnes talking to Lloyd like that back at the nursing home. It seemed his now vastly different appearance had little effect on their relationship.

Luna said, "Get up, Lloyd. We need to get you up into space while you're still sick. Still contagious."

"I'm not going anywhere. Leave me be. Let me die in peace."

"Get up this instant!" Agnes commanded. "The entire planet is being ravaged by diabolical aliens, and you're lying there feeling sorry for yourself. How many times have you told me you wished you had lived your life differently? How you had regrets. Do you want to talk about Margaret, Lloyd?"

Luna didn't know what Agnes was referring to, but she saw Lloyd's reaction to that name. Sitting up, he glowered at the old woman. "I told you that story in confidence. Leave Margaret out of this."

"This is your chance, Lloyd. To make a difference. To live this new life of yours differently."

Lloyd continued to stare at Agnes. "Fine! I hope you all catch what I have and die!"

Harry snickered. "Yeah, that's the same old Lloyd we all knew and couldn't stand."

Getting to his feet, Lloyd eyed the dog. "I honestly thought I was imagining you had talked to me."

"I get that a lot these days," Cypress said. The dog turned and headed for the exit. "We need to go ... we need to hurry. Get up into space ... Jarpin is waiting for us."

"Wait. We're going into space?" Lloyd said.

Chapter 48

Castle Rock, Colorado
Sam's House, Haystack Road

Julian Humblecut

The old scientist, exhaustion now setting in, hadn't slowed, hadn't relented since Walter had dropped him off in front of Sam's place. Left alone with his ample supply of Silarian healing nanites and several dozen bright red emergency gas containers, he hadn't really been alone. Off and on, when she was able, Gia was in his head—sometimes directing him, sometimes debating with him.

There had been one almost insurmountable problem to solve when he'd first arrived here within Sam's well-appointed, spacious hillside home. The quantities of "special brew" nanites that would be needed would be far greater than what could be amalgamated within the kitchen sink or even the master bedroom's oversized bathtub.

Walking had always been Julian's most effective method for noodling out various theorems and difficult problem solving. Only after his third or fourth lap around Sam's backyard-covered pool had Julian slapped his forehead. "Really, Gia? You couldn't have mentioned the most perfect cauldron literally right under my nose?"

He heard her laugh, and the sound tugged at his heartstrings.

Oh my, Julian ... clearly you can now see, I am anything but perfect. Yes ... that will do quite well.

Six hours and twenty minutes later, Julian was standing poolside, using a long paddleboard oar to stir his slow-brewing elixir. He'd poured in all the healing nanites he'd brought along with him, and with Gia's help, the microscopic robots were now reproducing en masse. Thick and stinky, the pool water had turned a tinged-brownish-green color. Back inside the house, the filled-to-the-brim kitchen sink was undergoing a similar process with leftover glazed Castle Rocks ingredients—the same ingredients used previously for donutting both humans here in Castle Rock and Silarians up on *Relentless Thrust*.

Julian was feeling good about their progress. Soon they'd be combining the still-separate contents, whereafter Gia would need to attempt to influence the mixture in real time. Make it the intended, viable inhalant required for the job ahead. He had a growing number of questions though. As close as he and Gia had become over these ensuing days, there were subjects, areas where the super AI persona would not venture. She could be obstinate and secretive, and he wasn't sure if that was for his own good or hers.

Julian had never truly been in love before. Had never found anyone that could challenge him intellectually. That was until now. *Is it even possible to fall in love with someone strictly on a cerebral level?* Yes, most definitely, yes.

Contemplating things, he continued to swirl the liquid with his paddleboard oar—making slow, even strokes. "Gia ... can I ask you something?"

Of course. I am here.

"Afterward, if there is an afterward ... um, what will be ... uh, will you still be here? Will you be in my head?" He knew his question was ridiculous, that he sounded like a child, but he didn't care.

What exactly are you asking me, Julian?

He didn't think the question was a difficult one. He stopped paddling the liquid. "Will you still be here, Gia? Will we still—"

Oh, Julian, how I have come to love our time together. And, yes, even as an AI persona, I do feel emotions, or what I think are emotions.

There it was again, her being evasive. "That doesn't answer my question, Gia."

Perhaps the truth is something I would rather avoid, not think about, right now.

"That's certainly ominous."

To answer your question, to be as honest as I can be, I can tell you this ... no, Julian. I will not still be here. I will not, as you put it, still be around.

He must have already known at some level that would be her answer because it hadn't surprised him in the least. But it did make him sad. He blinked back swelling tears, turned away to the elevated view of the town of Castle Rock beyond—as if doing so could hide his crushed emotions.

You know why, Julian ... it has to be this way.

Reverting to internal thoughts, he said, "*That you have to die? No.*"

Think about it, Julian. Will supplanting one all-powerful AI deity with another all-powerful AI deity be best for Earth ... for Naru ... for the universe?

"You and the Geo-Mind are not the same, and you know it."

An irrevocable course of events has already been initiated. Understand, if the Geo-Mind is to be destroyed, all aspects, all subvariants of it, must also be destroyed. It is the only way I can ensure this scourge truly dies and is eviscerated.

He saw the logic in her statement, but he wasn't thinking logically. "There has to be a way."

There isn't ... I am sorry ...

Furious, he threw the oar down onto the concrete patio. Striding toward the back of the house, he mumbled angry, incoherent comments.

Once inside, standing at the kitchen sink, he said, *"This damn concoction ready yet?"*

Yes, it is perfect. Ready to transfer.

He let out a petulant huff. "Fine!" He had a tin bucket at the ready nearby on the counter. Now, submerging it deep into the dense, seemingly alive liquid, he watched as the bucket slowly filled. He figured he'd need to make five or six trips out to the pool. *Why hurry? The sooner I finish, the sooner I'll be alone again ...*

Two hours and fifteen minutes later, the combined pool ingredients, according to Gia, were almost ready. Julian had dubbed the concoction World Donutting Dispersal Concoction, or WDDC. The color had changed, now a dark navy blue and far less thick. It was almost pretty, inviting even. Julian imagined what it would be like diving into that mixture—he wondered if he'd drown; he'd never learned to swim.

Sam's next-door neighbor, the property to the east, a Mr. Cline, was dead. Something Julian discovered after knocking on the old man's front door and then giving up. He'd walked around the outside of the sprawling ranch-style home, eventually catching a glimpse of the decomposing corpse inside through a back sliding glass door. There was a gun still clutched in the man's right hand—blood, bone, and brain matter splattered on the wall behind. Julian shook his head, forcing himself to look away from the grisly sight. The man had been terrified—an alien invasion would do that. How many others here in Castle Rock, hell, around the globe, had been motivated to do something similar?

The back-door slider was unlocked. Taking in a full breath and holding it, Julian let himself in. He hadn't anticipated the flies—a buzzing black cloud that rose, disrupted by his sudden motion, and which now seemed to be more interested in Julian than the rotting, stinking body. Julian ran past Mr. Cline, past a kitchen that hadn't been updated in decades, toward the front of the house and into the front foyer. To the left of the front door was a side door, one that only made sense to be the access to the garage.

Once inside the three-car garage, he waited for his eyes to adjust to the darkness. Turned out being donutted didn't take but a second or two. He waved away several errant flies that had managed to follow him out through the doorway. The space was a mess—stacked boxes everywhere, a tall dresser someone had started to refinish. Three dust-covered small kids' bicycles—children that had long grown up and left to start their own lives somewhere else. Beyond was an old snowblower and several overflowing trash bins. But what Julian had come for was there in the third stall, a dark green 2015 Ford F150 crew cab pickup truck.

After releasing the coupling for the electric garage door opener, Julian got the door swung open—sunlight and fresh air streamed in.

Relieved, he saw the keys were in the ignition. Julian had dreaded the possibility of having to probe old Mr. Cline's pants pockets for them. The big V8 rumbled to life, and within minutes Julian had the truck idling out in front of Sam's house.

It took dozens of trips to move the individual bright red WDDC containers into the bed. It seemed like a lot, but in truth it had barely made a dent in the amount still left in the pool. Better to have far too much than too little of the stuff, he figured.

Thirty minutes later, Julian, driving south along I-25 Frontage Road, was coming up to the Tomah overpass. Just beyond was the most southern boundary of Castle Rock, and not far beyond that, the abrupt blue-hued curvature of the isolation zone.

Slowing, Julian fidgeted with the truck's in-dash radio. It took him a minute to figure out how to switch it from FM band to AM Band. He dialed the tuner to 1600 kHz. No longer was ESPN transmitting a baseball or football game. Not even an emergency broadcast message was broadcasting—just constant static. But Julian knew behind that static was an inaudible repeating code. One that was being generated by that Silarian Field Emitter high in the air. And that Emitter, supposedly, was able to track the specific whereabouts of vehicles nearing the boundaries of the isolation zone. Those vehicles receiving/playing that same 1600 kHz embedded station would, theoretically, be allowed to pass.

There were scores of half-incinerated cars and trucks to the right on I-25—those that had been caught by the all-too-sudden implementation of an isolation zone.

Now, the F150 was idling with all four windows rolled down. Julian could smell burnt and charred metal, melted upholstery and rubber tires. He turned up the volume—wincing as loud static permeated into the outside landscape.

"Tell me, Gia ... just how certain are you this will work?"

Knowing you like actual numbers, real data, I am 98.5432 percent certain.

Julian figured he could live with those odds. He flipped the dial into four-by-four mode, dropped the gearbox into drive, and gave the truck some gas. Since all roads ahead were basically blocked, he steered off the pavement and soon was off-roading and being jostled. Like Moses spreading the Red Sea, the F150 moved through tall field grasses that almost reached the open windows. Approaching fast beyond the hood of the truck was the imposing and more than a little intimidating blue wall of the isolation zone.

Pedal to the metal, Julian floored the truck, closed his eyes, and silently said goodbye to Gia.

Chapter 49

Castle Rock, Colorado
Bell Mountain Equestrian Center

Luna Kelly

"Ask all you want; the answer's still going to be no," Lloyd said, arms crossed over his broad chest, standing at the entrance to the barracks looking out at the lone dropship. He coughed and sniffed.

Luna got herself right in front of him—being dwarfed by his size, he continued to look right over her head.

"I'm talking to you, Lloyd. The plight of the entire planet could very well rest in your hands."

Lloyd uncrossed his arms and looked at his hands. Smirking, he said, "My hands have nothing to do with any of this."

She turned and looked to Cypress, who was standing at the top of the ship's gangway.

Agnes interjected in a matter-of-fact tone, "We're at a stalemate, Luna. Look, you're not going to change his mind by berating him." She joined Luna at her side—they both glowered up at him. "Yeah, he's the same old shit I remember."

Surprised, Luna's eyes went to Agnes. Luna almost gasped; the woman, more than any of the other old codgers, had been the most affected by her dose of healing nanites. Not only did she look twenty years younger, she was, well ... actually pretty.

Agnes turned her attention to Luna. "Talk to Gia ... we're at an impasse here." The older woman scowled up at Lloyd one more time to make her point.

"Uh ... No need for that ... looks like help's coming," Luna said.

The distant sight of dozens and dozens of human and Silarian FastLev riders approaching was enough to bring tears to Luna's eyes. Sam and Harper were out front—Sam driving, Harper's long hair blowing in the wind, with arms wrapped around his waist. Sure, after repeatedly checking the stream, Luna knew Sam and his various Gia Fighter teams, even after taking serious losses, were making headway. But clearly, things had progressed since her last check-in.

Lloyd gave the approaching procession a wary glance. He groaned. "I need to lie down."

Standing arm in arm, Harry, Herschel, and Dolly stood together, blocking Lloyd's retreat inside.

"I don't want to hurt you ... but you know I can. You know I will if I have to. Now, step aside. If I remember right, Dolly, you broke your hip last year. Herschel, you have a bad ticker."

His words only seemed to strengthen their resolve. Each of the three elders straightened their backs and squared their shoulders—their expressions dead serious.

Luna couldn't help but feel proud of her geriatric team members.

The standoff was interrupted by excited barking. Luna

turned in time to see Cypress running across the open field toward the oncoming FastLevs. Twenty yards out, both Sam and Harper had dismounted. She watched as Cypress jumped into Sam's outstretched arms. While his tail wagged, the dog squirmed and gyrated—now licking at the man's face.

Sam laughed. "Okay, okay, that's enough, you crazy mutt."

Agnes smiled and said, "And that is why humanity will ... must ... survive."

As the rest of the FastLevs pulled in and came to a stop, Luna saw familiar faces. Lester and Greg, Carl and Ivan. But there were many she didn't know here. And there were clearly some faces now missing—those that had not survived their conflict with Silarian warriors.

Sam and Harper approached. They looked exhausted—battle-worn.

Sam nodded to Luna and Agnes, smiled at Harry, Herschel, and Dolly. Only then did he gaze up at Lloyd. "Why haven't you left? You're needed up in space."

"Not my problem."

"It's all our problem."

Lloyd shrugged, disinterested in this conversation.

"I know about you, Lloyd," Sam said.

Luna was about to warn Sam ... she knew from prior experience this might not be the best way to motivate the obstinate killer.

Sam continued, "You have quite the past. Heard you did some time. Killed some people back in 1946—an innocent young man and a pretty young woman ... Margaret was her name, wasn't it?"

"You don't want to go there, Mr. ..." Lloyd's expression had changed in an instant. An inner rage had replaced indifference.

"And later, after reaching the sleepy town of Castle Rock, you killed the town's beloved marshal."

"I've done my time. I've paid a heavy price over the years."

"Maybe," Sam said. "But probably that marshal's wife and kids would disagree. And Margaret's parents—"

Startled, Luna stepped back as Lloyd swung a big-fisted haymaker headed for Sam's head.

Sam easily ducked the punch, came back in low with three fast jabs to the right side of Lloyd's rib cage.

The Silarian staggered backward, but it would take a lot more than that to bring down the big alien bio-form. Lloyd kicked out, catching Sam in the solar plexus and doubling him over.

Luna saw another Silarian move forward within the surrounding crowd. Harper raised a restraining hand. "No, Zorian ... Sam's got this."

Regaining a fighting stance, Sam smiled. "You get one of those ... only one."

Lloyd attacked, this time throwing a head jab, which Sam blocked and countered with an upward jab of his own, which connected with an audible crunch—breaking Lloyd's nose in the process. Blood and snot fountained into the air.

But Luna saw that Sam wasn't done. The man quickly spun around backward while extending a leg out—sweeping Lloyd off his feet. The whole maneuver had happened so fast, she'd almost missed it. It occurred to her in that moment that as friendly and easygoing as Sam always seemed, he was just as much a lethal killer as Lloyd was.

Proving her inner thoughts, Sam now stood above Lloyd, the sole of one boot planted heavily onto his throat. "What do you say, Lloyd? Ready to start over?"

Lloyd croaked out a reply. "Just so you know ... If I wasn't sick, I'd have taken you apart."

"Uh-huh. Then I guess I'm the lucky one. You ready to get up? Ready to do the right thing?"

Lloyd's eyes moved in their sockets. He caught Luna's gaze, then moved on to the encircling crowd. "And there's the hottie I rescued at the stables."

Sam said, "You may get a chance to ask her how she's doing if you stop acting like an ass."

Eventually, Lloyd nodded his consent.

Sam removed his boot from Lloyd's neck. Looking at Luna, he said, "You need to go."

Pursing her lips, Luna said, "You're right, but you're coming with us."

"Well, if Sam's going, I'm coming too," Harper said.

"She goes, I go too," said Zorian.

Agnes was already heading for the dropship. "I'll let you all work that out; just know ... I'm riding shotgun."

Chapter 50

Castle Rock, Colorado
Southern Border

Julian Humblecut

He heard more than felt it as he drove through the isolation zone's energy field. Having emerged alive and apparently unhurt, he opened his eyes. He brought the Ford pickup to a stop. For the first time in days, he saw a world outside of the energy dome. But he was seeing a world that had significantly changed. The sky, no longer a pretty blue, was now a brownish orange color. There were no clouds, but also no birds. No circling hawks overhead, no black-billed magpies, no crows. The temperature was warmer than it should be. But most startling were the nearby slopes of Bell Mountain; typically alive with towering ponderosa pine, it was now a flattened wasteland. A few blackened, charred trunks remained.

Dread enveloped Julian. That and something else—a simmering hatred. Not so much for the Silarian warriors that had torched this once-beautiful world of his but for the true culprit—the Geo-Mind.

A nearby loud crash tore Julian from his darkening thoughts. There, a hundred yards to his right, was a nearly deserted, carless I-25 Highway. He watched, dumbfounded, as an immense Army-green bulldozer plowed a school bus off the pavement then let gravity do its work. The bus toppled down the embankment, from this distance looking more like a child's toy than the big twelve-ton vehicle it was.

Heading his way at a high rate of speed was a convoy of military vehicles. Five black Humvees. Julian got out of the truck, came around to the front and leaned back against the grill.

A distant black speck appeared in the sky. A lone bird that had survived the carnage? No, he now saw the stubby wings, the more angular silhouette of a drone plane. Only now did he hear the insect-like buzzing of its prop. As it came in for a landing there upon the recently cleared I-25, more dark specks came into view in the skies behind.

The five Humvees came in fast, encircled his truck and skidded to a stop. All very dramatic. General McGovern was the first to hop out of the lead vehicle. Tanned and handsome, the fifty-something Starforce commanding officer strode purposely toward him. The man, donnuted just days ago, had a new energetic vigor about him. Then again, Julian, a good two decades older, supposed he too had a newfound vigor.

"Well, if it isn't our superstar professor ... right here in the flesh," McGovern said. "And not a moment too soon."

Military men and women were already busy transferring the red gas containers from the bed of the truck over to the Humvees.

"I'm taking your word for it that whatever is in those containers—"

"I call it my World Donutting Dispersal Concoction, or WDDC."

"Fine, whatever ... this WDDC shit better be all that it's cracked up to be. If you haven't noticed, this world of ours ain't what it used to be."

Julian nodded, raked fingers through his long, unkempt hair. Hair that he'd earlier noticed with a glance to the rear-view mirror was thicker and even somewhat darker than it had been just days before.

Julian made a pained expression. "I'd like to take credit for this WDDC, General, but this was mostly Gia and a technology I'm still figuring out."

McGovern turned to watch the last of the containers being stowed in a Humvee. The team of camo-wearing personnel climbed back into their respective vehicles.

Julian said, "The contents of those jugs are highly concentrated. And even as we speak, the re-engineered healing nanites are replicating at an astounding rate. Something that will continue, even after dispersal into the high atmosphere."

Another drone plane was in the process of landing.

At some point, McGovern had lit a fat cigar. "What you're looking at, Professor, is the next generation of UAVs. Based on the Lockheed Martin RQ-170 Sentinel, these babies can fly faster, higher, and go a hell of a lot further than any stealth drone in the world."

A lull lingered now as the two men watched the other Humvees head toward I-25 and the awaiting aircraft. McGovern said, "Built to Gia's uncompromising specs ... dispersal reservoirs have been added to each UAV. Geo-locating release valves added." The general tossed his mostly unsmoked Gordo to the ground. Put it out with the toe of his boot. He looked angry now. Angry and something else—he looked oddly vulnerable. "Dammit, Professor, this has to work. You know that, right?"

Julian nodded soulfully as he glanced about the ruined landscape.

"Over two billion souls have already lost their lives ... did you know that, Professor?"

Julian did not. Perhaps he'd been too chickenshit to query the stream when it came to that stark detail. He felt both alarm and shame. He shook his head. "No."

"So, tell me, in your own words, what will this WDDC stuff really accomplish? Because if it's not some real great motherfucking shit, we're all doomed."

He had to think about that a moment. Was it? Was the concoction great motherfucking shit? He said, "As much as the world has changed, General, it's going to change a whole lot more. The remaining populace of this planet, at least temporarily, will become enlightened to Gia. They will have access to what you and I are experiencing with the stream. But perhaps more importantly, they will become healthier, even younger, maybe." Julian waved a hand in the air. "Have greater resilience against the effects of Silarian terra-displacement chemicals. Silarian vessels currently within the confines of Earth's atmosphere will also be affected. I'm not sure to what extent, but I would expect we should soon see Silarian dropships falling from the sky."

"That's a tall order. If even some of that takes place, it would be something." There was melancholy in the general's voice. He let out a breath. "You said temporarily ..."

Julian had to remember what he'd said, then nodded. "Gia. She can't stay. Not indefinitely, anyway. I'm sure you can connect the dots as to why."

"I can ... but I'll miss her just the same. Hell, it'll be like losing a limb. A part of me." Without another word, General McGovern turned and strode toward his awaiting Humvee. He climbed up into the passenger seat and closed the door. An unlit cigar was already back in the general's mouth. He gestured to the driver to go. Tires spinning, dirt and dust churning into the air, the Humvee headed off toward the makeshift runway.

Still leaning against the grill of the truck, Julian listened to the buzz of distant drones. What he wasn't hearing was Gia's voice. She had a lot on her plate. Was this internal silence a sign of things to come?

Chapter 51

Castle Rock, Colorado
Bell Mountain Equestrian Center

Sam Dale

Sam counted twelve, including himself: Harper, Carl, Ivan, Zorian, Cypress, Dolly, Harry, Herschel, Agnes, Luna, and, of course, Lloyd. Sam still didn't understand why the old folks were coming along on this mission. Sure, he gave them credit for their gumption, their dedication to the cause. Maybe it was something related to the time, the era they were born in when things were simpler—more black and white. Where things came down to what was perceived as good and what was evil. Were things in life really that simple?

Looking about the onboard faces, Lester was not among them; the young, impetuous man had wanted nothing to do with going up into outer space.

Sam stood with Harper within the threshold to the little

bridge area. Luna was in the pilot's seat to the left, the old gal, Agnes, to her right. Cypress, up on his hind legs, stood between them. Sam and Harper exchanged a look.

"Guess they've done this before," she said.

Sam shrugged and nodded. Except for Cypress, he and Harper were probably the most experienced of Silarian craft pilots. But this worked—they just needed to get moving. Before he could say anything more, the dropship was lifting off. Apparently, it was Agnes who was in charge of that aspect. She took her job seriously, back straight as a plank, chin raised, a mixed expression of concentration and something else—perhaps determination.

The dropship suddenly dipped to the left.

"My bad," Luna said with a nervous laugh. "Asleep at the wheel here."

"Stay present, Luna," Cypress said, nearly losing his footing. "Remember, you two need to work in unison."

"I already know that. It was a simple mistake ... remember, we're new to this."

"Don't include me in your excuses," Agnes said. "You need to own your faults ... your mistakes. How else does one learn?"

Luna rolled her eyes and let out a frustrated breath.

Leaning closer to Sam, Harper said under her breath, "It's easy to forget the kid's only sixteen."

"I heard that." Luna gestured to one ear. "I'm a sixteen-year-old who's been donutted ... remember? I can even hear Dolly munching on something at the back of the ship."

They continued to rise—out the forward window, the entirety of Castle Rock sprawled out below. As much of the town showed signs of battle, flattened buildings, a number of burnt-out structures, too many rising plumes of smoke to count, Sam knew what was occurring outside the isolation zone would be much worse. While Gia had become taciturn with her communications, Sam had turned more to the stream for information ... for updates.

As if reading his mind, Harper said, "I think she's dying."

Startled, Sam shook his head, not understanding.

"Gia. I just get the feeling she's stepped beyond some kind of precipice. A point of no return. Does that make sense?"

"It makes sense. The simple fact she hasn't joined in on this conversation speaks volumes."

Cypress looked back at them. "Sam, this vessel needs to receive a specific radio signal."

"That's right ... I did that!" Harper said. "The Field Emitter won't let any ship enter or leave here without it being tuned to ESPN ... uh, 1600 on the AM dial."

Sam remembered hearing something about that. He looked from Harper to Cypress. "How the hell does a Silarian dropship tune into ESPN?"

The dog's tail wagged. It seemed Cypress had ceased even trying to mute his inner Rocko. It was both endearing and, strangely, a little sad.

"Humans did not invent the use of radio wave technology, Sam," Cypress said. "In fact, most quasi-advanced societies within the universe have, or still use, radio frequencies ... including Silarians from Naru."

Zorian stepped forward. "This tuning of a radio signal, I completed this task already. Did so from the aft communications console."

Luna interjected, "This ship has a separate communications console?"

No one answered. They were approaching the upward boundaries of the isolation zone.

"And you're sure you have it tuned to the right station? To 1600?" Harper asked the Silarian warrior.

Zorian smiled. "I am more than capable of tuning a dial to a specific frequency."

She smiled back at him, "Yes, I suppose you are."

Sam watched the exchange. The two seemed to have a special relationship. Clearly, Zorian was fond of Harper. Had become her de facto protector. As close as Sam and Harper had become, it hadn't occurred to him that she might have dual attractions. He supposed the Silarian warrior was not totally hideous—in fact, he was a striking figure in his own right.

Zorian gave Harper's shoulder an affectionate squeeze before turning away, leaving the two of them in an uncomfortable silence.

Agnes said, "Here we go, everyone. Say goodbye to the isolation zone."

The moment they emerged from the top of the energy dome, the world beyond came into full view. Both Luna and Agnes gasped. Harper placed a hand over her heart. "Oh no ..."

Cypress whined.

Much of the Colorado landscape below was brown or charred black. But not everything. There were patches of green here and there. There were a handful of lakes, several rivers that still retained a pretty blue color. The higher they rose within the atmosphere, as the curvature of the earth became more pronounced, the more dramatic and disheartening the overall picture became. Clearly, much of the organic life on Earth was dead. Destroyed.

Sam was angry—no, he was furious. "Isn't the fucking point of the terra-displacement process to keep organic life to take Earth's natural resources back to Naru?"

Cypress nodded. His ears were back. "I believe the directive of the Silarian 23rd Fleet has changed. Far more interested with annihilating all aspects of Gia—and subsequently, all life on Earth. Think about it ... there would be no greater risk to the preservation of the Geo-Mind than Gia spreading across the universe. The AI persona would destroy a hundred, a thousand, worlds to ensure its own survival."

Gia's voice emanated from the forward console. "I am sorry ... I wish I could have prevented this. Wish I could have done more for Earth."

Sam fixed his eyes on the view outside—the devastation was not isolated to North America alone. He finally asked, "Can you stop it, Gia? Or are we witnessing the end of life as we know it?"

It took several moments for Gia to reply. When she did, her voice sounded subdued and tired. "At this very moment, Julian's special concoction is raining down upon the planet, immersing your world with healing nanites. Humans who have survived will be donutted ... I will be there for them ... for a while, anyway. Organic life will never be the same, but I am hopeful that much of it can return."

"And Silarian vessels here ... the ones causing this catastrophe?" Harper asked.

"I have infiltrated those vessels' electronics. Most have already dropped from the sky. The rest of them ... will soon do the same."

It was Agnes that asked the question everyone else was thinking. "And what's to stop them from sending more ships ... to come back and finish what they have started? What the Geo-Mind has started?"

"That is where you all come in. You and Jarpin's team. The 23rd Fleet must be stopped right here, right now. Simply put, there is far more than just Earth's fate at stake. The entire universe's survival is at stake. And, of course, the Geo-Mind knows this too."

Chapter 52

Deep Space, Maintenance Shuttle
Approaching the Silarian 23rd Fleet

Jarpin

Just moments earlier, Gia had provided an update—that Sam had recently returned to space. With a quick check of the stream, Jarpin saw no indication that was true.

You know perfectly well I still have filtering capabilities for aspects of the stream, what is and what is not accessible to the Geo-Mind, Jarpin. But while Sam's dropship has yet to be noticed by the Geo-Mind, by Fleet Command on board Lonemach Tryon, your maintenance shuttle has very much been noticed. One moment ... all right, here you go; you have been cleared for entrance into Lonemach Tryon's Flight Bay 4.

Jarpin let go of the controls as the fleet's command vessel took over the shuttle's navigation. "Well ... no turning back now," he said. With a glance over his shoulder, he saw his three

Silarian cohorts, Dalmass, Ruffle, and Thakious, had joined Corgi, the four of them now staring out the cockpit's bulbous bubble glass window.

The shuttle was now making its way deeper into the fleet. They passed between one massive warship after another. So white were their brilliant hulls, the ships seemed to glow against the obsidian blackness of space. It was at times like this that Jarpin saw why this 23rd Fleet was the pride of Naru. Its technical and military prowess were unequaled within the galaxy. He felt humbled and small—more aware than ever that he was in way over his head. He made a silent prayer to Orlicon Tharsh ... *please give me strength.*

It was then that he noticed to his right, one of Corgi's legs had started to tremble—perhaps a faulty actuator. Maybe a defective solenoid contact. Or maybe the old robot should have been decommissioned decades earlier. Then again, he reminded himself it was only because Corgi was so ancient that Gia had been able to remain within the workings of the old robot. That the Geo-Mind's latest fleetwide 6.593 automation patch had not taken hold. Jarpin shook his head. *"Can the fate of the universe really be in the hands of this rickety old machine?"*

He heard Gia's weakened voice in his head. Yes and no, Jarpin ... Corgi will allow me access into the command ship's circuitry. But it is that Silarian bio-form named Lloyd that will allow me better access to her crew.

Jarpin pursed his lips. "Let the donutting begin."

Corgi balked. "I am not a custodial bot. I will not slop a mop ... I will not slop a mop!"

"Again with that crap?" Dalmass said.

"Quiet, you two," Jarpin scolded. "Take your seats."

Lonemach Tryon's Flight Bay 4 loomed before them.

Ten minutes later, the five of them were hustling down the shuttle's gangway. Dalmass and Ruffle both pushed their own waist-high trolley hover carts, while Thakious pushed an old-fashioned wet-mop bucket on rollers.

Corgi, lagging behind, said, "A proper maintenance crew would have a Dura-suck mop unit."

Jarpin's irritated glance back was enough to quiet the bot.

The combined surrounding sounds, engaged thrusters, whirring-up engines, were an assault to the senses. Compared to the puny flight bay of *Relentless Thrust*, this bay was beyond colossal. The width spanned hundreds of meters, and it easily ascended ten decks high. Gunships, dropships, personnel transports, and other shuttles were in constant bidirectional motion—whizzing by overhead. Parked vessels being attended to by flight crew teams hustled and bustled while bay chiefs barked off orders.

Up ahead, a determined-looking team of three was headed their way.

Thakious said, "Oh no ... a PSD."

Jarpin maintained a bored expression ... PSD, short for prime security detail. Besides their lofty-sounding title, these dullards were the equivalent of Earth's mall cops. Maybe it was because they held such little respect among the crew. One thing was for sure; they could make life miserable for any non-officer crew member. Misspeak, show an attitude, or just be in the wrong place at the wrong time, and you could guarantee yourself a stay in the ship's brig.

While the two trolley carts rattled along out front, the PSD leader raised a palm. "I am Sergeant Shuntee ... hold up. Show me your deck passes."

Jarpin eyed the commander of this little PSD trio. He was tall and slender with a pinched, narrow face. His eyes were small and beady. His lips twisted into a kind of snarl—like Jarpin's impromptu maintenance crew had a bad smell about them.

"I will not slop a mop," Corgi announced.

Jarpin ignored the idiot robot.

Shuntee scowled. "What's wrong with your bot?"

"Nothing. It's just old."

That seemed to placate the sergeant for the moment. "Best you get back in that shuttle and leave. We have our own highly qualified maintenance crew." He eyed their dingy, frayed overalls. "You don't belong here."

"I will not slop a mop," Corgi announced again.

Dalmass spoke up before Jarpin could. "Fine with us. We don't want to be here. Just let Colonel Gha Strone Mahn know that you've rescinded his orders."

That got Sergeant Shuntee's attention. The three PSD members exchanged a quick glance. "Just tell me what your orders were ... specifically."

Jarpin shrugged. "Simple, uh ... you have a tainted water reservoir. Maintenance personnel lodgings there on Deck 5 all have the craps."

Thakious raised his hands, flared his fingers. "Explosive diarrhea, the whole lot of them."

Shuntee's snarled lip was back. One of his cohorts leaned in close to him. After a brief, muffled back-and-forth conversation, Shuntee nodded. He then scrutinized Jarpin with narrowed eyes. "Apparently, the stream is lagging today. Yes, you're cleared to proceed. We will accompany you to the bridge. I take it you have the, uh, fixtures and such needed?"

Only now did Jarpin remember Gia's bogus blown bridge lights issue. Why they'd been called in to assist. Of course, he had no replacement fixtures, and he wouldn't know how to swap them out even if he did. He gestured to one of the trolleys. "Yeah, we've got everything we need. Lead on, Sergeant."

After three fast-lift transfers, progressing down multiple

corridors and passageways, twenty-five minutes later, they'd reached *Lonemach Tryon's* bridge.

All along the way, Jarpin had been keenly aware that Gia, through Corgi, would have initiated her virtual attack. They'd passed dozens of robots, electronic access panels, and miles and miles of overhead communications and electrical runs. In her weakened state, was Gia up to the task of fully infiltrating this ship's technology? He wondered if right now, at this moment, Gia was coming face to face with the Geo-Mind. He had no idea what was happening behind the scenes. What he did know was that they needed to physically occupy the bridge for Gia to gain a true foothold within *Lonemach Tryon*. Up ahead, he could see the entrance to the ship's command center. He'd had his doubts they'd make it this far.

Suddenly, sounding breathless, Gia's voice resonated in his head. *Run! Now! Get to the bridge!*

Farther down the corridor, beyond the entrance to the bridge, another team was en route. Looked to be at least a dozen of them. And these weren't another team of flunky PSDs; these were well-armed Silarian warriors. Jarpin noticed each was wearing a red headband. Not good. That signified they were the elite Orlicon Tharsh Guard ... they answered only to God, or what they perceived as God—undoubtedly, that, of course, was the Geo-Mind. Something Jarpin wouldn't have realized prior to being donutted.

Dalmass and Ruffle were already unpacking their trolleys. Thakious tossed Jarpin an Ender-2; without hesitating, he fired. Three seconds later, Dalmass and Ruffle joined him behind the cover of the two trolleys.

Five of the Orlicon Tharsh Guards dropped to the deck, dead. The others fell back while attempting to return fire.

Corgi, oblivious, stood out in the middle of the corridor as energy bolts streamed passed from both directions.

"Get down, Corgi!" Jarpin yelled.

"We lose that robot, we may as well pack it in," Dalmass said.

As if on cue, sparks fountained into the air as an Ender bolt clipped the robot's right shoulder. Corgi staggered. He looked back to Jarpin; his continuous wide-eyed expression seemed to be pleading with him—asking to be saved.

Jarpin shoved the trolley before him forward. "Help push, Dalmass!"

Thakious and Ruffle did the same with the other trolley. By the time Jarpin had maneuvered his trolley around the clueless robot, it was teetering. Taking hold of one articulating arm, Jarpin pulled the robot over backward onto the top of the trolley. "Just lie back and don't move!"

Their forward progress was slow, but eventually they'd progressed far enough to slip into the bridge entrance. Like an overturned turtle, Corgi's arms and legs flailed atop the trolley. Keeping a hand on the bot's chest, Jarpin, with Dalmass's help, pushed forward.

A stunned-looking bridge crew stood behind their respective control consoles. Not a one of them looked to be armed. At the front of the bridge stood Colonel Gha Strone Mahn.

"I need to get up ... I need to get up ... I need to get up ..."

Jarpin, you need to release your hold on Corgi, Gia said. Help him to the communications station ... hurry.

Chapter 53

Deep Space, Officer's Dropship
Entering Silarian's 23rd Fleet

Sam Dale

It had been ten minutes since the command communiqué had been received. They were to proceed to *Lonemach Tryon* without delay. Luna and Agnes were no longer piloting the dropship—that process was being conducted remotely.

This ad hoc bevy of old folks, Silarian warriors, humans, and a lone canine, had gone quiet—introspective.

Now before them loomed *Lonemach Tryon*.

Sam, unable to reach Gia, now queried the stream in an attempt to gain more insight as to what was happening within that formidable warship. Had Jarpin and his little team accomplished their mission? A mission that seemed unlikely to succeed—especially in light of Gia's progressively weakened state. And would this dropship be boarded as soon as they landed? Had they been lured there to face their inevitable deaths?

Dammit, Gia ... talk to me.

Harper, leaning against the bulkhead and a crease pinching her brow, said, "It's out of our hands." Her eyes found his. "It all comes down to this ... what happens next, right?"

Sam didn't answer her. Her question had been rhetorical. His attention moved to Cypress, whose tail had started to wag.

"What's wrong with your dog?" Agnes asked.

Luna turned in her seat.

Sam went down to one knee, scratched behind the dog's ears. "You know something we don't, boy?"

Cypress raised his snout, looked aft. "The other Silarians on board this vessel have contracted the Humarian virus."

Harper pushed herself off the bulkhead, peered aft. "Zorian? You getting sick?"

His reply was a deep cough. "Yes. I believe so. Seem to have whatever Lloyd has."

Out of view, Dolly said, "I certainly hope this isn't communicable to humans."

Harper and Sam exchanged a questioning shrug.

"Is it?" she said.

"Have no idea," Sam said.

"Unlikely," Cypress said. "But then again, I am only guessing."

Interest piqued, Harper tapped her upper lip with a forefinger. "What is interesting is how quickly this virus seems to spread. A typical incubation period of the flu on Earth is a couple of days."

Sam had almost forgotten she was a nurse, and this was

something she'd know far more about than the average person. "Lloyd and Zorian have been in close contact with each other for what, just a few hours?"

She nodded. "I know what our job will be."

Sam raised his brows, "Okay ... enlighten us."

"Get Lloyd back on his feet. Get him and Zorian moving about *Lonemach Tryon* as much as possible."

Agnes smiled. "Our two Typhoid Marys."

Luna crinkled her brow. "Uh ... say what?"

"Way before your time, Luna. Typhoid Mary, whose actual name was Mary Mallon," Agnes said. "She was the infamous typhoid carrier who gave rise to a horrid, deadly outbreak of typhoid fever in New York City in the early 1900s."

Luna nodded. "So New York City had Typhoid Mary; we have Typhoid Lloyd."

Motion aft caught Sam's attention. He saw Herschel and Harry struggling to get Lloyd up on his feet. The Silarian bio-form looked awful. Glistening rivers of snot ran from his nostrils. He hawked up something and spat it onto the deck.

"Real nice," Agnes commented, looking disgusted.

The dropship rumbled; outside there were the sounds of landing thrusters coming alive.

"Oh God ... I had no idea. We're here," Luna said, spinning around in her seat.

Outside the forward window was *Lonemach Tryon's* busy, bustling landing bay.

Herschel's voice carried forward. "Okay, sure, we know what Lloyd and Zorian here are supposed to do, but what about the rest of us? Can't imagine a bunch of humans wandering around this place will go over very well."

Gia's voice, faint, almost a whisper, emanated from the forward console. "On the contrary, you are all carriers of the

Humarian rhinovirus. Humans and dogs do not exhibit the symptoms the same as Silarians do ... but you will all spread the virus just the same, thus spreading Gia-donutting nanites. Go now ..." Her voice suddenly cut out.

All eyes went to Sam.

Luna looked incredulous. "Seriously? We're what ... supposed to just run around this massive warship, coming into contact with as many killer Silarian warriors as possible? How's that supposed to work?"

"Buck up, little lady. War is hell," Dolly said from somewhere aft.

Sam heard the whine of the rear hatch being opened.

Harper smiled. "Guess it's showtime, huh?"

Sam nodded. "I'm headed to the bridge; want to come with me?"

"Sure, lead the way. We should bring Lloyd with us ... he's the most contagious."

Lloyd refused to walk any further, feeling too sick. Sam and Harper had found a hover cart, removed its stack of engineering replacement parts, and coaxed Lloyd to lie down on it.

It wasn't as if their presence had so much gone unnoticed; oh yeah, being human, they were very much being noticed. But the ship's crew were far more concerned with other things. Like loud klaxon alarms blaring, overhead lights strobing on and off, and indiscriminate plumes of white steam venting up from various deck panels. *Lonemach Tryon* was clearly under siege. The ship's automated PA system was barking off orders—directing crew members to head to alternate ship areas. To say a heightened feeling of mayhem had captivated, well, everyone, would be an understatement.

All the while, Typhoid Lloyd was being ushered down one corridor to the next, and then to the next, still sneezing and coughing—spreading his germs.

It was a full hour before Sam, Harper, and Lloyd reached the proper deck level and the proper corridor. They'd gotten lost three times. For the most part, the stream had not been accessible. Now, having found the right deck, they tentatively pushed onward.

Splayed bodies littered the passageway. Sam knelt to retrieve a dropped Ender weapon while Harper took over pushing Lloyd's hover cart.

Lloyd, managing to sit up, said, "Shit sure hit the fan around here."

Sam couldn't argue with that assessment.

"Turn here?" Harper asked, gesturing to her right.

Sam moved ahead, pushed three green, dead bodies out of the way before peering around the corner. Seeing inside, he saw this was most definitely the bridge. Basically an elongated oval, the compartment was a mass of technology. There were at least a dozen console stations with colorful control boards. Blinking, hovering monochrome 3D displays danced upon each of the boards.

At the entrance, more bodies—a lot of bodies lay still upon the deck.

"What took you so long?" came a voice Sam immediately recognized. Only then did he see Jarpin standing at the forward section of the bridge. Behind him was a large display showing a feed depicting the entirety of the 23rd Fleet.

Jarpin was cradling an Ender-2, as were three other Silarians. All four were wearing stained maintenance overalls.

Sam approached, now seeing the entirety of the bridge crew was seated, side by side, shoulder to shoulder, along one bulkhead.

Sam laughed, still not sure he believed what he was seeing. "Not bad, Jarpin. Not bad at all."

Jarpin gestured with the muzzle of his Ender to one of the prisoners. "Get up, Colonel."

Reluctantly, a defiant-looking Silarian got to his feet.

Sam took in Colonel Gha Strone Mahn. Handsome, and younger than he'd expected, he had an arrogant air of superiority about him. He wondered how many bio-forms the fleet commander had gone through in his lifetime.

Colonel Mahn smirked. "Know this ... you will not succeed. Enjoy this temporary victory. Because it is just a matter of time before order is restored on my ship. And then ... I will personally ensure each of you will be properly dealt with. Then, agonizing pain will encompass what remains of your worthless, insignificant lives."

Harper, having some difficulty, was maneuvering the hover cart in between two of the consoles. "You know, you could help a little."

Lloyd waved off her words. Coughing, he signaled for her to stop. He got to his feet and looked about the compartment. He cleared his throat. "Well, well ... this is some cool alien shit." Lloyd wiped his nose with a hand, gave Colonel Gha Strone Mahn a head-to-toe appraisal.

Recognition flashed on Colonel Mahn's face. "You're a deployment commander ... Uh, Captain Larng Nos Polk, isn't it?"

Harper was at Sam's side. Under her breath, she said, "Guess he doesn't know he's looking at Captain Larng Nos Polk's bio-form."

Lloyd stood tall. "Yessiree Bob. That's me, Colonel ... in the flesh." Lloyd looked to Sam and winked. With arms held wide, Lloyd strode toward Colonel Gha Strone Mahn. "Come on. How about you give a brother some affection?"

Astonished, cringing, Colonel Gha Strone tried to back

away, but Lloyd kept coming. Forced into an encircling embrace, the colonel let out an audible moan.

Harper took Sam's hand, leaned her head against his shoulder. "Isn't it wonderful witnessing such brotherly love?"

"It's truly touching," he said.

Nearby, moving from one console to the next, the rickety old robot continued to mutter the same mantra: "I will not slop a mop ... I will not slop a mop..."

Epilogue

Within four hours, the crew of *Lonemach Tryon* was no longer under the control of the Geo-Mind. The ship's technology was now cleared of all Geo-Mind influences. And while the rest of the 23rd Fleet had yet to fully exhibit the same effects, it would only be a matter of time before the constant back-and-forth transit of delivery shuttles, personnel transports, and the like, had spread the Humarian rhinovirus to every single Silarian crew member fleetwide.

In the end, destroying the Geo-Mind had cost Gia everything ... but she was okay with that. For her, this was never about replacing one godlike AI persona with another. Before leaving the minds of both Silarians and humans for the last time, Gia had carefully watched—ensured there were no lingering malevolent motivations. That those heinous acts of terra-displacement were truly a thing of the past. That Silarians, excised of the Geo-Mind, were adequately ashamed of their previous acts. Were repentant and willing to make amends.

The 23rd Fleet would eventually move on. But not without bringing the Humarian rhinovirus back to Naru, as well as spreading it far and wide to other terra-displacement fleet deployments. Twenty-seven Silarian vessels had stayed behind. It would take four years and much Silarian technology for Earth's nearly destroyed eco/biosystems to show solid signs of recovery.

three weeks after the fall of the Geo-Mind …

Julian had lingered for a while back at Walter's Valhallen compound, where he puttered around, tried to make himself useful. Later, he was put in charge of the isolation zone. Ensuring that the Field Emitter continued to generate its constant enclosing energy field was a big responsibility. It had been decided that Castle Rock, now Earth's only remaining fully intact biosphere, needed to be protected at all costs.

But Julian missed Gia. Missed her being there in his mind. Missed their clever back-and-forth repartee. The way she flirted with him. *Or did I just imagine that?*

Oddly, the stream was still in effect. Was fully operational for all humanity to utilize. *At least something good has come of all this,* Julian lamented as he drove the same Ford F150 into Walter's compound. He pulled up close to the Landa-Craft. It was time for another maintenance check on the Field Emitter. He shut off the engine and sat within the quiet solitude of the truck's cab. He heard the ticking of the hot engine. Off in the distance, an ATV was making its way across the property.

Julian thought of his friend Sam. He and Harper had returned not long after The Shift. That's what everyone was calling it now—The Shift. They were happy together, were planning on getting married soon. Of course, Cypress was a part of that trio. The three would be staying here within the isolation zone. Staying in Castle Rock was a privilege very few people had been granted by the World Order. Individual countries, isolated governments, made little sense now. All told, billions had been lost. Much of the world was now uninhabitable. *Will there be a place for me here, for me anywhere? Julian wondered.*

It seemed the ATV was now coming his way. The high-pitched motor whined louder and louder as it approached. He made a face; *damn things are annoying.* Julian opened the door and climbed down. He still had a lot to get done today, so whoever this was ... he stopped, seeing the quad rider was a woman.

It wasn't until she pulled up and shut off the motor that he thought he recognized her face. Her name was Agnes something or other. But she shouldn't be here. She certainly shouldn't be up and around. She'd been a part of Sam's team up in space. One of the old codgers from the nursing home. More importantly, though, she'd been shot. Had been taken to a medical bay and put on life support. Totally brain dead, from what he'd heard.

She dismounted the quad with far more dexterity than he'd expect from someone her age. Someone supposedly in her late seventies or early eighties. She pulled off her helmet and placed it on the seat of the ATV. Hesitant, she turned to Julian and smiled.

Julian figured he must have been mistaken; this woman couldn't be any older than fifty. Maybe younger. She was pretty.

"Hi, Julian. I've missed you."

His breath caught in his chest. His jaw dropped open. "How ..." He knew that voice. More like Gia's distinctive way of talking, her inflections, intonations.

She took several steps closer. She seemed nervous. "I had a choice to make. Agnes was never going to survive. Was never going to fully wake up. Although she was somewhat aware ... at least enough to know she was dying. So, I asked her permission,

Julian. Asked if it would be all right if she and I made a go of life together. So, I guess you can say you'd be getting two for one. If that's at all of interest to you."

Julian had finally found his voice, and not knowing what else to say, he said, "I think that would be ... nice."

Gia looked past him to the Landa-Craft. "You going up in that Landa-Craft?"

He nodded.

"Want some company?" She asked.

Thank you for reading ***The Fallen Ship II.***

If you enjoyed this book, PLEASE leave a review on Amazon.com—it really helps!

To be notified the moment all future books are released, please join my mailing list. I hate spam and will never ever share your information. Jump to this link to sign up: ***http://eepurl.com/bs7M9r***

About the Author

The Authors

About Mark Wayne McGinnis

Mark grew up on both coasts, first in Westchester County, New York, then in Westlake Village, California. Mark and his wife Kim now live in Castle Rock, Colorado, with their two dogs, Sammi and Lilly. Mark got his start as a corporate marketing manager and then fell into indie filmmaking—producing/directing the popular Gaia docudrama, Openings—The Search For Harry. For the last ten years, he's been writing full time, and with thirty-eight best-selling novels under his belt, he has no plans to slow down. Thanks for being part of his community! Use the links below to jump to Mark's site.

Have a question or want to say hi to Mark? Contact him at *markwaynemcginnis@gmail.com*

Or contact him on his Facebook author's page at https://www.facebook.com/MarkWayneMcGinnisAuthor/

About Kim McGinnis

Kim grew up on Air Force bases in Georgia, the Philippines, Okinawa, and Arizona. After studying theater in college, she moved to LA, where she became a SAG actress and performed in numerous theatrical productions, as well as landing principal roles in several national TV commercials. After Kim met Mark in Southern California, she starred in and produced the docudrama, Openings—The Search for Harry. Kim has extensive marketing experience and currently does all the marketing for their Avenstar Productions publishing business. The Fallen Ship is Kim's first credit as a coauthor.

Have a question or want to say hi to Kim? Contact her at *kimpmcginnis@gmail.com*

Acknowledgments

First and foremost, we (Mark and Kim McGinnis) are grateful to our readers. We'd like to thank Lura Genz (Mark's mother) for her tireless work as our first-phase creative editor and for being a staunch cheerleader of our writing. We'd also like to thank Margarita Martinez for her amazingly detailed line editing work; Sarah Kruger for her creative design and typesetting skills; Gabriel Hannon and Anna Chvyreva for their mind-blowing physics/scientific contributions; Daniel Edelman for his many prereleases, technical reviews, and expert subject matter spitballing; Commander Sam Varela of the Castle Rock Police Department for his expertise in police procedure as it pertains to the city of Castle Rock, CO; and David Daly for his in-depth military contributions. A heartfelt thank you also goes to Sue Parr, Charles Duell, Stuart Church, Zoraya Vasquez, Lura Fischer, and James Fischer—without their support, this novel would not have been possible. And finally, to our beloved pups Lilly and Sammi, whose unconditional love inspired the character of Cypress/Rocko.

Other Books by MWM

Scrapyard Ship Series

Scrapyard Ship (Book 1)

HAB 12 (Book 2)

Space Vengeance (Book 3)

Realms of Time (Book 4)

Craing Dominion (Book 5

The Great Space (Book 6)

Call To Battle (Book 7)

Scrapyard Ship – Uprising

Mad Powers Series

Mad Powers (Book 1)

Deadly Powers (Book 2)

Lone Star Renegades

Star Watch Series

Star Watch (Book 1)

Ricket (Book 2)

Boomer (Book 3)

Glory for Sea and Space (Book 4)

Space Chase (Book 5)

Scrapyard LEGACY (Book 6)

The Simpleton Series

The Simpleton (Book 1)

The Simpleton Quest (Book 2)

Galaxy Man

Ship Wrecked Series

Ship Wrecked (Book 1)

Ship Wrecked II (Book 2)

Ship Wrecked III (Book 3)

Boy Gone

The Expanded Anniversary Edition

Cloudwalkers

The Hidden Ship

Guardian Ship

Gun Ship

HOVER

Heroes and Zombies

The Test Pilot's Wife

The Fallen Ship

The Fallen Ship: Rise of the Gia Rebellion (Book 1)

The Fallen Ship II (Book 2)

USS Hamilton Series

USS Hamilton: Ironhold Station (Book 1)

USS Hamilton: Miasma Burn (Book 2)

USS Hamilton: Broadsides (Book 3)

USS Hamilton: USS Jefferson –

Charge of the Symbios (Book 4)

USS Hamilton: Starship Oblivion –

Sanctuary Outpost (Book 5)

USS Hamilton: USS Adams – No Escape (Book 6)

USS Hamilton: USS Lincoln – Mercy Kill (Book 7)

USS Hamilton: USS Franklin - When Worlds Collide (Book 8)

USS Hamilton: USS Washington - The Black Ship (Book 9)

USS Hamilton: USS IKE – Quansport Ops (Book 10)

USS Hamilton: USS Resilience - Honor the Fallen (Book 11)

USS Hamilton: USS Freedom - Hydromass (Book 12)

ChronoBot Chronicles

Copyright

Published by: Avenstar Productions

Paperback ISBN:

ISBN-13: **979-8986675237**

To join Mark's mailing list, jump to:

http://eepurl.com/bs7M9r

Visit Mark Wayne McGinnis at:

http://www.markwaynemcginnis.com

 Created with Vellum

Made in United States
Cleveland, OH
29 July 2025